THE ARK

You are far more powerful than you have been led to believe

Ian C. Jervis

ISBN: 1497470102
ISBN-13: 978-1497470101

Dedication

To my God the Father, mighty Yahweh, maker of all things of purpose. You are my refuge, my strength, source of all knowledge, my friend and my Saviour. Without You nothing has purpose. Thank You, I love You.

To my wife Lisa, my inspiration, my true love. You make my life fantastic in all aspects. Without you this book could never have been written. You make my walk with God complete, like the triple braided cord, You, me and Him. I love you.

CONTENTS

FOREWORD

In truth, two people have written this book, one being myself in putting it all together, but also the love of my life, Lisa, who has been the main contributor to this story.

Although this book will be found in the fiction section of your bookshop or online book store, many of the occurrences in The Ark have happened in some way. Some have been dreams, some have been visions and a few have been actual real life events. I will leave it up to you, the reader to decipher.

I hope and pray that you will not only enjoy this book but that it will be a blessing in your life and will inspire you in your walk with Him.

Blessings,

Ian C. Jervis

Chapter 1

You Are Not as Powerful as You Have Been Led to Believe

It was hard for Lisa to concentrate. The kids, happy to be home after a long day at school, had just tipped out the bucket of building blocks and were thrilled at the noise it had made, screaming at each other as they scattered the blocks to flatten the pile. The TV was blaring with an action cartoon, as an alien life form had captured the hero, holding him to ransom to try and steal from him the key to the universe.

"I'm trying to read, boys!" Lisa complained, but as usual when they were in full flow, they totally ignored her request to calm down and carried on with their high-volume banter. She shuffled in her chair, sitting more upright, her head bowed down staring at the book on her lap and continued to read with an even more intense focus, trying to battle through all the noise and distraction. She found herself staring at the same passage in her bible, over and over again. The words were seeming to jump out from the page; almost separating themselves from the rest of the passage, drawing her in. It was as though she couldn't read past those few lines. The more she looked at them, the more they seemed to radiate, almost pulsating in front of her eyes.

The passage was from the book of Matthew, where Jesus was talking with the rich young man about entering the kingdom of heaven. It read, 'Jesus looked at them and said, "With man this is impossible but with God all things are possible."'

She repeated them under her breath, only her lips moving as she soaked up the words of her Saviour. She started to day dream.

She suddenly found herself back in her childhood, listening to her teacher in primary school, shouting at her in front of the class:

"You're a failure, Lisa. If you carry on like this, you'll never amount to anything! You're useless!" The teacher's stern voice echoed around in her head over and over again, along with the merciless laughter of her so-called classmates. She felt the trauma, embarrassment and humiliation of the whole episode as though she was right back there in that dimly lit, dingy classroom.

The classroom transformed into the kitchen of the house she grew up in and she was standing there, as a teenager in front of her parents having a finger wagged in her face, being told by her father,

"You're a thorn in my side!" She felt the pain, hurt and frustration of those times, all those years ago, as though she was reliving it right there and then.

The face of her father evolved into the accusing, angry grimace of her drunken husband, bellowing at her as a young adult. She could smell the beer on his breath as he shouted into her face,

"Why did I get stuck with you? Why can't you look like her?" he yelled as he forcefully prodded and pointed at a glamour model on the overturned page of a men's magazine.

Again, the feeling of inadequacy and unworthiness felt as real in her mind as it did at the time. Her heart pounded with anguish as she sat there in her chair, blankly staring at the bible on her knee; the pressure and stress of the pictures in her mind felt like

2

more than just a past event. She could hear the familiar sound of the voice in her own mind confirming what these people had told her.

"You're a failure"

"You'll never achieve anything"

Suddenly she awoke from the reverie with a start as the alien on the TV screamed at the hero, who was bound to a pillar.

"You are not as powerful as you have been led to believe! Just give in!" The alien's words seemed to reverberate around in her head. She looked down at the bible on her lap.

"With God all things are possible."

Then she looked back to the TV as the alien continued to attempt to intimidate his captive, knowing that if he could just make the hero doubt himself, he could overpower him.

She felt as though a revelation was unfolding before her very eyes, that with God she could do more with her life, more than she had ever thought possible! Could it be that she had been held back from realising her own potential? Could it be that she, just like the hero, had been made to doubt her own abilities and had all those negative instances in her life been an attempt to keep her from becoming the person she was meant to be? Could it really be that to God she was significant and capable of achieving so much more - that He had a genuine plan for her; a calling on her life?

Suddenly, it all started to make sense. In one fluid movement she dropped her bible, stood to her feet, put her hands over her mouth and gasped.

"Oh, my goodness! Of course!" she said out loud. "That's it!" The boys turned and looked at her.

"Are you okay, Mummy?" Josh asked, concerned at his mother talking to herself.

"Yes Josh!" Lisa replied enthusiastically. "Better than ever!" As she felt herself returning to Earth, she smiled at her boys and in her usual calm, motherly voice, reassured them both that Mummy was fine. Happy with the fact that all was well and back to normal, the boys continued their game, the TV still blaring in the background. Lisa had been touched by something truly powerful, something that she had never in her life experienced before.

The reason she had been reading her bible intently and trying to concentrate on it so much that afternoon was because at her bible study group last week, everyone had been asked to read and reflect on a passage and discuss it when they got together again, which was to be that evening - and as usual, Lisa, being so busy, had left it until the last possible moment.

*

Lisa Jeffreys was an attractive twenty-nine-year-old, with dark, almost black hair, brown eyes, a fair complexion and a slim figure.

She met Dan, her husband, in her late teens and against the advice of her mother, got married before turning twenty, within a year became pregnant with Joshua, so she never had a career or even had the chance to think about one. She didn't regret anything but always felt that she should achieve more in her life than she had so far.

Dan, worked at the local hospital as a porter during the week and at weekends he helped out at local shop. With all the hours he worked, they didn't get to see each other a great deal, which suited them both. Whenever he did come home he seemed to be drunk or in the process of getting that way, so life together wasn't much fun. In fact, he would often get violent if she dared to say anything about his drinking or their financial circumstances, so most of the time she kept her head down and tried not to aggravate the situation.

Looking back, it wasn't really any surprise that her marriage was failing: all of the dreams that she'd had before she married Dan were clear warning signals which she chose to ignore. She and Dan fought constantly. It was obvious that they weren't meant for each other but they had been together for so long that marriage just seemed to be the next step. Lisa hadn't even taken Dan's surname; she remained Lisa Jeffreys while he was Dan Thomas.

Maybe her mother's advice was right and she should never have married him - but then she wouldn't have her precious boys. In Lisa's mind, divorce was never an option because then she would have had God against her. At least as it was, even though she was unhappy with her marriage, God loved her. That's what they told her at church anyway.

Both boys, Josh and Luke, were of primary school age and her love for them was paramount in her life. She always took great care in ensuring they had everything they needed even though, materialistically, they didn't have very much.

They all lived in a seaside town on the West coast of Wales, where Lisa had lived since her parents moved there when she was thirteen; a place where everybody knew everyone and everyone's life was everybody's business. Nothing much ever happened in Hightown - in fact, a broken greenhouse window once made the front page of the local paper. Although Lisa had suffered some turbulent times there, it was home. It was a place she loved.

Her house was just one of twelve identical houses on a small estate. The house was small and plain, nothing to write home about, but Lisa never complained or even thought about complaining. Somehow, she had always managed to make this tiny house in the middle of the town feel special, certainly to the people who knew her.

On the outside, Lisa seemed to be a very quiet and mild person. Inside, however she held a quiet confidence and a strong faith to which she had clung to many times during the challenge's life had thrown her way.

One of her greatest treasures was her passion for the truth, something she picked up as a child, overhearing her Dad praising her to a friend about her trustworthiness. So that was the benchmark that he had unknowingly set for her as a child, to which she still lived up to. She used the word 'transparent' to describe herself. "What you see is what you get. She expected the same of others and always found it painful if she found out that someone had lied to or hidden the truth from her."

But there was a secret place in her heart where she held on to ideals and dreams that she had carried from childhood to present day. She'd always dreamed of doing something great with her life but never quite knew what. She had a passion to reach out to people and make a difference in the lives of others. How she would ever do that, she did not know, but a feeling deep inside would often remind her that there was more to come. Over the years, however, even though her faith remained strong, some of her dreams had begun a slow fade.

Lisa and the kids would always try and go to church on a Sunday. It was the little bit of freedom she loved and looked forward to every week. It got her out of the house and it was one place where Dan would never be seen dead in, never mind alive, and so she had a warm, safe feeling there; it was a real sanctuary for her and the boys. It seemed worlds away from the routine at home.

Recently she had started to go to the bible study group, which she had kept quiet from Dan. He was always late home on a Wednesday so she didn't see the point in talking to him about it because it would only end in an argument. So, on study night she would get a babysitter for a few hours and have some time away from the boys to herself with friends.

Lisa was determined that she was going to remember the events of that afternoon. Was it God giving her this revelation? It had to be, surely.

She decided to write everything down. She remembered that she had a little leather-backed notebook that someone from church had bought for her last Christmas, which she hadn't had the

6

opportunity to use. It was now going to have a purpose. It was going to be her book of God experiences; at least she hoped it would be.

Many times, she had heard stories and testimonies from people at church, who always seemed to have such tremendous things happen to them but she had never really experienced anything herself apart from feeling emotional during worship from time to time and a knowledge that God was real and loved her. Maybe this was her time.

She was scribbling down the details of the events that afternoon when the doorbell rang. It was Sophie, the baby sitter.

"Hello Lisa!" said Sophie brightly, stepping inside. "How are you today?"

"Fine thank you, Sophie," replied Lisa, smiling, always pleased to see her trusted babysitter.

"You're here early."

"It's the same time as always, Lisa, six-thirty," answered Sophie, looking at her watch, wondering if she had got the time wrong.

"It can't be," Lisa cried unbelievingly, looking over at the kitchen clock. "Oh, my goodness, it is! Come on in, I've made dinner for you and the boys, it just needs warming."

Sophie hung her jacket up in the hall and said, "So, where are the little princes?" Lisa replied,

"Oh, they're in the lounge saving the universe from an evil alien as always!" They both laughed. Sophie made her way to the lounge to see the boys while Lisa hurried upstairs to get changed.

"Wow, where have I been?" she said to herself, glancing again at the clock on the wall on the way.

As she searched her wardrobe looking for something appropriate to wear for that evening she flicked through all her pretty dresses, a wave of sadness came over her. She had always tried to look good for her husband hoping that he would notice but somehow, he never did. There had been a short time when they first met when she seemed to be the centre of his world but the romance quickly dissolved and hadn't returned. She thought about all of the times that she had begged Dan to set aside some time so that they could go out for an evening or away for a weekend but he always seemed to have something else to do.

Sometimes she would get dressed up to surprise Dan when he got home from work; she would book a babysitter and a table at a restaurant. When he got home she would have his bath ready so that he could go relax and get dressed up to enjoy some time alone, hoping that it would bring back that spark which had been missing for so long.

But Dan would always say, "We're not teenagers anymore, Lisa!" or something similar to put her down and make her feel stupid. One time, he came home very late after Lisa had prepared a romantic meal just for the two of them and turned the lounge into a candle-lit, romantic haven. She did everything that she wished he would do for her. When he eventually got home, he burst through the door and almost fell onto the hallway floor, obviously having had one too many. He managed to stay on his feet only by grabbing the newel post at the bottom of the stairs. He gazed into the lounge and looked around at everything she had done. He laughed mockingly.

"Get a life, Lisa! Haven't you got some friends or something else to do? Let me set the record straight here, sweetheart, so that we can do away with all this rubbish!" he said arrogantly, slurring his words. "If it wasn't for those two lads I would have left long ago!" The words cut like a dagger to Lisa's heart and to that day he had never taken any of them back.

She recognised the flood of self-pity that was trying to wash over her and assertively pulled out her favourite dress and said,

"From now on, Lord, I am going to be the best I can be for you! I'm done with crying over what I don't have or what cannot be fixed and I'm going to praise You for what I do have! I have You! You are all that I need. From now on I am going to see myself through Your eyes, not through Dan's, not through anyone else's. You are God! You take the time to speak to me, a mere human, to You I am a princess! I love You!"

Her sadness turned into praise and she felt a warm sensation flood over her whole body. As she fixed her face in the mirror she even noticed something different about the way she looked. Her eyes sparkled and she had a look of confidence that she had never seen before. There was an air of confidence and strength about her whole appearance. For the first time in a long time, she looked on the outside how she felt on the inside.

She smiled as she looked in the full-length mirror, turning one way then the other, feeling good about herself. Something from the inside was happening to her and she totally approved.

As she walked down the stairs she could see Sophie and the boys wrapped in blankets, engrossed in a film.

"Bye, Sophie! Bye Boys!" she shouted as she opened the front door.

"Bye!" came the trio of voices in unison, not moving from their positions glued to the TV.

As she closed the door behind herself and got the car keys from her bag, another little contented smile occupied her face. She was excited about going tonight and seeing her friends again from church.

What had happened that afternoon was still forefront in her mind and the big question she was asking herself now was whether she should say anything at the bible class or just keep quiet about the whole episode. Part of her wanted to tell all but another part of

9

her was a little scared. She was still relatively new to the bible class and usually didn't say a great deal at all, only responding when she was asked a direct question.

Regardless of whether she shared anything at all with the group that night she felt that something important was going to happen and she did not want to miss it. Walking from her car to Tom and Jan's house she had a spring in her step that she hadn't noticed since she had been a child. She felt great!

Tom and Jan Philips, who hosted the bible study, were a couple in their mid- to late-fifties. Tom had retired early from his engineering job and had earned enough to keep Jan at home to raise their two children who had now flown the nest. They were very loyal to the church establishment and were personal friends of the pastor and his wife. The type of people who nurtured and protected their reputation in the community at all cost, extremely concerned with what other people thought of them and their possessions. They were both always well-groomed and immaculately dressed and inadvertently made you feel slightly beneath them when you were in their company. Friendly, never the less.

Lisa rang the doorbell.

"Lisa!" exclaimed Mrs Philips, as she opened the door. "Come on in! You look lovely, tonight!"

"Thank you, Mrs Philips, I feel great!" replied Lisa.

"How has your day been?" asked Jan politely.

"Well actually it was quite amazing," responded Lisa enthusiastically. It crossed her mind to say something about her day right there and then but Mrs Philips had closed the door behind her and was already walking off at speed down the parquet floored hallway with her back to Lisa, not meaning to be rude but obviously preoccupied with other things. "Oh well," Lisa said to herself. "Perhaps I should keep it to myself anyway!"

She wandered into the main room where there were about

twenty people, some sitting and some standing but all chatting. She sat down on the first convenient chair and looked around the room. She knew everyone there to some degree. Some she knew well from living in Hightown most of her life and others she had met at previous classes. She said hello to the people who took the time to acknowledge her and shared niceties with the people on the chairs either side of her before Mrs Philips burst in and called everyone to attention with several loud claps cutting through and immediately silencing the ever-snowballing hubbub in the room.

"Excuse me, everyone!" she announced in her well-spoken, eloquent, very English accent, "Can I have your attention, please? I want to introduce Charles to you all! It's his first night tonight, so make him feel welcome! Carry on!"

Everyone mumbled hello to Charles and he sat down on a chair on the opposite side of the room to Lisa. A few people near to him got up to shake his hand, mumbling a few welcoming words to him and Charles, being an obvious gentleman, half rose out of his chair to reciprocate them.

For some reason Lisa felt quite strange when she looked over at Charles. There was something about him that seemed comforting and familiar. Did she know him from somewhere? She found herself staring at Charles while her mind searched through the archives of her past. He looked over at Lisa and mouthed "Hello," at which point she realised that she had been staring intently at this man for quite a while and he had obviously noticed her doing so! She looked away immediately without responding.

"What's wrong with me?" she thought, telling herself off. "How rude! Don't do that again!" The meeting began and Tom Philips stood up to pray. He asked God to be involved in the meeting and to speak to everyone in the group that night to which everybody mumbled 'Amen' and opened their bibles.

11

As Tom shared with the group it wasn't long before Lisa found her mind wandering from his words and onto the events of the day. She was so amazed and yet felt so privileged that God Almighty, the maker of the heavens and earth, had been communicating with her. But why her? Surely, He would use people who had skills of some description and not little old Lisa who had never really amounted to anything?

She tried to focus on the study but found herself getting frustrated with what Tom was talking about. It just seemed so irrelevant. She had hoped that the study would throw light on what God had been saying that day, whereas all it was doing was distracting her thoughts. She knew she should be focusing on what was being said but each time she looked up at Tom, who had a real skill at turning what could be a simple sentence into a novel, she visualised herself leaping from her chair and screaming, "Stop rambling and get to the point!"

She found herself glancing over at Charles again. Her glance turned into a stare, trying to work out where she had seen him before. There was something about him that intrigued her. Each time her stare was broken by Charles looking up at her and each time she would beat herself up inside telling herself to stop staring at the poor guy. This was followed every time with a brief repentance, telling herself that it was no wonder that God wasn't speaking to her tonight and making promises to herself that she was going to concentrate and listen to every word that Tom was saying. She looked up at Tom, who immediately smiled and looked back at her and said,

"Lisa, you first! Share with the group what you have got from this evening."

She stared at Tom, who smiled back at her with a smug look on his face, knowing that she hadn't been paying attention to his talk. She felt herself starting to blush so she bowed her head and

12

sent out a quick prayer.

"What on earth has he been talking about? Lord, help me!" She lifted her head slowly, met Tom's gaze confidently and said,

"What I've learned tonight, Tom, is that God is good, full of mercy and grace. He is faithful and true and He loves me! I also learned that I am a bad Christian with the attention span of a goldfish!"

The room was silent. Tom stared at her, his smile fading. She looked over and saw Charles with his head in his hands. His shoulders were shaking as he was trying to suppress his laughter.

"Yes, thank you Lisa," said Tom. A smile came back to his face as he continued his interrogation. "So, what did you learn in self-study this week?"

Lisa cleared her throat and said,

"I learned that God is so amazing that he can even speak to you through a cartoon alien!" The room erupted with laughter, which bothered Tom because he was supposed to be in control and he wanted a serious reply. Comedy was not his strong point and he didn't quite know how to deal with a woman with a sense of humour, so he quickly moved on to his next victim.

When he had picked on a few people the meeting came to an end. Some people had cups of tea and coffee and some started to leave. Charles, being the new guy, had attracted a small crowd around him. People were asking him questions about himself and his recent arrival in Hightown. Lisa discovered quite a lot about him from just listening to his answers to other people's questions. He was new in town, he was single and he worked in management at the local food manufacturing plant. But none of the questions they asked and the answers he gave satisfied Lisa's curiosity with Charles.

Tom came over and sat down by Lisa's side and asked her how her self-study had really been that week.

13

"Are you sure you want to know?" she replied.

"Of course," he responded, "that's why I asked."

She plucked up courage and started to relay what had happened that afternoon. As she talked and got more and more enthusiastic about the events of the day she noticed a glazed expression creeping across Toms smile laden face. Even though he appeared on the outside to be listening, even nodding and agreeing occasionally, it became increasingly obvious that he wasn't really paying attention to what she was saying. At one point she was sure he was fighting off a yawn.

She cut her story short, realising that she shouldn't be offended because she had actually done the same thing to him in a roundabout way, during the study, so she asked him about his day. Amazingly he was able to tell her all about his day without any sign of weariness.

"Have you met Charles?" Tom asked.

"Not really," Lisa replied.

"Then come on over." Tom led Lisa to the other side of the room.

"Charles, I'd like you to meet Lisa Jeffreys. She is new here too! Lisa, Charles, Charles, Lisa," reported Tom and deposited her with the new guy.

Charles was easy to talk to, seeming to take a genuine interest in Lisa and what she had to say for herself. She explained that she had lived here most of her life so for Tom to say she was 'new' wasn't totally the case. All the time they talked Lisa searched her mind, to try and figure out what it was with him and whether she did know him from somewhere in her past. She was just about to ask him as to why he looked so familiar when Tom interrupted their conversation and introduced someone else to Charles. It was as though he was saying, "You've had him for long enough, now let someone else have a go!"

14

Lisa sidled out of the way and took her coat from the back of her chair. She felt it time to leave. She put on her coat and said 'goodbye' to the remaining people in the room but her small voice was completely drowned out by the laughter and lively conversation of the group of stragglers surrounding Charles, totally enthralled and engrossed in his story.

Just as she was about to close the front door behind herself, Charles came dashing out to her.

"I don't know if this will mean anything to you right now," he said, "But God wants me to give this to you!" He handed Lisa his business card. She gave Charles a warm smile and replied,

"Thank you, Charles," and put the card in her bible and closed it. "I have to go now, Goodnight Charles."

Before he could say anything else she turned and walked down the path and jumped into her car. As much as she would have liked to continue their conversation, she didn't feel it appropriate to be standing there, the two of them, alone, having only just met. She reversed out of the drive and sped off toward home.

"What's wrong with me, Lord? Who is this guy?" she thought to herself. She felt bad that this man had fascinated her so much. Why did she feel drawn to him? She was a married woman and planned to stay that way even with a non-participating husband.

"Why did he give me his card!" she said to herself, getting a little agitated. "As if I would want to call someone I don't know any way!"

"Forgive me, Father!" she prayed under her breath and a feeling of peace fell on her, a feeling of warmth and comfort, that God was in control and that she was safe and secure in Him. She slowed down and took it all in.

"Thank you, Lord," she whispered. "Thank you."

She turned onto her street and could see her home in front

15

of her at the end of the street. It looked so cosy, sat there all lit up; her home. She pulled up into the driveway, got out of the car and went into the house.

"Hi Sophie!" she shouted as she put her keys on the polished wood hall table. "Has everything been okay?"

"Yes, great!" replied Sophie. "I fed the boys and put them to bed. They have been as good as gold."

Lisa responded, "You are truly an angel, thank you so much."

Sophie replied, "No problem! I'll see you next week?"

"Yes, I think so. I'll let you know if not," said Lisa. She thanked her again and Sophie left.

Lisa closed the door after watching Sophie walk home and went into the lounge and flopped into her soft armchair. She sat there for a moment contemplating all that had happened that evening. She put her bible down on the coffee table, it fell open just where she had placed Charles's business card. She leaned forward and picked up the card. It looked very professional and formal. Just a simple plain white with an embossed border and the name 'Charles Michaels' across the middle with his title and phone number.

She flipped the card over.

She sat back in the chair.

On the back, scribbled in blue ink, were the words, 'You are far more powerful than you have been led to believe!'

Chapter 2

Back at Church

By Saturday Lisa was desperate to talk to Charles about the card with the message but two things kept her from calling him. One was that, being a married woman, it didn't feel right to be calling a strange man that she'd only met once, even if he was a Christian. That was how Lisa always operated. Secondly, even though she was bursting at the seams to talk to him about what he had written on the back of his card, she was fairly convinced that she should play it cool and wait to see him in church on Sunday.

During the last few days, questions were constantly rolling around in her mind over and over again: What if he doesn't come to church on Sunday? What if he works on the weekend? Should she call Tom and Jan to see if they knew whether Charles was going to church on Sunday? If she did though, she would have to explain why she needed to know and then have to tell them the story so far and she wasn't that keen to talk to share that with Tom and Jan. They probably thought that she was a little crazy as it was without embellishing the situation.

Eventually she concluded that she should just wait until Sunday and see if he went to church and if he didn't, then give him a call. The problem was that the same questions kept revolving around her head because she would be reminded of the whole thing by the fact that she was constantly thinking about it!

This was the vicious cycle that she had been caught up in since Wednesday evening. To remedy the situation, she would get

17

the hoover out and dust everywhere. She cleaned out Henry the goldfish and just did about ever chore around the house that she possibly could.

The boys even asked her if someone was visiting because Mummy usually only cleaned to that extent when somebody was coming.

As she was dusting the woodwork for a second time that day, the air thick with the scent of furniture polish, she came to the bookcase.

"Read a book!" she said to herself. "Hopefully that will keep my mind off things!" She looked along the shelf at all the titles. Nothing seemed to grab her attention, until she got to her bible. It was then she realised that since that Wednesday afternoon she hadn't even looked at the word, so she took it off the shelf and just stared at it, wary about opening it up for some reason, a little afraid, in some way, of God not speaking to her and yet at the same time actually fearful, for some reason, of Him doing so.

She sat down in the lounge in the armchair; the boys, engrossed in the TV sat cross-legged in front of the screen just a few feet away. She could feel her heart pounding with excitement and anticipation as she held the bible to her chest.

She closed her eyes and prayed softly, "Father, speak to me through your word."
Before she had even finished her sentence, words were passing in front of her eyes like one of those scrolling adverts in the post office. The words simply said, 'Luke 18:27'. It was so real.

Although Lisa had been a Christian for a long time, memorising scriptures wasn't one of her strong points. She opened her bible and flicked through the pages having no idea what she was about to read. Instantly a doubt came into her mind. Where had this vision come from? Was it her own mind playing tricks on her or was it truly God communicating with her?

Cagily she opened the pages of her bible and whispered to herself, "Matthew, Mark, Luke," remembering the order of the gospels she had known since Sunday school. She found the book of Luke and proceeded to search for chapter eighteen.

As she did she heard the softest voice in her head say the words,

"It's the same, Lisa!" As soft as they were, she felt the words resounding in her head and overwhelmed her spirit. Her heart rate increased. She could feel excitement brewing up inside her.

"What is the same as what?" she asked out loud, causing Josh to turn and look at her,
somewhat concerned at mummy talking to herself again. Lisa continued to search... chapter 16, 17, 18! Verse 24, 26, 27... there it was! She read to herself, 'Jesus replied, "What is impossible with men is possible with God!"'

"Oh my God!" Lisa cried. "Oh my God!"

The boys both turned away from the TV they had been so engrossed in and stared at mummy. They had never heard her swear before. They often heard 'Oh my God!' said on TV many times but never from the mouth of their mother.

Lisa, seeing how shocked they both were responded to their look of horror and said,

"I wasn't swearing at God, Joshua, Luke, I was telling him how fantastic He is!"
That satisfied the boys and they smiled at each other and turned back to the television as if nothing had happened. Lisa fell to her knees. Any doubt that she had before had now been totally stripped away. God Almighty, the maker of Heaven and Earth, was talking to her.

She had never experienced anything like this. If He had ever tried to talk to her before she didn't know, but now she knew that this was Him. Bewildered, she knelt on the floor, not knowing what to do or say. God was telling her the same thing again. The passage and things that had happened on Wednesday and then the card from Charles, and now this!

Suddenly she felt the need to bow her head in submission and lift her arms. She knew she was in His presence. It was amazing. She could feel Him in the room with her. It almost felt like she was basking in a warm glow of energy; an immense power that she had never known before. It was beautiful. So powerful, yet gentle.

She held her hands as though ready to receive something. A warmth came to her hands and she felt something in her hand, as though she was holding a pebble off the beach on a sunny day. She opened her eyes and looked at her hands. There was nothing there to see but she could certainly feel it.

The power gradually subsided leaving her with a feeling of gratitude. Tears fell down her cheek, as a broad smile enveloped her face. She felt that God had given her something, equipping her. For what she had no idea. She got up off her knees and went into the kitchen and sat at the table. She felt drained and yet totally exhilarated. Her notebook lay in front of her on the table. She opened the pages and read the scribbled notes she had made before. She took the small pencil that lived in the spine of the notebook and began to write.

Words just seemed to flow from her hand. The story of meeting Charles, his card and then what had happened today. As she wrote, she could see the connection with everything that was happening. It was becoming obvious that God was speaking to her but she wasn't fully sure what He was saying. She questioned prayerfully under her breath,

"What are You saying Father? And why do I need to be powerful at all?" Lisa desperately wanted a reply. But nothing. What did He want her to do? She needed to talk to someone, but who?

There was no point talking to Dan; he would just laugh at her and call her crazy. What about her Pastor?

"Maybe," she thought but then she realised that she had never really had a proper conversation with him, so maybe not. "Tom and Jan?" She dismissed that thought very quickly. "What about Charles?" And as soon as she thought about Charles, the whole thing about calling him started again, which was the very reason she had picked up the bible in the first place - to try and distract herself.

She came to the same conclusion as before: that she should wait until church to speak to Charles. After all, it was Saturday night now and church was in the morning. It felt like waiting for Christmas morning on Christmas eve as a child; every minute seemed to be a fully conscious one. She sat back in the cosy lounge with her two boys, noticing the 'tick tock' of the clock on the wall, over the sound of the TV, as the pendulum swung from side to side, each second seeming to drag on and on.

She was startled by the sound of a key in the door. It was Dan. An automatic knot of tension tightened in her stomach as she wondered what kind of mood he was in. He went into the kitchen and grabbed two beers from the fridge and staggered into the lounge, the smell of cigarettes and alcohol following him. He took the TV remote, slumped in the chair and turned the channel over to find something for himself to watch. The boys turned and stared at him in disapproval at their programme coming to such an abrupt end.

"Time for bed, boys!" Lisa intervened, avoiding the danger of any possible trouble. "Come on, let's go!" They were such good boys, hardly complaining at all about their entertainment for the day ending so suddenly. Lisa took them upstairs and got them ready for bed.

It was sad for Lisa that she couldn't speak with her husband;

she longed to be able to just have a conversation with someone close so that she could really pour her heart out.

She came back downstairs and sat on the sofa. She looked over at Dan in his chair, watching the football repeats with a can of beer in his hand and an already empty one on the arm of the chair. She found herself questioning why they had let things get they were between them. What had gone wrong? Was she the reason for their lack of a relationship?

He turned to her and blurted out,

"What are you looking at? What have I done now?"

"Nothing! sorry!" Lisa replied apologetically. "Nothing."

She got up off sofa and quietly left the room, whispering, "Goodnight, Dan," as she left, to which she got a grunt in reply.

As she got ready for bed all she had on her mind was the events of the last few days. Was she going crazy? In the past she would have questioned her own sanity but she had hard evidence. She had the card from Charles and all that she had written in her notebook. She thanked God for it. She looked at the card intently and the notes she had made before snuggling down to sleep, excited about the day ahead.

***

In the morning when she arrived at the church, by the look of the car park she was one of the first there. She sat in the car for a brief moment, closed her eyes and asked God for the strength and wisdom to achieve all she needed to that day. Then she helped the boys out of the car and walked across the car park towards the main entrance. Sam, the security man, unlocked the doors as they approached the foyer and joyfully shouted,

"My, my, Lady Lisa, you are here early today and don't you and your boys look smart!" He always called her 'lady', saying that she should have been one but she just lacked the manor house.

"It's a special occasion, Sam!" replied Lisa, playing along with him.

Sam teased her, "So, who are you meeting up with, eh?"

"Just God, Sam, just God!" Lisa laughed.

"Amen to that Lady Lisa, Amen!" chuckled Sam.

"Actually, Sam," Lisa continued, "I'm waiting for a friend who is coming here for the first time today, so I'm going to put the boys in the crèche and wait here with you if that's okay? Are the nursery leaders here yet?" He replied,

"They certainly are, Lisa. I'll wait with you, my Lady!"

"Thank you, Sam?" Lisa replied with a smile, walking away down the corridor.

The boys ran off to play with the massive selection of toys in the crèche and Lisa said her hellos to the ladies there and then walked back to the entrance.

She stood there with Sam for the next twenty-five minutes with no sign of Charles anywhere. She watched every car that arrived and checked several times in the sanctuary too. Still no Charles. She had a sinking feeling that he wasn't going to be there for whatever reason. Maybe she had put him off going to church by the way she had sped off when he handed her the card or maybe Tom and Jan had just put him off church forever. Whatever it was, he wasn't there and it was certainly frustrating her. She needed to speak to him!

"You'd better go in, Lisa!" Sam remarked. "Looks like you've been stood up!"

"Very funny, Sam!" said Lisa with a half-smile. "I will in a moment, I'm just going to go to the ladies room, let me know if anyone else arrives and if they do could you put them at the back?"

"Of course, Lady Lisa, of course!" Sam agreed and bowed in his usual manner as Lisa went off down the corridor.

She went into the ladies room and into a cubicle there. She looked around the bare walls and noticed there was a small area of graffiti at the top of the cubicle wall. Her first thought was that of disgust, wondering who would deface the walls of a church, especially in the ladies? But then curiosity got the better of her. Being only five feet four inches tall she couldn't read it from where she stood, so she put the toilet lid down to stand on it so she could take a closer look. She let out an audible gasp in sheer shock and surprise.

"What!" she cried. "It can't be! Oh God! What is going on?" Almost unable to believe what she was reading, she read the words out loud. "You -" she hesitated, "- are far more powerful than you have been led to believe!"

She didn't know what to think. Straight away she thought Charles must have been in the ladies toilet, writing on the wall!

"What is the matter with the guy?" she thought. "Why in here of all places?" She had a picture in her mind of Charles, a tall, sophisticated, well-groomed guy with a marker pen, sneaking into the ladies and vandalizing the wall. It didn't take many seconds for her to realize how crazy that thought was.

What was going on? She looked at it over and over again, inspecting it closely as though looking for clues. As she was studying the script, it suddenly struck her that Charles had never stepped foot in that church building before - at least, she knew that this was his first Sunday. It couldn't have been him unless he had crept into the ladies room mid-week to do the dirty deed. It just couldn't have been him, but if it wasn't Charles then who was it?

More questions filled her mind.

She washed her hands and looked at herself in the mirror. She looked shocked, quite pale. She sat down on a chair in the rest room trying to pull herself together. The next second, she heard voices in the corridor, getting louder and coming towards the toilets. She got up quickly and hurried out, only to meet the pastor's wife, Sally, and the church secretary at the door. Sally sheepishly glanced at Lisa, hardly able to look her in the eyes. Lisa mumbled a quick "Hiya!" so as not to appear rude and hurried off down the corridor without turning around. Still shocked by the writing on the wall, she headed for the main door.

As she approached Sam still waiting at the doors, it struck her how odd Sally seemed to be with her. She was normally so friendly with her and always had something to say.

Sam remarked, "Are you Okay, Lady Lisa? You look like you have seen a ghost!"

"Something like that, Sam," Lisa replied. "I think I need some fresh air!"

She pushed the door open and stepped outside into the sunshine of that beautiful, crisp spring Sunday morning. Sam went out with her and enquired of her health again.

"I'm fine, Sam, really. I just need some air!" Lisa insisted. Sam, still not convinced, stood with her and held her arm. Lisa smiled and said,

"Really, Sam, I just need to see Charles!"

"Charles, is that who you're waiting for?" asked Sam. He paused, thought a moment then said, "You don't mean Charles Michaels, do you?"

"Sam! Do you know Charles?" asked Lisa, in a surprised tone of voice.

"Why yes, Lady Lisa, he's my nephew! He's just moved into town. He's the new manager at the food plant down at Dover Street," Sam informed her. "You should have told me who you were waiting for. He told me he wasn't going to be here this morning. He has to sort out some rotas down at the plant but he's going to be here for the evening service."

A feeling of relief and frustration hit Lisa immediately. Relief in that at least Charles hadn't left town and frustration because now she had to wait another six hours before she could talk to him.

"So, you're the young lady he asked about, who he met at the bible study the other night?" said Sam putting two and two together. "Now that makes sense. He was very impressed with you!"

"I don't know about that, Sam, but I do know that I need to talk to him about something urgently!" Lisa continued. "Please don't say anything to him if you see him, I'll come down later and see him then."

She took a deep breath of fresh air and said, "Sam, I think I'm going to get the boys and take them home. I'll catch the message tonight."

She spun around and marched off down the corridor to the crèche, reappearing a few minutes later with a boy in each hand.

"See you later Sam, God bless!" said Lisa walking briskly to her car.

"God bless you too, Lady Lisa! Bye boys!" shouted Sam. They waved back and got in the car.

She arrived home to be greeted by Dan cleaning his pick-up truck.

"Oooh, look at you!" he laughed. "All dressed up for church? If I didn't know you better I'd think you were seeing someone!"

Lisa walked straight past him, not responding to his attempts to wind her up and went inside the house with the boys.

She paced around for most of that afternoon, not knowing what to do with herself. She couldn't figure out what was going on. As she went about her usual Sunday routine all she could think about was what God was suddenly doing in her life. She realized that for God to arrange for a few words to appear on a toilet wall

26

was hardly 'parting the Red Sea', but the fact that this was another message from Him to her was still astonishing.

"Why me?" she kept asking herself and God at the same time. "Why choose me?"

Lisa wrote everything down in her notebook, which was now starting to get quite exciting. Then she hid it away in her closet; the last thing she needed was for Dan to find it and make fun of her for it. He would be sure to question her on Charles's card and what was her relationship with him, as innocent as it may be. She just didn't need the hassle. There were more important things to be dealing with.

Dan went off to work without a goodbye and Lisa got on the phone to call Sophie.

"Can you come tonight for a couple of hours? Oh great! Thanks. See you at six. Bye!" was the brevity of the conversation with the angelic babysitter and Lisa headed upstairs to get ready again. She noticed herself in the mirror, looking much more confident again and it brought a smile to her face. Life was getting so exciting for Lisa. She couldn't wait to see what was going to happen next.

Sophie arrived and went into the lounge with the boys who let out squeaks in unison as they saw their number one teenager buddy. Lisa gave the boys a kiss, picked up her keys and left the house. Out again and on a mission!

She stopped for petrol on the way to church and while filling up, she noticed a pick-up dash past which looked just like Dan's. She looked puzzled for a second because, if it was Dan, why wasn't he at work? The shop he worked in was nowhere near here!

Her quandary was interrupted by a man tapping her on the shoulder and saying,

"Your tyre is down, Lady! You'll need to change that! Would

you like any help?"

Lisa put the petrol gun back and went to the front of her car and looked in despair at the flat tyre and cried,

"Oh no! Why now! Oh, could you? Thank you so much!"

Now she was going to be late. It felt like somebody didn't want her to go that night and it took what seemed an age to change the tyre but in twenty minutes it was done. After thanking the man, Lisa sped off down the motorway towards the church. She parked and ran towards the building blipping the alarm fob of her car on the way.

She could see Sam standing at the door of the church with a tall, suited man. She slowed her trot down to a casual walk so as not to seem too eager.

It was Charles! At last!

"He is real and not just a messenger from God," she thought to herself. Everything inside her wanted to run up and give this man a hug as though he was a long-lost friend, but she resisted and played it cool.

"Hello again, Sam," she said calmly.

"Hello, Lady Lisa. Twice in one day, God must be really getting to you!" Sam replied, teasing as usual.

"Hello Charles, good to see you again," Lisa said shaking his hand.

"And you, Lisa! Sam says you would like to talk to me about something?" Charles replied. Lisa looked at Sam, knowing that she had asked Sam not to say anything but he just smiled back at her with his cheeky grin and a 'job done' air about him. She turned to Charles.

"Oh yes, Charles, shall we?" continued Lisa as she directed him down the corridor away from Sam, so as not to be overheard, towards the main doors of the Sanctuary. They stopped just outside the double doors, where they could hear the service going on. She looked at him and said,

"It's about the words you wrote on the back of your business card. You said that God gave them to you?"

"Oh yes, I'm sure of that," said Charles. "Although what they mean to you, I have no idea. I'm just the messenger, you know!"

"Oh, okay," replied Lisa disappointedly. "I thought you may have been able to throw some light on the whole subject."

"Not really," he said as he held the door open for Lisa to go in to the service. Lisa thanked him and they went in and found a couple of seats at the back.

The message was nearly over so it was hard to really get into what the speaker was saying and Lisa wasn't very interested anyway. She sat there recovering from the disappointment of Charles's lacklustre response. She had so hoped for more from him than just, 'I'm just the messenger.' She wanted to talk everything through with somebody sympathetic to her thoughts.

She kept thinking but what about the ladies room? And the bible readings? Maybe she was making far more of this than it really was. Maybe it was just coincidental. All this was spinning around in her head when everybody stood up and applauded. The message was over and everyone started to sing the last song, whatever it was. Lisa got up quickly and said a short sharp goodbye to Charles. He made a vain attempt to say something, but Lisa was gone. She went straight past Sam without saying a word to him and ran off across the car park to her car. She jumped in and drove off down the road towards home.

"What a waste of time that was!" she cried out as she drove. "God, what is going on?"

Chapter 3

Sheep on a Train

The battle in her head was raging. Surely these happenings couldn't all be a coincidence! She drove past the end of her road and down to the lake, needing some time to think about everything. It was only a few miles away from home and it always seemed so peaceful there.

She stopped by the waterfront and switched the engine off. She rolled her window down. It was so silent and still. Nothing could be heard other than the sound of the water lapping against the shore.

As she sat and stared into the ether, tossing around the events of the last few days. She felt so alone with the whole thing. The words from Charles's card and the toilet wall kept going around and around in her mind. She desperately needed to talk to someone about this but it seemed like there was no-one now.

She had hoped to confide in Charles but now she felt that even he wouldn't take her seriously. She felt confused and a little bewildered. Apart from God, she had no-one to talk to. She sat there for a while, chatting away to God when she suddenly felt the urge to go home. Maybe Sophie needed to get home; it was a school day tomorrow, after all. She thanked God for listening and started the engine, reversed away from the lake and headed towards home.

As she pulled up onto the driveway outside the house she noticed that Dan wasn't back from work yet, which was a relief because she didn't really want to talk to him right now and have to deal with any of his smart remarks. She put the key in the door and went in.

Sophie got up from the sofa in the lounge when she heard the door open and came to meet Lisa in the hall. "Hello Mrs Jeffreys, have you had a good time at church?" asked Sophie politely, clutching something in her hand.

"Yes, thank you," replied Lisa. "Has everything been okay while I've been out? Have the boys gone to bed okay?"

"Oh yes, they have been great as usual!" replied Sophie. "The only thing is though…" She left a deliberate pause and in a questioning tone of voice, which grabbed Lisa's attention immediately.

"What, Sophie? Tell me!"

"Well…" continued Sophie. "A man dressed in a suit showed up about twenty minutes ago, asking for you. I told him you hadn't returned from church yet. He looked a little stressed, Lisa, like it was kind of urgent. Anyway, he gave me this and asked if you would call the moment you go back.

"So here!"

She handed Lisa a familiar business with the name 'Charles Michaels' with the words Call me! and an 'x' written on the back.

"Who is he, Lisa, or is it none of my business?" she enquired.

"Oh, don't worry, Sophie, it's just someone from Church but I can't think what he wants. Oh well, I'll give him a call in a minute and find out," Lisa replied and smiled at Sophie. "Did you bring a coat?"

Sophie took the hint and got her things together. Lisa handed her a £20 note.

"Wow thank you, Lisa!" said a grateful Sophie, it was twice as much as usual.

"That's fine, Sophie," replied Lisa, "I may be needing you

more than usual."

"Anytime!" said Sophie, and they said goodnight.

The door closed behind Sophie and Lisa frantically searched for the phone. She eventually found it in the lounge under a cushion and looked at the number on the card and started to tap in the numbers on the phone keyboard, then stopped and hung up.

What was she doing?
Who was this guy?
What if he was just hitting on her?

It certainly didn't seem like it but if he was, she would give him a piece of her mind. She had to call! She had to find out what was happening! She started to dial again. She completed the number and put the phone to her ear.

It was ringing. She felt really nervous about calling. She wasn't used to calling men for a start, and particularly ones that she hardly knew. It felt sort of wrong but right at the same time. She needed to talk to someone. Who else did she have?

"Hello?" answered a female voice.

"Oh!" responded Lisa, expecting Charles to answer. "Is that 340 404?"

"Yes, it is," replied the woman. "Do you want to speak to Charles?"

"Yes please, if he is there?"

"He sure is! Hang on I'll get him for you." She heard the woman calling Charles and then a muffled response from a man's voice.

Who was this woman?
What was she doing at Charles's house?
I thought he was single?
Is he a complete liar?

A myriad of thoughts went through Lisa's mind in what must have

32

only been seconds. Charles's deep, slightly out-of-breath voice interrupted her questions.

"Lisa! How are you?" and before she could reply, he hurriedly continued. "I'm so glad you rang, I need to speak to you! There's more to this than you think, but I've been trying to wrap my brain around some things myself, which is why I couldn't say too much about it on Sunday! Can we meet up somewhere, as soon as possible?"

"Well," replied Lisa hesitantly. "Well, yes I guess so. When and where did you have in mind?"

She so wanted to ask him who the woman was at his house but felt she should leave that for now.

"Can we meet after work tomorrow at say six-thirty at the café bar on Holborn street?" said Charles with what sounded like a hint of desperation in the tone of his voice.

"Yes, I'm sure that will be fine as long as my babysitter can come. If there's a problem, I'll call. She put the phone down and immediately began to feel nervous. What was it about this guy that made her act so strangely! When she thought about Charles, she was almost intimidated by him but in another way, she felt at ease and very comfortable. Once again, her mind began to fill with questions. Who was that woman - was it his wife? Has he told her that he is meeting me? Does he really have something important to tell me or is he a creep? Should I be meeting him this way or should I call him back and tell him to meet me at church? But how do I wait that long!"

"Stop!" she said out loud, just as Dan came in through the front door.

"Stop what?" he questioned anxiously.

"Oh nothing! Nothing for you to worry about! I'm off to bed, goodnight!" Lisa said sharply on way up the stairs. She suddenly stopped in her tracks.

"Actually, Dan I do need to ask you something." And in one breath, as fast as her mouth would carry her words she said, "I know that you are going to think this is stupid anyway so I won't bore you with all the details but God has been speaking to me a lot lately and then as it turns out He has also apparently given somebody a message for me, they have asked to meet me tomorrow night but the thing is, it's a man. I didn't want to go without asking you or without you knowing, is it okay with you?"

Dan replied in an annoyed tone,

"Whatever, I don't care about all your weird God stuff. Do what you like, just leave me out of it. Can I go relax now?"

"Yes, sorry," she replied and continued upstairs. As she got ready for bed, Lisa's mind was filled with so many questions.

What did Charles have to do with any of this?

What was God saying to her and why on earth was Dan dressed so smart tonight? He never wears anything smart, never mind a jacket! And how come he didn't even show a hint of interest in the fact that she was meeting a man? In the past he would at least made fun of her or looked for an argument.

'Oh well, I need to sleep,' Lisa thought to herself and climbed in bed. As soon as her head hit the pillow she drifted off to sleep.

Hours later, Lisa woke and immediately sat upright. She looked over at the clock. It was 6am. She had been dreaming and it wasn't just any old dream. It had been very vivid. It just had to mean something but she had no idea what. Was God speaking to her in her dreams now?

She dreamt that sheep were travelling on the flat bed of a train and they were all sitting together as couples. As she watched the sheep sitting, chatting away, enjoying their journey, blissfully ignorant of three big black wolves who were waiting to attack the

34

train. They moved in on the train and one wolf attacked a sheep and devoured it. She even saw the sheep's feet sticking out of the wolf's mouth. Then she woke.

She heard the words in her head. "Tell Pastor Adams!"

Now she had even more on her mind. With everything else that was going on that she couldn't understand and now this. What was the dream saying? Was God trying to talk to her through the dream? Would she make a fool of herself if she told Pastor Adams? Should she tell Charles about the dream? Would he think that she was going crazy? Would that be the end of their friendship?

"Oh, my word!" she said to herself. "I have to get out of here!"

It was the beginning of half-term holidays for the boys, so she had the added thoughts in her mind of how to entertain them for the day. There was only one thing for it. It seemed to work every time she had a crisis or stressful situation.

"I'll go shopping!" she said assertively, and jumped out of bed. She showered, got the boys ready, then got dressed herself. They all had breakfast together and Lisa called Sophie to check she was okay for the evening then they all jumped in the car and headed off to Tolchester, or 'Big Town' as they affectionately called the only nearby town that contained what Lisa would describe as real shops.

Tolchester was about half an hour from Hightown but a pleasant drive along the coast; time well spent as far as Lisa was concerned.

She parked in front of the shopping centre and they walked off together into the myriad of shops, to partake in, what Lisa believed was therapeutic activities. The boys soon found themselves sporting matching cardigans and Lisa rewarded herself with a new top, a new bag, a lovely black-and-white dress, all for under £100, which was graciously paid for by her credit card. She had done particularly well, because part of the therapy and to truly gain from the trip, she needed to not only obtain new items but to see how much she could save as well, so as not to feel a well of guilt afterwards.

They were enjoying a spot of lunch together in the busy food court when Luke let out a loud shout of, "Daddy!" which startled everyone within a twenty-foot radius. He was convinced that he had seen Dan over by the coffee shop but no matter how hard they all looked none of them could see him again. He had either gone or Luke had been completely mistaken. Lisa was relieved.

"What would Dan be doing in Big Town?" she thought to herself. "He'll be at work!"

Dan had been behaving differently the last few days and even though things had been 'spiky' as usual between them, she had noticed that he seemed to be sober more often, which of course was a good thing but just not Dan. Then, of course, there was how he was dressed last night. Whatever was going on, though, she certainly didn't want him around while they were involved in shopping therapy. Luke must have been wrong.

Lisa finished her lunch, tidied the table and decided to head back home due to the expression on the boys faces when she mentioned 'round two'. They started to head towards the car.

Just as they were passing Lisa's favourite shoe store, a pair of heels sparkled at Lisa, grabbing her attention instantly.

"Wow! Look at them, boys!" she cried enthusiastically. "Don't you think mummy would look great in them?"

The boys were starting to get a little wriggly after what was, to them, a hard day's shopping, mixed with the fact that they were on their way down from the sugar high from lunch, their response was a little apathetic to say the least, but Lisa soon had them through the door and into the shop's own little play area.

"Could I try these in a size five, please," Lisa asked the shop assistant.

"Sure, won't be a moment," replied the chewing assistant and went into the stock room. Lisa sat down on a bench, watching the boys almost reluctantly playing and waited for the girl to return with her shoes.

"If you want them just bring them over to the till," the assistant said as she handed the box over to Lisa, who graciously relieved her of them, smiling as she did. What happened next could never be explained by Lisa apart from it having God involved in it somewhere.

As she sat there and leaned forward to fasten the straps on that gorgeous pair of shoes, she felt something physically being pushed into her back pocket.

She instantly stood up and cried out,

"Hey! Get off!" She spun around, not knowing what she would see, whether it was be one of the boys messing around or some pervert feeling her behind. As she stood there, a little taller than before, she was astounded! Nobody was there! The boys were still playing and the assistant was serving someone over at the till. There was no-one within twenty feet of her. She questioned an elderly man who was staring at her because of her shouting out.

"Did you see that?" she quizzed him.

"See what?" the innocent guy remarked.
Lisa asked again,

"Did you see someone put something in my pocket?"

"No madam, there's been no-one anywhere near you, not that I saw!" He grabbed his wife and hurriedly left the store. Lisa reached to her back pocket and felt a small rectangular shape of something in it.

Now, Lisa never used any of her pockets, especially the back ones. She always maintained that placing things in the pockets would spoil the look of her jeans. However, there was something in hers, right there and then. She tentatively put her hand into her pocket and pulled out a folded-up piece of paper. It had been folded many times. She started to unfold the paper. Thoughts were flying through her head.

What was it?

Was it a threatening letter from someone, or perhaps a ransom note? But she could see both of the boys playing with building blocks and if someone had kidnapped Dan, well, they could beg forever.

What on earth could it be?

She unfolded the last part of the paper and sat down sharply. It was a rough piece of paper, not dirty but just kind of well used, but on it was scrawled the words,

"You are far more powerful than you have been led to believe!" She could not believe what she was reading.

She sat there in the store, with those beautiful new shoes on, dumbstruck, feeling like the wind had been knocked out of her. She stared at the paper in disbelief, looking at the handwriting on it. Someone had written on that rough piece of paper.

Who? Was it God? Was that His written hand?

She slipped off her new shoes, hurriedly put on her old ones and headed for the till.

"Come on, boys! Quickly!" she shouted. "Time to go!"

She handed her credit card over to the assistant, tapped her pin number into the machine and left the store with a boy in each hand, loaded with bags. She dashed through the busy shopping centre, almost dragging the boys, running away from what she had no idea but she needed to get out of there, that was for certain.

She unlocked the car and lifted them into their seats, strapped them in and shut the door behind them. She sat in the driver's seat and breathed a sigh of relief.

She started the car and pulled out of the car park and onto the road to Hightown, wasting no time.

Her heart was racing again, as she drove down the road; her head full of questions and bewilderment. She looked at her speedometer. She was speeding! She never did that, especially not with the boys in the car. Realising how fast she was travelling, she slowed down and took a deep breath. She adjusted her rear-view mirror to see into the back of the car. The boys were fast asleep after their day of shops and sugar, completely unaware of their Mum's imitation of Stirling Moss.

When they got home, the boys ran into the lounge and turned on the TV. Lisa went into the kitchen, made herself a cup of tea and sat down at the kitchen table, bemused, not knowing what to say or do. She took the piece of paper and looked at it again. Immediately, thoughts flashed through her mind.

Who was responsible for this? It had to be God!
There was no-one else there!
What other explanation could there be?
Who would ever believe this if she told anybody?

She grabbed her black notebook and wrote down all the events of the day, from the dream about the sheep to how she felt about the events on her shopping trip. She put the piece of paper inside as a bookmark and closed it. She put it in her new bag to take with her later.

She started to calm down as she thought about possibly being able to share this with Charles and hoping that God had told him something that would begin to make sense of all of this. To occupy herself she began trying on all her new clothes. It was a

39

wonderful distraction from all the craziness of the day that she'd had.

Her personal fashion parade made time pass quickly and it would soon be time to leave. She was almost ready when she felt the urge to pray, so she sat on the corner of the bed, hung her head, closed her eyes and spoke to her heavenly Father.

With her hands clasped between her knees she asked for guidance, strength and the right words to say. She asked Him to be with her and stay by her side throughout the hours ahead. She felt a warmth and a comfort which can only come from God, that caused her to smile with a knowing confidence that He really was there with her.

"Bless you, Father. In Jesus' name, Amen."

The timing of the doorbell couldn't have been better and hurried down to open the front door. As expected it was Sophie.

"Look at you, Lisa!" exclaimed Sophie, looking her up and down. "You look fabulous! That dress! And look at your shoes!"

"Why, thank you, Sophie," replied a beaming Lisa. "New today! I'll just pop upstairs and finish getting ready then I'll be off."

"Doing anything special tonight?" Sophie shouted after her running upstairs. Lisa shouted back, knowing that this could be one of the most important meetings of her life,

"Not particularly!"

Chapter 4

The Dream Explained

Lisa was feeling nervous again. As she drove down Holborn Street heading towards the café bar, she realised that she was going to have to tell Charles everything. She didn't want to appear foolish but she was going to have to go through all her experiences with him, lock stock and barrel.

"He must know something to say that there's more to this than I think! Yes! He must!" she agreed with herself. She knew it was time to relax and stop stressing about it all. God was involved and one thing she knew was that her heavenly Father was with her and that He loved her.

She could see the café bar ahead on the left.

"Here we go!" she said to herself and pulled into the car park and parked up. She could see Charles waiting by the door for her.

"Wow, a gentleman!" she thought. "So rare!" She smiled to herself and got out of the car and walked towards the entrance where Charles was waiting.

He looked immaculate! It was exactly 6:30 p.m. She was right on time, but he was early.

"Lisa! So good to see you!" said Charles, shaking her hand, formally.

"You too, Charles." Lisa replied. Charles opened the door for Lisa to go in and they were instantly approached by a waitress who showed them to a table next to another couple.

"Can we have a more private one please," asked Charles.

"Of course, sir," said the waitress. "Follow me." She took them to a table in the far corner of the room.

"Thank you," said Charles. "That's perfect!"

Lisa felt like she knew this man so well, but she'd only met him twice and very briefly on both occasions. They sat down and studied the menus, passing small talk and niceties before ordering their food and drinks. There was a brief pause in their conversation and Charles, lowering his voice a little, got more serious.

"Lisa," he paused. "There are important things we need to talk about." Lisa thought to herself,

"Tell me about it!" but she just smiled and nodded and let Charles continue.

She was more desperate to hear what Charles had to say than to tell her side of the events. After all, she knew her story. It was his she wanted to know about and how all this might make more sense.

The waitress brought their food and drinks, which they thanked her for. Charles continued,

"God has some great things for you, Lisa. You need to realise why I gave you my card with that message on."

He told Lisa that God clearly spoke to him about giving that message to her and that the first time He had spoken to him was months ago.

"And He insisted that I give you those exact words! I don't even recall writing the words on the card! I note down lots of things that inspire me, maybe it was one of those notes. Anyway, I pulled the card out of my wallet one day and I knew I had to pass this message on to someone" he said. "God had told me that I should take the transfer to Hightown that I'd been offered and that once I had done that, I needed to look for a young lady at a bible study group."

Charles smiled as he related. "I remember questioning God about which study group I should go to and how I'd recognise you! Oh dear, my lack of faith!"

Then Charles looked at Lisa and said,

"But I just knew it was you, Lisa, the moment I laid eyes on you. I can't explain it, somehow, I just knew!" He laughed. "But it's fortunate that there aren't too many bible classes in Hightown!" He told her how he'd gone to her church first, purely because his uncle Sam worked there and he didn't know anywhere else. He said,

"Sam put me in touch with Tom and Jan and the rest is history."

"Thank you for that, Charles," Lisa replied. "It's so good to hear your side of this whole thing but you should eat a little now before your food goes cold! I have a lot to tell you, but I am totally impressed and thank you for your obedience to God! Not many people would do what you have done!"

She went on to passionately express the whole story, from the bible passages standing out and the alien cartoon right up to the incident in the shoe shop, only to be interrupted by the waitress checking on their food and drinks. Charles was amazed as Lisa relayed her story. He hadn't realised what God had been doing with Lisa at all. He listened intently, only interrupting her occasionally in response to God's miracles and on the odd occasion to make his excuses.

"Well I couldn't really say anything at Church because there were too many people there and if any of this should have been overheard by anyone else, well, you know, sometimes Christians can be very judgmental." They laughed and giggled like a couple of teenagers relating all their stories and events.

"And I thought you'd been in the ladies toilet scribbling on the wall!"

Lisa felt so much better. She had been able to get everything off her chest with Charles and more importantly, she now had a 'partner in crime' whom God had obviously called to be there with her. They were both on a mission now. To do what? They had no idea.

The subject of Lisa's dream was high on the agenda. Charles felt it a matter of urgency that she should relay the dream to Pastor Adams. Lisa admitted that she was frightened to, but in the end agreed with Charles and said she would make an appointment with him in the morning.

Neither Lisa or Charles really knew what to say about the messages of being more powerful than she had been led to believe but they both agreed that it was God's doing and He was emphasizing this to Lisa, for some reason, even though this was a message for all people and not just for her.

Lisa confessed to Charles that she had been put down by somebody or something most of her life and even though she felt she was made for better things; she never really thought her life would ever amount to much.

"So, why me?" Lisa asked Charles. He replied,

"Well, my answer to that would be, why not you?" He deliberated. "Look Lisa, I believe this: God looks for people who have the right heart. It's your availability he wants, not your ability. When you look at the scriptures you can see many great men and women who had exactly the same question. Moses had a long list of excuses as to why he shouldn't or couldn't set Israel free from slavery in Egypt. Then, there was Abraham, Noah, David, Isaiah, Jeremiah, Peter, Matthew, Paul and loads more were all used by God because of one thing: their hearts!

So, Lisa, you're no different. Right through the ages you can see God using ordinary people with extraordinary passion. He knows you inside out. He knows you can do whatever He's asking you to do and has picked you because you have the right heart."

"Wow, you should be a preacher, Charles, thank you." They both laughed. Charles carried on.

"Just keep praying and doing as He says. Let me know what's happening and I'll keep you informed if I get any else." They finished off their meals and got up to go to the till.

Lisa went to the ladies while Charles was paying and while she was in there, remembered one more question she needed to ask Charles. He was just putting his wallet away in his pocket when she came out of the toilets.

"Charles?" she asked quietly. He replied,

"Yes Lisa, what is it?" She paused, not wanting to upset him, but she had to know. She asked,

"Who was the lady that answered your phone the other day?"

"Mrs Brown? She's my housekeeper. Why?" replied Charles with a puzzled expression. The relief on Lisa's face must have been visible. Somewhere deep inside she'd had the thought that he must be with somebody. She had overheard a conversation at the bible class where he'd said he was single, but for Lisa, it was hard to trust men, certainly with the experience she'd had with them. All she'd ever known was disappointment and being let down by Dan, so it was hard for her to believe that he would be any different. She answered,

"Oh no reason really, I was just checking that you hadn't got a secret wife stashed away! I mean, if you're married it's fine, but I don't want any secret meetings, you know? So, I hoped that you had told your wife, I mean the one that you don't have… you know what, I'll just shut up now."
They both laughed.

"Hardly!" said Charles holding the door to let Lisa walk

45

through.

"Thank you so much for such a great evening," Lisa said as they walked from the building.

"Goodnight Lisa," said Charles.

"Goodnight Charles," Lisa responded. Charles leaned forward to kiss Lisa on the cheek but before he could, she had turned away and was walking towards her car.
She got in her car and gave him a little wave as she left the car park.

"Bye Lisa," whispered Charles to himself as he watched her drive away. "Lord, that's some woman!"

***

At home, Lisa said goodnight to Sophie, watched her walk home and closed the door behind her.

The house was silent. How lovely it was to have a little peace and quiet. She made herself a hot chocolate and sat down in the lounge and contemplated what had happened.

"How did this ever happen to me? What does God want me to do?" she asked herself.

She was willing and ready, albeit, a little scared and was dreading the thought of calling the Pastor the next day but she knew that it had to be done. It was amazing to her that God would ever choose her to do anything for him, but if that's what He wanted of her, she would be faithful to Him.

It was getting late; almost eleven. Time for bed. As she cleared a few things in the kitchen, she whispered,

"Thank you, Father, for blessing me and the boys so much. I am here for you, always. I love you."

"And I love you," whispered back that now-familiar voice in her head. She climbed the stairs with a smile on her face and peace in her heart.

As she got to the top of the stairs she noticed the two boys in their room. The door was open and she looked in to see them both sleeping soundly. What a peaceful sight it was. A joy to behold.

She also noticed that Dan's door was open. They slept separately these days; it was much easier with his drinking habits, and in reality, their 'marriage' was pretty much over. The light was off. She glanced in, noticing that his room was empty, bed still made.

"He must be working late or at a bar somewhere," she thought to herself and went to her room.

When her head hit the pillow, she felt all she could see and hear were those words, 'You are far more powerful than you have been led to believe.' She fell asleep with them running around and around in her mind like as though it was being fixed into her brain; into her very soul.

She woke before the alarm clock and again instantly recalled a dream that she'd had during the night. It was the sheep and wolves again only this time, somehow weirdly, the sheep that was being attacked and eaten looked familiar. She also recognized one of the wolves that was helping the big black wolf, that devoured the sheep. This wolf was much smaller and weaker, almost like it was an assistant to the big wolf. Again, the words 'Tell Pastor Adams!' were in her head.

She jumped out of bed, got dressed and rushed downstairs. She made herself a coffee and went to get her address book out of the telephone table. There it was: The Pastor's number. She cleaned around the house a little, firing arrow prayers up to her father in heaven, mustering up the courage to call. Eventually she went over to the phone and picked up the receiver.

"Oh well, here goes!" she said out loud to herself and dialled the number. As the phone rang at the other end she found herself feeling anxious. She was asking herself why she felt that way with certain people, when the Pastor answered the phone with a cheery,

"Hello, Pastor Adams speaking!"

Lisa replied. "Hello Pastor, it's Lisa Jeffreys here."

To which he responded,

"Hello Lisa, what can I do for you today?" She continued, "I need to come and see you about something as soon as possible. When would you be able to fit me in? I know you're very busy but I feel it's important." He replied,

"Okay, how about later on this afternoon, say Three o'clock?"

"That would be great! Would it be okay if I brought the boys with me? It's half-term, you know." she asked hopefully.

"Of course, or they can go in the crèche, there's always someone there!" answered Pastor Adams, and the appointment was made. She put the phone down with a sigh of relief. Quite why she had been so worried she had no idea. He seemed such a nice man to talk to.

She went upstairs to wake the boys and dressed but as she went past Dan's room she noticed that his bed was still made. This meant that either Dan had gone to work early and changed the habit of a lifetime and actually made his bed or he hadn't slept in it, and knowing Dan as well as she did, the latter was the obvious answer. She asked herself,

"Where has he been? What is he up to?" then answered herself, "I guess he was drunk and stayed over at one of his drinking buddies!" It was most unusual, even for him, not to let her know. Something seemed wrong, but she wasn't going to let it concern her too much as she had such a lot to try and achieve that day.

On her way to church the boys seemed extra playful in the car. Lisa kept trying to picture the conversation with Pastor, in her mind and trying to figure out what would be a good way of starting the conversation. In the end she decided to just say it as it was. God was telling her to do this, so a pastor would surely understand that and not worry about the eloquence of the messenger. She was finally happy with that, after arguing with herself all the way down the road.

"Quiet, boys! We're here now," said Lisa firmly. No-one could have heard them, as they pulled onto the car park of the church, but she always liked them to be well mannered. The way they behaved in public, she believed, was a reflection on her.

They walked across the car park, down to the entrance and pushed open the front door. There were a few people milling about around the crèche area, so Lisa thought it would be a good idea and beneficial for all concerned, if the boys played in there. There was a young girl at the crèche reception, who signed them in and so off they ran.

Lisa was still a few minutes early, which was normal for her; she would always rather be early and wait, than be late for anything, so she decided to pay a visit to the ladies before seeing the pastor. For two reasons: one being the thought of seeing the pastor made her slightly anxious and secondly, to see the graffiti on the wall again.

She thought she had chosen the same cubicle as before, but there was nothing on any wall so she had a peek in the other two cubicles in there. Nothing! The walls were spotless!

"Maybe I'm in the wrong ladies room!' she thought to herself and went to look for another. She was sure she had chosen the right one first time but she could have been mistaken. The second ladies room was the same. The walls were as clean as new paint. She rushed back to the young girl on crèche reception. "Excuse me but are there other ladies rooms on this level?" she asked her hurriedly.

"No Mrs Jeffreys, there's just the two," replied the girl. "There are two more on the upper level and several more in the office section, but just the two here. Are they not working?"

"No, they're fine I'm sure," Lisa laughed. "It's okay I was

just wondering, thank you!" She thought for a second and asked again. "Erm, I don't suppose you know if they've been re-painted since last Sunday?"

"No. they haven't, Mrs Jeffreys," answered the young girl. "But they will be done again after Christmas."
Lisa smiled and walked away. This would have normally seemed very odd, but with all the happenings of the last week she was beginning to become accustomed to strangeness.

"Wow!" she thought to herself on her way through the corridor towards the office section, "God must have just put it there for me that day! Amazing! I wonder if anyone else saw it?" She knew the answer to the question but put her mind on the task ahead.

She went into the office area and met one of the secretaries at the desk.

"I have a three o'clock appointment with Pastor Adams," she said to the secretary, who replied,

"Mrs Jeffreys, go on through, Pastor is waiting for you."

She walked to the door marked 'Senior Pastor' and timidly knocked on it.

"Come in!" a voice shouted from in the room and she opened the door. Pastor Adams was sat behind his desk. He smiled at Lisa and said,

"Come in and sit down, Lisa, it's nice to see you. Tom and Jan mentioned that you have just started going to their bible study group recently." This was one reason she didn't really like the size of this church. With it being quite large it didn't have the intimacy that smaller churches have sometimes.

"Erm Yes, I've been going for about six weeks now, it's really good."

"Yes, right, good!" replied the pastor, almost embarrassed. "I'm sorry, we have a lot of people here, I lose track sometimes.

Now," he continued, clearing his throat. "What can I help you with?"

Lisa debated with herself. Should she say that she has been having dreams or should she come right out with it and tell him what God told her to say?

"God has been speaking to me through some dreams in the last few days and has told me to tell you about them."

She spoke with an authority that she didn't recognize in herself but to her amazement, as soon as she said, "God has been speaking…" Pastor Adams leaned back in his seat and folded his arms. A frown came on his forehead as he listened. She obediently related the dreams she'd had in great detail, not giving opinion just the facts. The more she talked, the more Pastor Adams seemed to be uncomfortable; squirming in his chair; resting on one arm and then the other. At one point he even looked at the ceiling.

Then suddenly, he abruptly interrupted Lisa and said sharply,

"Look! Mrs Jeffreys, whatever you think you've dreamt about is nothing to do with me or any of my flock! Excuse me for saying this but I am the man of God here! If He's got anything to say about me or any of my flock, He would have told me first, don't you think? Why would he speak through one of my congregation about something that was nothing to do with them? I am the appointed Pastor of this Church and that's the way it works!"

Lisa was shocked by his rudeness but still tried to appeal to him and said,

"I understand that, Pastor, but I really felt that the fact that the sheep was familiar, really stood out, it felt like God was trying to say that I knew the person who was about to be devoured and that…."

He interrupted again,

"Mrs Jeffreys! I'm afraid I have to insist!" He almost snarled

51

and said,

"When I asked you if I could help you with anything, that's what I meant. I didn't expect you to be advising me on how to look after my Church! Now let's end this right here, shall we?! I'm very busy, as you know, and I have a lot of people to see today, so I'll bid you good day if that's okay with you?!"

"Yes, that's fine," replied Lisa, talking as fast as she could, as Pastor Adams was already on his feet and making his way around his desk to show her out, "But just to let you know that it was God that told me to tell you or else I would never have said anything!"

"Goodbye Lisa," said Pastor Adams nonchalantly. "I hope to see you soon." He held the door for her and closed it behind her even before she could say goodbye back.

His attitude completely stunned Lisa.

"Are you alright, Mrs Jeffreys?" enquired the secretary as she walked back through to the reception. "That was quick!"

"Yes, all sorted, thank you," replied Lisa quietly.

Not only had his attitude taken her by surprise, but it really disturbed her that, in her eyes, Pastor Adams was a man way 'up there' in terms of being close to God and from her understanding of scripture, he should be a representative of Almighty God on earth. She felt completely brushed aside by his tone, body language and the words he spoke; as though what she had to say was pointless and meaningless. She knew that the way the Pastor had behaved was not the way the Father is with us. In her opinion a pastor is a shepherd and should care for his flock and not bash them over the head with his superiority to try and make his 'sheep' feel inferior. The rod and staff were to protect the sheep from wolves and danger, not to wallop them.

She collected the boys from the crèche, thanked the leaders there and walked them outside to the car. It was a beautiful day and so she decided to let the lads have a little play on the swing park at the back of the church. She sat on a bench and watched them playing and went over in her head what had just happened. She was supposed to deliver the warning to Pastor, which she did, but she wasn't expecting the result she got.

"Oh well," she said prayerfully. "I'm sorry, Father, if I did anything wrong to upset Pastor Adams. I really didn't mean to, but I have delivered the message!"

Something caught her eye over on the staff car park at the rear of the church. It was Pastor Adams carrying something to his car. He opened the trunk of his Mercedes and put in the object he had been carrying. She looked closer and noticed it was his golf clubs. She felt anger build up inside her.

"Yes, you have got a lot of people to see today, haven't you, Pastor?" Lisa whispered under her breath and smiled. She called the boys as loudly as she could, causing Pastor Adams to turn and see her. He quickly jumped in his car and closed the door. Josh and Luke reluctantly came to her and they walked around to the front of the church and got in their car.

As she drove home she thought to herself,

"So, what now? What happens now? I need to tell Charles! Yes! That's it, tell Charles!"

Chapter 5

More Than She Bargained for at the Supermarket

As much as she wanted to call Charles there and then she decided to play it cool and call him after six when she knew he would be home from work. She took a detour from the road home to do some grocery shopping at the supermarket in town near to the cafe bar on Holborn street that they visited the previous night. It wasn't her local store but she just felt like keeping her head down a little and didn't want to see anyone she knew or have a conversation with someone that may ask her a personal question of any kind.

What had happened with Pastor Adams had surprised her and she felt emotionally bruised and battered. It hurt her that a man in his position wouldn't even listen to what she had to say or take any of it on board. She did however have a peace about her that she had delivered the message. The fact that she had been so rudely brushed off was his problem and not hers. She had done her part and that was all she could do.

It was nice to wander around the aisles for a while with her precious boys just doing the things that mothers do. It had been so crazy lately that she really enjoyed the normality of a little food shopping, especially in a store where people didn't instantly recognise her.

Living in Hightown, as in any small town in Wales, was very much like that. There would always be people around that knew you and all your business and although she would never want to change that, it was nice to have a little respite from it for a short while.

Ironically, just as she was queuing at the checkout keeping the boys hands off the impulse buyer's chocolate bars by the conveyor, she noticed Sally Adams, the pastor's wife, just two people in front, paying for her goods.

Lisa turned her head quickly away and made out that she hadn't seen her. She didn't want to speak to anyone at the moment, especially the wife of the man who had just been so rude to her.

She gazed anywhere and everywhere she could, other than towards the checkout but when she heard a familiar 'clank' of bottles as Sally's goods wobbled down the conveyor, she turned her head slightly back and rolled her eyes towards Mrs Adams. Her eyes seemed at maximum stretch to get a peek at what she thought she had heard.

It was just as she'd thought; Sally Adams had amongst her groceries three bottles of white wine, which were about to be 'bleeped' by the girl on the till. She turned her head slightly to relieve her eyes more than anything but also to get a better look. Then she noticed that not only did she have three bottles of wine amongst her items but also a four pack of beer about to go through as well. Not that Lisa was against having a drink, but she knew that Pastor Adams was teetotal, or at least, that's what he'd said anyway and he had even preached against the evils of alcohol and other addictive substances many times. It seemed very strange that Sally would be a drinker herself in a home that she assumed was so 'anti'.

After today's incident at the church, she didn't know what to believe about Pastor Adams anymore, but she did know that she shouldn't judge Sally, whatever the reason for the booze. She could be buying it for someone else anyway and what was wrong with a little wine.

"Who am I to think or say anything!" she thought and

turned away again so as not to be seen.

Thankfully, Sally took her goods and left without noticing her. It could have been quite awkward. It was, however, really difficult to keep a smile off her face. Even though it was none of her business, she couldn't get it out of her mind. The question of who the beer was for, kept revolving around her head. One thing was for sure, she could never imagine Mrs Sally Adams, first lady at a large church, chairperson with several organizations and Patron of various charitable groups, supping a can of beer in front of the TV watching Match of the Day.

She could be wrong, of course, and like she kept reminding herself, who was she to judge? The fact that she wanted to have a good chuckle at this whole incident made her think even more about how bad she, herself was and that she needed to repent of how much she had enjoyed those thoughts.

Driving home was much more cheerful than the drive down, but should she tell Charles about Sally or would that be just gossiping? Maybe it was more significant than she had first thought. She needed to pray.

She arrived home and let the boys into the house and brought her groceries in. On the second trip to the boot of the car she heard a familiar young voice shout her name.

"Hi Lisa!" It was Sophie, the babysitter. "Do you need me tonight?"

What an angel this girl was. It was something Lisa had been contemplating on the way back from the store; did she need Sophie again tonight and if so, was she asking her to babysit too many times these days? This had answered her question for her.

"You know, I just may!" Lisa shouted back. "I'll give you a call, if that's okay?"

Sophie waved and carried on down the street.

56

What was going to happen tonight? She certainly needed to speak to Charles as soon as possible and face to face would be ideal.

"But what if he's doing something else?" she thought. "Surely, he has a life outside of dealing with me?"

Life was becoming a never-ending stream of questions in her head that she was having to deal with, so different from what it used to be, being a mother and, in her eyes, a failed wife.

She got the last of her groceries into the house and started to put them away in the kitchen cabinets, when the phone rang. It was Charles. It was great to hear his voice.

"Lisa! I was hoping you were at home. I had to call; it's been on my mind all day! How did you get on with Pastor Adams?" he blurted out, without taking a breath, answering another question she'd had in her mind about him not having time for her. She replied,

"Oh! Well, it was interesting to say the least but, Charles, is there anyway, I can talk to you in person rather than over the telephone? I need some advice!" Charles said quickly,

"I was hoping you were going to say that… same place, eight o'clock?"

"Sounds great!" replied Lisa enthusiastically and they hung up. It was incredible for her to think that she could be out two nights consecutively but she knew this was God's work and it needed to be done, plus she really enjoyed that she could at last share her thoughts with someone on the same wavelength.

Sophie agreed to come around early as she had homework to do and she loved to play with Josh and Luke before they went to bed. Lisa sat down in the lounge with the boys and watched cartoons with them for half an hour. They were the apple of her eye and really all she had, so she liked to get involved in their lives as much as she could, even if it was watching superheroes on TV

57

sometimes. Their father was never around, so she had to play his role too sometimes, even though she knew that they needed a man really. She did too.

She cooked dinner for Sophie and the boys, then went upstairs to shower and got ready for the evening. Since this whole episode had begun she had found herself going out so much more than usual.

She questioned herself about whether or not this was right. Her motive was simply to pursue the path that she believed God was leading her on and it seemed that Charles was playing a part in God speaking to her.

The doorbell rang and Lisa ran down the stairs to let Sophie in.

"Maybe I should have a key cut for you, Sophie," Lisa joked. They laughed together. Sophie went in to see the boys who were jumping around the lounge in their pyjamas, excited to have Sophie with them again. They loved playtime with Sophie and having her put them to bed was always a great adventure. They too seemed to be really enjoying this last week or so. They loved Sophie and it was really exciting to be running around with Mummy.

Lisa grabbed her things, shouted goodbye to the kids and left the house. She felt like her life had purpose now. Just being with Charles was exciting and she was really enjoying his company. She couldn't deny that deep down she was developing a connection with him and she knew that she couldn't hide this from God. She prayed while she drove that God would deal with any improper thoughts or feelings that she may have for Charles and that He would bring this friendship to a close in His timing. One thing Lisa was totally confident with was that God loved her and wouldn't allow anything to happen that would hurt her but she also knew that the enemy would love to use this against them in some way to try and ruin God's plans and all that He had been doing.

As she pulled into the car park of the café bar, there was Charles, waiting for her at the door. As she approached him, he opened the door for her. They greeted each other and went in to meet exactly the same waitress that was there last night. Lisa hoped that she wouldn't recognise them.

"Would you like the same seats you had last night?" the waitress asked.

"Oh well!" thought Lisa.

"Yes please!" said Charles and she led them to their seats. Lisa felt good about being with Charles again. Dining out, apart from taking the boys to a fast food restaurant, was an experience she had never really known before. How she wished that she could share such experiences with Dan, but she knew it was never going to happen.

A part of Lisa felt certain that God had connected Lisa and Charles, but, she was uncomfortable with the fact that she was meeting with him so often and developing a bond with him.

They ordered their food and drinks and as soon as the waitress had taken their menus away, Charles wasted no time.

"So, tell me! How did it go? I've been dying to know all day!"

"Not so good really, Charles. To be truthful with you, it was horrible!" She relayed the whole story, blow by blow. She could see by the look on his face that Charles was getting more and more upset as the story unfolded.

"My goodness!" he said sympathetically, "That must have been awful for you. Poor you!"

When she relayed the part about the golf clubs, he hung his head in shame.

"I cannot believe that is the reaction of a man of God, to a Dream! Does he not realize that if it hadn't been for a dream our Saviour could have died as a baby! Not that God would have

59

allowed that to happen but it was a dream that Joseph had that told them to leave Nazareth where they were living at the time and go to Egypt!" Charles was furious. "I feel like giving that man a piece of my mind, Lisa, but I know that's not the way!"

"No, it isn't," Lisa agreed. "But whether I am going back there is another matter."

"Well," replied Charles. "I'm with you, whatever you decide. What about bible class tomorrow, do we go?"

"I really don't know what to do for the best that's why I wanted to talk to you in person," Lisa continued. "We would have been on the phone for hours!"

"Yes!" laughed Charles. "And I wouldn't have been able to see your lovely face!"

It went quiet. Charles's statement had shocked them both it seemed. Lisa looked down sheepishly just as the waitress came with their food. They thanked her and picked up their cutlery.

"Anyway, let's eat," she said.

"Yes, let's," Charles replied. They ate in silence for a few minutes, neither of them knowing what to say.

"How's your steak, Charles?" asked Lisa after a few minutes, to break the awkwardness.

"Oh fine," replied Charles. "How's the chicken?"

"It's great, thank you," she answered with a smile. After a few moments Lisa said,

"Charles?" He swallowed his food and replied,

"Yes?"

"Something else happened today too." Before he could reply she continued. "And I don't want you to think bad of me or anything and I'm not judging anyone or trying to be a gossip and just tell me if you think I'm being wrong in being concerned about what I saw but I have to…"

"Just tell me, Lisa," replied Charles. "I wouldn't think any of

60

those things anyway."

"Well I know you are new at this church and may not realize how much Pastor Adams is against alcohol but…"
Lisa paused and Charles stepped in again,

"Oh yes! That's right! He told me when I had a meeting with him when I first arrived, that he was once an alcoholic himself and considers himself to still be in recovery! He won't have it anywhere near him or his house. Why?"
Lisa seemed quite startled at what Charles had said.

"I did not know that," she said. "So that kind of makes what happened even more mysterious!" She went on to tell Charles all about seeing Sally buying drink at the store and now with what Pastor Adams had told him, she felt something was going on and it was not good.

Just as she related this whole story to Charles the dream came back into her head. It was like God was revealing something to her as they sat there talking.

"The dream!" Lisa whispered loudly and emphatically. "The sheep that was being eaten that looked familiar! It's…"
Before Lisa could say another word, Charles interrupted again,

"It's Sally, isn't it?" Lisa didn't reply. She figured that was enough said. A smile came on Lisa's face and it wasn't to gloat that Sally Adams was doing something wrong, it was that for the first time in her life she had someone who thought like she did.

What Sally was up to was another matter that they couldn't do anything about as yet, but to know that someone else was definitely on her side was amazing.

They carried on eating their meals and passing small talk for a while.

"You know something, Charles," Lisa began.

"What's that, Lisa?" replied Charles. Lisa carried on,

"I thank God for you!" There was a small pause. "I think without you I would have gone crazy over this whole thing!"

61

They smiled at each other.

Charles broke the silence and the eye contact.

"Lisa, I think we should carry on going to church but not be seen together, at least arriving or leaving anyway. We should just behave like nothing has happened and we just know each other through church." She nodded. Charles continued. "And to the bible study, for now at least. That way we can keep our eyes and ears open for a while without being suspected of knowing anything. Also, I think that there is more to this than we realize. We are still missing something." Lisa agreed.

It was nice to have somebody decide for her for once and, of course he was right. She looked at Charles and asked,

"Do you think this dream and what is happening with Sally is the reason for the messages?"

"Oh no!" replied Charles assertively. "This is only the tip of the iceberg! A test to see if you're up to it. You're going to go onto much bigger and better things, I'm sure!"

Lisa was not sure how to take that. She laughed to herself after Charles's comment. Either Charles was trying to butter her up or he knew something that she didn't. God must know what she was capable of, surely, and if so, what was ahead?

They spent the rest of the evening just talking about their backgrounds; where they were from and the life events that had led up to this time. It was so refreshing to be able to talk about herself for; her hopes, her dreams and her faith.

Charles paid again, insisting on it and they left the café bar. "So, I'll see you at Tom and Jan's then?" Charles said as they walked towards their cars. This time he didn't even attempt to give her a goodnight kiss. He had messed up enough for one night.

"Oh yes!" said Lisa. "And keep Mum!" They laughed and went on their separate ways.

Chapter 6
A Walk in the Park

The next morning, Lisa woke and sat up instantly. She felt different; great, but different. She couldn't put her finger on it but something had happened to her during her sleep that she had never experienced before. She had been dreaming again, only this time she couldn't remember anything, but she felt like she had been actually given something. She could only describe it as a feeling of empowerment, as though she'd had something revealed to her spirit or being given something that her conscious self wasn't aware of.

She sat there for quite a while trying to figure out what was going on. She looked herself all over. She looked normal. She went to the bathroom and looked in the mirror. Everything was as usual although she did notice something. She looked vibrant and healthy; not that she had been ill or anything but she was now in her late twenties and occasionally would notice the odd grey hair, which she would immediately remove with disgust. She never normally looked this good just after climbing out of bed.

She bounced downstairs and got on with all the normal things of her day; washing, cleaning, feeding children, washing children and all the rest of the things that occupied her normal day. Nothing was different but it just felt good. She couldn't take a smile off her face or at least she felt like she was smiling.

"God? Is this you? What have you done to me?" she asked, as she hoovered the lounge. Whatever it was, she knew was good and she thanked him for it.

Even though the whole day was just a regular day, there was so much peace and joy in her heart and she got more done than she felt she had ever done before. All day she praised God in her mind and when she was alone, told Him just how awesome He was. She knew she wasn't alone.

When she read her bible that day in preparation for the evening session at bible class, things just stood out like they never had before and made so much sense to her. She looked at the pages; at the bible as a whole and felt a love for the scripture and a comfort that she had never felt before.

As the end of the day approached, all she could think about was getting to bible class, it was the one place she felt 'safe' meeting with Charles. She longed to be able to exchange reports of the things that God was saying and doing in their lives but she knew that meeting him anywhere else could eventually arouse suspicion and she did not want to give anyone any cause to point the finger at them.

As she was giving the boys their dinner, she realised that she hadn't seen Dan for ages. His bed was made and hadn't been slept in again. She wouldn't normally see him a great deal anyway and since he had taken the second job at the store, it was even more the case, which didn't really bother her but this was the second night he hadn't been back home at all. That was unusual, even for Dan. The more she thought about it, the more she worried. She was his wife and felt responsible for his well-being, even if it wasn't reciprocated.

She was sure that he must be drinking heavily to have stayed out two nights in a row and that had to be bad for his health. She tried to call his mobile but it was switched off and went straight to the answer phone, so she decided that she would make a point of catching up with him later and check that he was okay.

By six o'clock she was ready to go to the bible study. The doorbell rang and of course, it was Sophie. After the usual greetings and orders for the night, Lisa left the house.

She looked at the car and thought,

"No! I'll walk! It's not much more than half a mile and the exercise will do me good." She was feeling great and if she arrived a little late it wouldn't be a bad thing, and would certainly keep any possible suspicions away concerning her and Charles because he was bound to drive and be early too.

She wasn't looking forward to the actual meeting at Tom and Jan's; she loved to study the word and of course, Charles, her friend and confidant would be there, but she hated all the paraphernalia that went along with it all.

As she walked, she reflected on all the things that had happened since the last time she went to the bible class. It had been amazing and all in just seven days. She was beginning to feel that she

really was more powerful than she had been led to believe. She thought about her 'previous' life, visions passing before her eyes about how people had put her down through her early years, bullying at school, teachers not being exactly positive, and many other traumatic events that had stayed with her all those years.

Then, of course, she'd got married and it all had gone downhill from there! It was amazing how she had been then, compared with how she was feeling right now; 'Chalk and Cheese'. Almost two completely different lives.

Amazingly though, as she looked back she could see how everything that had happened, good and bad, had got her to this very point in her life. Again, she thanked and praised God.

By the time she arrived at Tom and Jan's she was nearly ten minutes late. She rang the doorbell. "Just be yourself!" she whispered to herself. Jan answered the door.

"Lisa! Do come in," she shouted and stood back from the door to let her in. "We're just about to start! We've got a full house tonight!"

"Oh great," Lisa replied and walked through to the main room.

It was indeed full. All the chairs and stools were taken. Some people were standing and some were sitting cross legged on the floor. Lisa found a space on the floor near to the fireplace where there was a cushion. She grabbed it and placed it on her lap. She felt comfy like that.

She looked around for Charles. He was nowhere to be seen. Where was he? She took her bible from her bag and waited for the meeting to start. "What's going on? Why are there so many people here?" she thought to herself. It was soon to become obvious. Tom came into the room and got everyone's attention. He prayed and thanked God for all the people there and asked Him to be part of the meeting which Lisa always agreed with.

Voices could be heard in the corridor. The door opened and a windswept Charles crept in apologetically. He must have had the same idea about being late.

"Amen," echoed around the room at the end of the prayer and Tom remained standing waiting for Charles to find a place. Tom smiled uncomfortably as Charles settled on the floor opposite Lisa
with his back to the couch. Tom stood on the piece of floor that was vacant in the middle of the room between Lisa and Charles.

"Well, good evening everybody!" Tom started with a somewhat uneasy smile on his face; anything disorganised made him feel edgy and he hated anything that made him look at all foolish. He continued,

"We are very fortunate this evening to have a special guest to talk to us!" Lisa pricked up her ears along with all the 'oohs'. "Will you all please welcome..." Tom announced, increasing the intensity of his voice, "...our very own Pastor Christopher Adams!"

Everybody stood up and applauded.

"You have to be kidding!" Lisa cried to herself. She tried to look for Charles but he was lost in the crowd.

Pastor Adams 'milked' the crowd for a while before beckoning people to settle down.

"Take a seat! Take a seat!" he told everybody and after a scuffle everybody returned to where they were.

Lisa hung her head in disbelief, then looked up to see if Charles was looking her way. He was looking directly at her. As he did he smiled sympathetically, squinted his eyes and gave her a 'be strong!' stare, then looked up at the Pastor, who was just about to begin.

"Get a grip!" she thought. "This is nothing! Just act as if nothing has ever happened!" So, she lifted her head and forced a convincing smile towards Pastor Adams, who was now pacing around the small space in the middle of the room, telling some ice-breaking joke. She tried to look as interested as she could, which was difficult under the circumstances, considering it was only yesterday afternoon when she had delivered a message to Pastor from God, only to be brushed off as though she was a fool for doing so! Also, she suspected that his wife was up to no good and was about to be 'devoured' by a symbolic big black wolf.

The way he had spoken to her and lied about playing golf had certainly made her question this man who was now strutting around like a peacock, preaching God's word, just a few feet away from her.

She kept glancing at Charles, who was also smiling and trying to look interested, but he was doing a much better job of it than she was. One thing with Lisa, was that you could always tell what she was thinking. It was something that she was proud of and wasn't used to having to fake it.

Pastor Adams told everyone about the plans the church had got for the coming year ahead. How excited he was about the growth they were seeing and how they were going to have to have another service on Sundays and possibly even add a new wing on to the church. Somehow, even though it seemed all very positive, Lisa had a strange feeling about it all. She knew that this was not what God was wanting. Why she knew, she didn't know. She just knew.

Amazingly, Pastor spoke about truth and loyalty to him and the church and how happy and blessed everyone would be if they all gave more money than they currently were. He spoke about himself and the church for most of the evening and hardly mentioned God or Jesus in any of it.

One thing Lisa had never really understood was where all the money really went at this Church. To her they should have been helping the poor and needy; the widows and orphans, as it says in scripture. It always seemed to be so much about helping the church itself: more TV screens, new carpets here, new computers there, more programs, etcetera.

One of her favourite scriptures had always been Isaiah 58, which talks about the true fasting that God approves of. To Lisa, it always felt like the church had its own agenda and wasn't concerned so much with what God really wanted to do.

As she thought about these things and what the church really should be involved in she felt God saying,

"Be the answer!" She felt that He was saying that she should start her own ministry.

"You want me to start a church?" she said in her head. "Surely not! What do I know about running a church?"

Her thoughts were interrupted by Pastor Adams, who accidentally knocked Lisa's knee as he walked past her, marching up and down.

"Oh, I'm sorry Linda!" said Pastor, almost sounding genuine about kicking her.

"That's okay, Tony!" replied Lisa.

"It's Christopher!" snarled Pastor Adams.

"It's Lisa!" smiled Mrs Jeffreys.

Pastor glared at Lisa for a second with disdain, before continuing his 'pitch' to his flock. Charles looked at Lisa with a 'play it cool' expression to which Lisa grinned back in victory. They seemed adept at having conversations together by mere glances and expressions.

The more Pastor Adams went on about 'his' church, the more irritable Lisa got. She couldn't believe her ears when he started going on about false prophets and how people had come to him and tell him how to run the very church that God had apparently ordained him to run. Amazingly, even though it was obvious that he was pointing at Lisa as one of the false prophets, he never once looked in her direction. It was plain to Lisa that he was just trying to 'protect' the people in Tom and Jan's study group, just in case she had said anything negative to the group about her dream and how he'd dealt with it.

"Relax, Mr Pastor!" she thought to herself. "I'm not going to share your problems with anyone here!" She stared at him knowingly, with a broad smile across her face, while thinking,

"Wow! The nerve! What would everyone say if they all knew the truth of it!" Lisa looked over at Charles, who was looking directly at her, raising his eyebrows. He was amazed, as she was.

Everybody applauded when Pastor Adams finished, especially Lisa, who managed to do so with an edge of sarcasm, but was glad that he had actually finished. People stood up as they clapped, completely taken in by it all.

Tom wrapped up the meeting, thanking Pastor Adams and inviting people to take refreshments and hang around. He added that if they were fortunate enough they could maybe even grab a second of Pastor's time.

A large bunch gathered around the Pastor, laughing at his witty banter, hanging on to his every word. All Lisa could think about was how to escape. As she stretched her back, she looked over at Charles. He was on his own so she shuffled over to him.

"If I leave now, can you pick me up in a few minutes?" Lisa asked Charles, "I walked here."

"I can't," Charles replied, "I walked too! That's why I was late!" They laughed.

"I was late too!" chuckled Lisa. "Just not as late as you!"

They both looked around the room, smiling and nodding at people who met their glances, pretending to join in the elation of having their Pastor present. Lisa whispered,

"I need to leave now, it's getting dark but maybe we can talk on the phone?" She said her goodbyes and left.

It was nearly dark outside, which made Lisa feel a little uncomfortable, but she whispered a little prayer under her breath and set off down the street towards the shop. It seemed to get dark very quickly and Lisa was relieved to hear her name being called from a recognizable source and the sound of somebody running towards her.

"Hey Charles, it's good to see you, I hate walking on my own in the dark!" she laughed.

"I know! I couldn't let you walk home alone. Although, I'm like you," laughed Charles. "I may be six foot but I'm a big chicken really!" They both laughed as they continued along the street towards the coffee shop which they could see just ahead.

"Do you fancy a quick coffee?" asked Charles, as they came out of the shop. "I have a few things to tell you."

"Well, ok, I guess so" replied Lisa and they went to the coffee shop, ordered drinks and sat down at a table.

"Lisa," Charles began. "When you left… you should have heard them talking!"

"Why, what were they saying?" demanded Lisa. Charles continued.

"Well, I overheard Tom, Jan and Pastor Adams being less than complimentary towards you. The reason he came tonight was because of the meeting with you." She smiled,

"Well it did occur to me during his 'false prophet' talk."

"It certainly was!" said Charles. "And another thing, they think you are a troublemaker and are just kicking off because of your apparent failed marriage! I could not believe what they were saying! He also told other people, too, that someone was trying to cause trouble from within the church. He didn't say your name but certainly Tom and Jan knew he was talking about you. It was incredible! Why has he reacted like this to your dream, Lisa and what does it have to do with your marriage?" Lisa shrugged her shoulders.

"I've no idea but it's certainly stirred something up!" She thought for a moment, looked at Charles and said, "Accusations, Charles, accusations. You know where they come from!" said Lisa referring to the Enemy. "Maybe we're doing something right and someone's not pleased!"

She changed the subject by telling Charles all about how she'd woke up that morning; about her day and how great it had been; how empowered and healthy she was feeling and how she felt so much more equipped to deal with things. She was of course hurt by what they had all been saying but wasn't surprised and in no way was going to let small minded people affect what she was doing.

"God told me to tell the Pastor and that's what I did. Whatever God wants I will do! And there's something else that I haven't told you yet because it is something that at first, I did not fully understand. I still don't for so many reasons. As a married woman I can't keep meeting with you privately, but I do believe that God has connected us for a reason! I'm not sure why yet, it sounds strange given the circumstances but I am going to continue to pray and ask Him to show me more." she said and finished her coffee. Before Charles could reply she said,

"Shall we go now, Charles?" They got up to go and Lisa tried to pay but Charles wasn't having any of it.

"When you're with me, Lisa, I pay! So, don't try that again! That's the way I was brought up and that's what's right!"demanded Charles.

"Okay, okay!" Lisa laughed, backing away from the counter. "Have it your own way!" She was always thankful to Charles, as money was always tight in her home as it was, without having to find extra money for coffees and meals out but she concluded,

"Thank you, anyway."

"You're totally welcome, Lisa," Charles replied, paying the waitress. He took his change and they walked outside.

The walk back to Lisa's house, took them through the park, which is a lovely place to be in daylight but not a good place to be at night and definitely not a place to be if you're alone and female, but she felt safe with Charles.

About halfway through the park they passed a group of youths fooling about, so they speeded up a little and headed for the lights of the avenue ahead. All of a sudden, there was a barrage of shouting and two of the guys they just had passed jumped Charles and another one grabbed Lisa around her neck and held something sharp to her back. Charles put up a struggle but Lisa screamed and shouted,

"Charles! Stop! He's got a knife!"
Charles immediately stopped fighting. The youth with the knife screamed at them,

"Empty your pockets! I want rings and jewellery, everything!"

"Okay! okay! No problem, just keep calm!" shouted Lisa, and went to take her purse from her bag. Charles took his wallet from his inside jacket pocket, to take his cash out.

Suddenly, Lisa grabbed the youth by the wrist he had the knife in, twisted it behind his back and in one fluid movement disarmed him. She took a pistol out of her bag and held it to the temple of the youth's head.

"Get out of here you two!" she screamed at the boys holding Charles. "I don't want to use this thing but I will if I need to!" They let go of Charles ran, scampering through the park like two frightened rabbits.

"Let me go, let me go, lady!" cried the one who Lisa had in an arm lock. "I'm sorry, I'm sorry!"

"Think of this as your lucky day, kid!" Lisa shouted in his face. "Go home to mummy and thank God it was me you tried to rob! Go and get a job! And don't let me ever see you out here at night again! Now Go!"

She flung him down on the ground and he stumbled as he tried to get up and run at the same time. He ran off through the park, after his mates, yelping like a puppy.

In no time at all, it was silent. Charles stood there, mouth open, amazed at what he had just witnessed. Lisa sat on the ground; silent; bewildered at what had just happened. Charles sat down by her side.

"How did you do that?" Charles gasped, still out of breath.

"I have no idea!" replied Lisa in shock. "Charles, I don't even own a gun, where did this gun come from?" She shook her head. "How did I do all that?"

"I have no idea!" said Charles. "But I'm sure glad you can handle yourself."

"Handle myself? I couldn't fight my way out of a paper bag!" exclaimed Lisa. "Did that all just happen?"

"I think so!" said Charles. "Well, I was here and saw it with my own two eyes!" They both sat there stunned on the grass, unable to talk or offer anything of an explanation. Eventually, they got up and gave each other a hug.

"Honestly, Charles," Lisa reiterated, "I can't do what I just did. This isn't my gun and I…" She stopped suddenly as she lifted

73

her hand to look at the gun. It had disappeared!
Literally right there in front of her eyes. She didn't see it vanish but had felt it in her hand right up to the point she lifted it up to look at it.

"What?" she cried staring at her empty hand. "Where has it gone!" she cried. They both looked around the floor in case she had dropped but there was nothing, it had completely disappeared.

Charles took her by the hand and they quickly set off walking towards home.

They reached Lisa's driveway and Lisa insisted on dropping Charles off at his house. They got into the relative safety of her car. She reversed down the driveway and headed off down the road. Neither of them said a word to one another, both of them totally flabbergasted at what they had just witnessed.

When they arrived at his house, Charles asked Lisa if she would like to come in for a coffee but she refused. She smiled at Charles and admitted to him,

"I daren't Charles, but thank you!"

They said goodnight and agreed that they'd be in touch, both still feeling a little dazed. Lisa sped off down the road back home needing to get away from it all. She pulled up on her driveway alongside Dan's pick-up. He was home.

"Wonders never cease!" she said sarcastically and went in. She said goodnight to Sophie and followed her outside into the night air. Lisa watched her walk down the road to her house. When she had seen her go indoors she turned around and went back inside. She noticed that Dan had come home and gone to bed. Even though she wanted to check that he was okay, she felt mentally exhausted with all that had just happened and she couldn't take anything else he might throw at her.

She turned all the lights off, locked the doors and went upstairs. She got undressed and flopped onto the bed, exhausted. She lay there for a while, staring at the ceiling, still recovering from her ordeal in the park. She thanked God with all her heart and said,

"Talk about divine intervention, Father. You are amazing!" Then she climbed into bed and turned on her side to put out the light. There was a post-it note stuck on her alarm clock. It read. 'Well Done!'

Chapter 7

The Writing is on the Wall

As she woke the next morning, Lisa looked over at the clock and just stared at the post-it note that was stuck to it. Was it written by someone in the house or was it from the hand of God again? There was only one way to find out. She jumped out of bed and grabbed the note.

"Who has written this?" she shouted, for the whole house to hear. "And what does it mean?"
The boys came running into her room.

"Written what, mummy? Can we see?" cried Josh excitedly as they bounced up and down on the spot.

"Oh, it's nothing, don't worry!" she said. "Go and get dressed. Mummy's going to take you both to the playgroup today."

They both bounced off to the bathroom giggling with one another.

Lisa knew they couldn't have written the note and even if they had asked Sophie to write it, what could they mean by 'Well done' anyway? That was the boys eliminated off the list immediately.

The only other person in the house was Dan and it didn't look like his hand writing at all. Just then, Dan staggered into the room in his usual scruffy morning manner.

"What's all the commotion?" he asked sleepily.

"Did you write me a note last night?" Lisa asked, not showing him the note as she felt he would accuse her of something if he saw it.

"Note, what note?" said Dan, yawning as he did so, trying to wake up.

"Just say yes or no! Did you leave me a note last night?" Lisa shouted impatiently.

"Nope, it wasn't me, it must be from your lover-boy!" he laughed as he walked back out of the bedroom towards his own.

"Very funny!" she replied, following Dan out of her bedroom. "And tell me something else while we are actually talking to one another, where have you been the last couple of nights? I know we don't have much to do with one another anymore but you could at least tell me where you are and if you're coming home! I can't even set the alarm when we go to bed because I don't know if you're going to come in and set it off!" Dan apologized immediately,

"Oh, I'm sorry, Lisa! Things have been a bit crazy at work and I've been staying at Frank's house sometimes when I've had too much to drink."

"That's okay. I don't mind. Just let me know what you're doing or move in with Frank." Dan apologized again,

"I'm sorry. Forgive me."

"Of course, don't worry!" said Lisa, and she went into her bedroom and closed the door behind her. She felt better for saying something to Dan and getting it all off her chest but suddenly realized that in all the years they had been married, which was nearly ten years, he had never apologized to her. In the last minute he had, twice! Normally he would have just argued back, but he had actual been civil!

What was wrong with him?

Was he becoming human? …. Surely not? A part of her was thinking that there may be hope for this guy but on the other hand she was trying to figure out what he was up to.

Why was he being nice?

She got dressed and went downstairs into the kitchen. The boys were dressed, Dan was making the coffee. It was like a normal family. She stopped and looked around and realized how much she had missed being a family. She liked what she saw and wished it could have always been that way.

Was it possible that Dan could change and be the husband and father she had always hoped he could be? Could this be the start of an incredible testimony of a saved marriage?

"Maybe that's what God is doing!" she thought to herself.

She gave the boys' cereal and sat herself down with a coffee and a piece of toast.

"So, who wrote the note?" she asked herself as she munched on her toast. It was really an obvious question but it was still a challenge, even with everything that had happened recently, for her to automatically assume it was God. She'd seen Him perform many miracles in the bible and heard many testimonies from people but she'd never known of God writing notes for people. He could do anything of course, but it was still hard to accept.

In her head she heard a wonderful soft voice saying,

"Well done, my good and faithful servant, well done!" She smiled and said out loud,

"Thank you!"

"For what?" replied Dan, thinking she was talking to him.

"Not you! I'm talking to God!" laughed Lisa. Dan gestured palms-up to the boys and everybody laughed. It was a sound that hadn't been heard in the house for a long time. It seemed that everybody was happy.

Dan went off to work and Lisa immediately grabbed her journal and wrote down in as much detail as she could in the short time that she had before having to leave the house, the events of last night, from the episode in the park to the note that she found when she went to bed.

'Wow!' She thought to herself as she read her own words,

realising just how incredible and miraculous these events were. She had barely had the time or the chance to really take it all in but as much as she wanted to sit and ponder her thoughts, it was time to go.

She smartened the boys up a little to get off to the playgroup. She had an arrangement with the church that she could take them there whenever she wanted and just pay for the days they attended. This was ideal for her, as most of the time she liked to do things with them during their holidays but sometimes, like today, she felt she needed a bit of her own space.

It was amazing that she hadn't even thought about what had happened last night. In fact, she had been more occupied with thoughts of her family than she had with the fact that last night she had taken on a gang of muggers, disarmed a fully grown male with a series of incredibly strong, swift, aggressive moves that would have impressed any SAS team member, followed by producing, from her handbag, a hand gun that wasn't hers, that never actually existed, then holding the main offender at gunpoint and making them all scatter and run like frightened rabbits.

After she had dropped the boys off at nursery, she went to Big Town to do a little shopping. She didn't really need to get anything but she often loved to just walk around the shops and department stores aimlessly, just browsing. It was very relaxing for her. She had her favourite shops to look in and coffee houses that she would sometimes stand outside and smell the wonderful aroma. She looked at her watch and made the excuse that she deserved a grand cappuccino, and it was only when she was sitting peacefully drinking it, along with a 'naughty' brownie, that what had happened last night, and what she had been able to do, actually hit her. 'What must Charles be thinking?' she thought to herself and wished she could talk to him now.

She decided to send him a text and ask if he was okay after last night. Amazingly he answered immediately and asked where she was. The next thing she felt a hand rest on her shoulder.

"Well what a coincidence eh? We must stop meeting this way or people will suspect something!" laughed Charles and asked if he could join her.

"We really do! But we didn't plan it, so, of course! she said. "Sit!"

Charles did as he was told and ordered himself a coffee with the waitress. Lisa just looked at him.

"A real man of God," she thought to herself, hoping he wasn't scared of her, after last night's antics in the park. She wouldn't have blamed him if he was.

Charles sat down at the table and explained that he was having a day off that day. He explained,

"It's not too busy at work right now and if I don't use up some of my holidays, I can end up losing them! As a single guy it's sometimes hard to use up all my allotted holiday time."

For a few minutes they didn't mention the park incident. Lisa told Charles about the note, which, considering everything that had gone on, was no surprise to him although as he admitted,

"Everything that God does is always amazing."

She also confided in him how she was missing family life and how Dan had reacted when she confronted him.

"It's so not like him, you know," she reflected. "He's normally so horrible about everything. And today, for the first time in a long time we actually laughed together!"

Charles just sat there watching Lisa as she talked, trying not to look at her the way he truly wanted to. He watched her lips as she talked and he wondered what it would be like to kiss them.
He quickly returned to listening to Lisa's predicament and nodded thoughtfully.

"So," he said eventually. "Have you fully recovered from last night?"

"Do you mean in the park or from the bible class?" replied Lisa sarcastically. They laughed.

"Both, I guess," said Charles playfully. Lisa replied,

"I don't know quite what to think really, Charles, but what I do know is that wasn't me last night and I'm sure you know that."

"Well, yes," agreed Charles. "I'd always thought you were a very gentle creature, but I'll be careful what I say to you from now on!" They laughed again. Lisa slapped Charles on the arm.

"Hey you! Don't be cheeky!" she retorted. "You don't know what I've got in my bag!" As funny as it was they both knew the seriousness of the situation and if God hadn't intervened, they would have been robbed, mugged and possibly worse, and would have been having a day of hospital food and police interviews, instead of sipping cappuccinos in Lisa's favourite coffee house. There would have been no way on earth that Lisa would have ever tried to do what she did. The way she'd been brought up, she was taught to hand over the money or whatever and not to put up any kind of struggle, especially with somebody brandishing a knife. What God did was truly incredible.

"The funny thing was," Lisa continued. "I didn't actually do anything! Something took over! It was totally supernatural! I didn't consciously make any decision to do anything apart from try and calm down the whole situation."

It was getting time for Lisa to leave but before she left she decided that she would go to the bathroom. While she was washing her hands, she looked up into the mirror to check her make up. As she did she noticed something over her shoulder, in the reflection, that was written on the door of the cubicle directly behind her. It looked like a load of jumbled up letters. She looked again, trying to make out what it said but with it being back to front, she was unable to see what it said. All she could make out was that it looked like capital letters with a full stop in between each letter, like an acronym or something. She shook the wet off her hands and turned around. She looked at it with a puzzled expression, wondering what the letters could stand for.

Suddenly, with a sharp intake of breath she realized what it was. It was an acronym! It contained the letters,

'Y. A. F. M. P. T. Y. H. B. L. T. B. :)' She followed each letter and said out loud,

"You Are Far More Powerful Than You Have Been Led To Believe." God was telling her again.

"Hallelujah! Praise you, Father!" She smiled at the sign and thanked God for his encouragement. "I love the smiley face too!" she said to Him and walked out with a big grin on her face.

When she got back to the table, Charles remarked,

"You look pleased with yourself! What's happened?" Lisa replied,

"Well if you're brave enough to go into the ladies room you can see for yourself!" She described what was on the wall and as soon as she had said the words, Charles dashed into the ladies room.

There was a bunch of screams and shouts from the bathroom and Charles came running out, ducking, with his arms held over his head, profusely apologizing, being pursued by two elderly ladies, one hitting Charles with her handbag, the other with her umbrella. Charles didn't stop; he just carried on running out of the coffee shop.

Lisa paid for the coffees, apologized and ran after Charles, laughing at the top of her voice.

When she finally caught up with him, she could hardly speak from laughing so hard and running at the same time. Charles was a fast runner and ran much further than he needed to. The offensive ladies only chased him a few yards out of the shop but Charles ran down the street.

"Did you see the letters?" Lisa finally asked when she had caught her breath.

"Actually, I did, for a brief second before Attila the Hun and Genghis Khan saw me!" Charles laughed.

They walked back toward her car. "Thank you for being in town today, Charles, it's been great fun!" Lisa said, climbing into her car as Charles held the door for her.

"Thank you for being you!" Charles replied and closed her door.

She wound down the window and said,

"So long, pardner!" with an American cowboy accent, pointed a finger gun at him and pulled off in her car.

"Don't shoot!" Charles shouted after her, as she drove down the road. "And God bless!" He whispered to himself. "What a great girl you are Lisa Jeffreys!"

He walked back into town and carried on with his day, whilst Lisa went to pick the boys up from the church and headed back home.

It felt good to be going nowhere that evening and to chill out with the family, although Dan, of course, wasn't at home. She would have liked to have talked with him some more to try and find out why he was being nice to her that morning. The more she kept thinking about it, the more suspicious she became. However, she was prepared to give him the benefit of the doubt. Only time would tell.

She cooked tea for the boys and sat next to them as they ate. She heard a key turn in the front door and in came Dan. He dashed upstairs shouting as he went, saying that he was meeting Frank and having a drink with the boys.

"Usual stuff," Lisa said to herself as she got up to take the rubbish outside.

On her way round to the bins, she walked past Dan's pick-up and glanced inside. Quite why she did that she will never know, but on the front seat of his pick-up were three bottles of wine and a four-pack of beer.

83

"What? Has he started to drink wine?" she thought to herself, and then it struck her.

"Three bottles of wine and a four pack of beer!" she said. It was the exact combination of drink Sally Adams had bought a few days ago when Lisa saw her in the supermarket. She threw the trash in the bin almost without thinking. She was puzzled. Was that just coincidence? Her heart pounded. Crazy things started to flash into her mind. Was Dan seeing Sally Adams?

"No, surely not!" she argued with herself. "Not Dan and Sally!" As she pondered on her mixed-up thoughts, she remembered seeing his pick-up the other day when he should have been in work at the hospital. Why had he been so nice to her yesterday? Dan came out of the house, looking a lot smarter than he usually did when going out with Frank and company. She trembled as he came towards her, but she was going to say something, that was for sure! How much, she didn't know. She leant with her back on the driver's door of his pick-up, stopping Dan getting in.

"You okay?" Dan asked Lisa, who was clearly not going to let him in his car. She didn't answer his question but instead asked a couple of her own.

"You look very smart for a night out with the lads." She stared at him. "Is Frank going to be dressed the same?"

"I dunno," replied Dan nervously. "I don't tell him how to dress, but we're all meeting at a nicer place than usual! We're having a meal!" Straight away she knew he was lying; Frank Morello never went anywhere nice for a meal, and as for the rest of his mates…

"Right, so will we be graced with your presence over night?" she asked him sarcastically.

"No, not tonight, I'm gonna have a drink, so it'll be easier to stay at Frank's. It's not good to drink and drive, you know!" said Dan, trying to sound responsible.

"I can tell you're going to have a drink! I've seen it in your car! Have you started drinking wine now, or is that for Frank?" quizzed Lisa.

"Erm, some of the lads like a glass and we're back at Frank's for a card game after we've been out! What's with all the questions anyway?" he pleaded.

"Okay, I'm sorry," responded Lisa. "But can I ask you one more thing?" Dan sighed,

"If you must!" thinking he'd answered the accusations successfully.

Lisa played her trump card. Even though her heart was pounding, she asked him casually,

"What is Sally Adams to you?" Lisa stared him directly in the eyes as she said those words, looking intently at his reaction. Dan answered,

"Who? Sally who? I don't know what you're talking about, Lisa!" She didn't say another word. She looked his face up and down, reading him like a book. His mouth was lying again and she knew it. She stood up straight from leaning on the car and walked towards the house, her eyes fixed on his for a few seconds, making sure he could see and feel the dismay and betrayal that she felt.

"Lisa, what is with you?" he shouted back at her. She ignored him and went into the house, slammed the door, locked it and put the security chain on. From inside the house she heard Dan's pick-up start and the tyres squeal as he hurriedly reversed down the driveway. Then he drove off into the night.

Lisa went to see the boys, who were watching TV in the lounge, and she tried to make out that nothing had happened. After being married to the man for ten years and with him for nearly twelve years, she knew when he was lying. After all he had many times, and this certainly was one of those occasions.

"Dan and Sally Adams!" she kept repeating to herself over and over in her head. "How? Why?"

85

She stared blankly at nothing. The TV blared but even that didn't interrupt her thoughts. It was only when the boys snuggled up to her, one either side that she snapped out of it. They helped her
to realise that they were the important people in her family now, them and only them.

"I love you, Josh, Luke!" she whispered lovingly.
They replied in unison,

"I love you too, Mummy!" It was the straw that broke the camel's back and she sobbed right there and then with a son under each arm. They carried on watching TV but they both knew something was wrong. Lisa assured them that everything would be fine and that she was just a little upset about something and they all sat there and watched the rest of Ice Age together.

When it had finished she tucked them up in bed, said prayers with them and went back downstairs. She made some toast and a cup of hot chocolate and settled herself in the lounge to watch a chick-flick to help relieve the stress.

She wished Charles was with her but she wasn't going to call him because she knew he would be round at her house in a flash and she wasn't going to give Dan any ammunition, that was for certain.

As she watched her film and sipped her hot chocolate, she asked God for the strength and wisdom she would need to handle this situation she had found herself in. As she prayed, she cried out. Even though she was unhappy in her marriage, she hoped in some way, the family could find happiness and that things could improve.

That morning, for a brief moment, she had thought there was a glimmer of hope for them all, but that too was all a lie. She suddenly remembered her dream and the familiarity of the little black wolf. It was Dan.

Chapter 8

The Red Circle

It all seemed like a blur. The whole thing that God was doing in her life and now this with Dan.

It seemed like they had always been together and even though they had been unhappy for most of the time they had been with one another, she had always expected to be married to him. She was used to him being there sometimes, not being there a lot of the time and him being drunk most of the time. It was just the way it was being married to Dan.

What on earth was going to happen now? Was it serious with Dan and Sally or was this just a fling? Whatever it was, things were going to have to change. She couldn't live with this man anymore. She thought about Dan's behaviour over the last month and looking back, it now made sense.

She wondered whether or not Pastor Adams knew about everything. Was that why he behaved the way he did? She didn't think so, but she certainly wasn't going to say anything to Pastor at all; certainly not until she had more facts about the whole sordid affair. Was a divorce looming up? The thought was almost unbearable, but she couldn't see how it could end in anything else. "Just when I thought that God could possibly have a plan for my life, that glimmer of hope gets crushed. What would God ever be able to do with a divorced nobody?" She thought to herself.

Over the next couple of days, the whole subject naturally dominated her thoughts.

She found herself getting more and more frustrated. Dan hadn't been home at all and she needed to speak to him to find out about what his intentions truly were so she could get on with her life as a mother and now a woman with a God-given calling.

She called her parents, who were very sympathetic but not at all surprised. They didn't really know what to do or say to Lisa, apart from how sorry they were. They'd never been through anything like what she was experiencing right now. So, what could they do? One consolation, however, was that they offered her and the boys a roof over their heads if they needed it. Lisa thanked them but that wasn't her immediate situation, right now she just needed somebody's Godly help and support.

She wished she could call somebody at the church for help but that obviously was not an option. Other than Charles, the only other person she knew well enough was Sophie, but she was too young to be able to offer any advice, plus Lisa wasn't going to burden her young heart with her problems.

One thing was for sure though; she needed to talk to somebody. It would have to be Charles, but how was he going to react now? Would he now think that the door was open for him to step in with her? It was obvious that he liked her and although she knew that they had a special friendship that God was a part of, she wasn't going to jump head long into something she could later regret. This time she was going to let God have His say regarding all areas of her life.

She sent Dan a text message and to her surprise, he replied and agreed to meet up with her after his shift to discuss things between them. He agreed to come when the boys were at playgroup, to avoid any unpleasantness for them and even though they were used to Dan not being there, Lisa couldn't remember any time in their marriage that he had ever put himself out for them. He turned up at two o'clock and Lisa invited him into the kitchen. It felt strange, he had always come and gone as he wanted and now he was being invited to sit down.

"Coffee?" asked Lisa.
"Sure!" replied Dan. "Why not?"

It was a peculiar atmosphere considering this was his home but then it was peculiar circumstances.

While Lisa stood making the coffee she searched for the words to say to Dan. But her thoughts were abruptly interrupted when Dan came clean about everything with Sally. Apparently, they were in love and it just happened one day when the church had a stand in the local mall and Sally was doing some PR for them. That was her role as first lady to the Pastor.

Lisa made a sarcastic joke about her taking the whole 'Public Relations' thing a little too far. Dan gave her a wry smile and continued in his explanation of how she stopped him in the mall and asked him a few questions. Of course, he left his mobile number and she called him and that's how it started. That was about two months ago.

"Dan, stop," pleaded Lisa. She turned her back to him so that he could not see the tears fill her eyes. She rested her hands on the work top and hung her head. She didn't understand why she felt so troubled, she has known for such a long time that this relationship had died years ago. But each word that Dan spoke felt like a dagger to her heart and all hope of a miracle restoration of their marriage was crushed.

"Why?" she asked herself. "How could he do this to me?" Her thoughts began to spiral quickly, and feelings of utter betrayal soon turned to anger. Her mind flashed back to so many little things that had made her suspicious over the past few weeks. He had managed to hide it all pretty well from Lisa, in fact if she hadn't been in the store that day and noticed Sally with her booze and then spotting the same selection in Dan's pick-up she would never have suspected anything.

Realising that this train of thought was going to lead to either a heated and full-blown argument or her falling apart right in front of him, Lisa consciously put an abrupt halt to these thoughts. She lifted her head and looked up, out of the window.

"Father, help me," she whispered. Assertively, Lisa turned to Dan and looked him directly in the eyes.

"It's amazing how God reveals things to us!" she said. "Now, I have to leave soon to go and collect my boys. I need you out of here." Dan commented on the way out of the door,

"I'll collect my things bit by bit so as not to alarm the boys."

"I don't think they'll really notice that much," Lisa remarked.

"They don't really know who you are anyway." It was sad but true. "One question Dan?" Lisa asked with a puzzled expression on her face. "Has she told her husband?" Dan replied,

"She's going to, this evening!"

"That's going to be fun!" Lisa laughed sarcastically. As Dan was leaving she asked him where he was going to be living and he told her about the house the Adams's have at the beach and that's where he'd be until further notice. Dan got in his pick-up and drove away. Lisa thought to herself,

"Wow! You've got some fun ahead!" She sat back down in the kitchen to compose herself before she had to leave to go and pick up her boys.

She finished the dregs of her cold coffee and pondered on Dan leaving the house for good. She couldn't understand why she suddenly felt so deeply sad. She had suspected and prepared herself for this for years. There had never really been any true love between them, they barely even spoke to one another but somehow, that routine, being so familiar had almost become comfortable, even living with suspicion! But this was real, this was it.

"Can it really be over? Just like that? What now?" she thought to herself. The realisation hit her that her life was about to change dramatically. She now was going to be the sole provider for her boys. One thing for certain was that she was going to have to get a job or something. She hadn't worked for a long time and even though she wasn't afraid to work, she had got kind of used to the freedom she had but she knew that what she'd receive from Dan wouldn't allow them to live there but she made up her mind not to worry but to have faith and try to be positive.

"Still," she said to herself. "It'll be an adventure, that's for sure!" She picked the boys up from the play group and spent the afternoon with them. They went to the park, on the swings, fed the ducks and then ended up at one of the local burger houses, with cheeseburger, fries and a milkshake. They laughed and giggled all the way home about anything and everything. Lisa was determined that their life as a family was going to get better and not be affected in a negative way, by her husband and their father leaving their home. Being honest, she knew that if he saw them on something of a regular basis, nothing would really change for them.

As she drove home, and the boys quietened down in the car, reality hit her once again. She was faced with a choice: to find a place to curl up, cry and wallow in a pool of thoughts and regrets or draw on that inner strength which she could feel deep within the pit of her stomach, like a voice, strong yet a whisper, saying to her, 'stand up and carry on.' She knew that she would be well within her rights to go home, draw her curtains and give herself a few days or even weeks to grieve and recover. But something deep inside told her that closing the door quickly to all of this was the right thing to do. She had spent enough time crying. As harsh as it may have seemed for anyone outside looking in, she made a strong and firm decision to move on, and to do it immediately.

During the afternoon, she sent Charles a message to see whether he would like to meet up with her later on that evening. "Of course. Eight o'clock? Usual place?" was the reply to her message which she confirmed with a short and simple, "Yes."

When they arrived home, the boys got on with their usual antics and Lisa went upstairs. She had made her mind up to clear out Dan's room. To her this was taking a practical step to move forward and close the door. She put all his clothes and bits and pieces in bin bags and placed them in the garage so that when he next came he could just throw them in the back of his pick-up and be done in one go.

"Bit at a time - puh!" she said to herself as she threw another bag on top of the pile. Among his things, she found an old photograph of them both. She remembered that time very well, a brief time when they had a good time together. A tear ran down her cheek. She sat on the bed and tried to think about exactly where they had gone wrong. The truth though, was that it had been a complete mistake from the start.

"Why didn't I listen?" she whispered to herself. "Forgive me, Lord," she prayed.

Apart from having the kids there hadn't been any other memories that weren't negative ones. They'd never been away on holiday since they had been married and she couldn't recall the last time they went for a meal or even to a fast food restaurant together, not on their own or as a family. God had never been part of their relationship, and He certainly didn't have anything to do with them coming together either. She could honestly say, now that God was firmly in her life and in her decisions, if she had listened to God instead of her fear of being alone in the first place she would never have considered Dan as a partner in a million years. She wiped her face and reminded herself of the decision that she had made only a couple of hours ago and got on with 'de-Dan-ing' the house.

***

At eight o'clock, she pulled onto the car park of the café bar. She could see Charles in his usual spot, waiting by the door. Was he trying to impress her or was this just the way he was? One thing she knew was that God had definitely brought Charles into her life, so she decided to trust in Him and just enjoy their friendship. She wondered if God had sent Charles in advance of all of this happening so that Lisa wouldn't have to go through it alone. Either way she knew that He had been sent to her for a reason and whatever that be, she was thankful to have him in her life, now more than ever before.

She walked up the step towards Charles. It was great to see his smiling face again. He was truly Lisa's only friend. When she had been pondering earlier on who she could talk to, she was amazed at her sheer lack of true friends and although she hadn't known Charles for very long she certainly knew one thing and that was that she could trust him, at least as much as she could trust any human being.

"Hi Charles," she said as he held the door for her. "It's great to see you again."

"You too, Lisa, you too," he replied and followed her inside. The same waitress took them straight to their usual seat and took their orders.

"Charles, thank you for meeting up with me. I needed to talk with someone desperately," Lisa began.

"That's no problem," replied Charles, smiling. "You know I love to talk with you and we haven't talked since I was accosted by those two women at the coffee shop!" They laughed about and recalled the incident all over again. It was still as funny as ever. The laughter subsided and Lisa's face took on a more serious

93

demeanour. She said,

"Do you remember when I told you about the dream of the sheep on the train and how the little wolf seemed familiar too?" Charles responded,

"Yes, I do, Lisa. Why?" She continued,

"Well, I know now that the little wolf is Dan!" Charles looked puzzled,

"Carry on," he said.

Lisa cleared her throat and said with obvious emotion,

"My husband, Daniel Thomas, is having an affair with Sally Adams!"

"Wait, what? No way!" gasped Charles, sitting back in his chair, completely taken aback with Lisa's statement, "Are you sure?" Lisa told Charles all about the drink in Dan's pick-up and then his entire confession.

"Well you have surprised me! Are you okay?" Charles questioned sympathetically. Lisa assured him she was fine and continued with her explanation of what she and Dan had arranged to do.

They spent the next hour talking about the implications of the whole episode, not only for Lisa but what it could also mean for the church.

"As we sit here right now, apparently, she is telling all to Pastor," Lisa continued. "So, I can't imagine what kind of storm that is brewing but it's going to be a big one. I never suspected anything was wrong between Pastor and Sally - she was there nearly every Sunday. Oh, how the mighty fall!"

Even though in the last few days, Charles and Lisa had been very unhappy with Pastor Adams to say the least, especially after the last incident at the bible class, there was no way that they would have wished this on him. They knew he was going to be devastated. This was going to shock the whole church, not just the people involved. The life of a Pastor, they agreed, can be very much like living in a goldfish bowl and whether he could take any blame for her adultery or not, his life was certainly going to come under some scrutiny. Christians, ironically, can be some of the most unforgiving and judgemental people.

"I would not like to be in that place right now!" Lisa went on.

"Oh, I don't know," said Charles. "It might be fun to be a fly on the wall!"

"Shame on you, Charles Michaels," Lisa laughed, "Shame on you!"

They both agreed that one day it would be really nice, just to go out and have a meal and have some time together without some major controversy going on. Lisa choked as she laughed and ate at the same time. She drank a sip of water and said,

"This can't be good for your digestion."

Charles paid for their meals again and as they left they hugged each other in the car park, they had hugged a number of times before after church meetings, as people do. But this hug was different. Lisa, for the first time in a long time, felt safe. For a brief moment, she felt the turmoil of the last few days melt away. They agreed that they would be there for each other whatever happened in the days ahead.

Then they both got in their cars and drove away. For possibly the first time in her life, Lisa felt sure that this was one man, other than her own father that she could definitely trust.

***

The following day, Lisa was going through her finances looking at what commitments she had, and it was becoming increasingly obvious that she was going to have to either get a job as she had thought or sell her home and get something smaller and cheaper to run. Looking at the size of their mortgage and knowing the kind of money Dan was bringing in possibly both options might be required. Either way she knew that she would be fine. It was time to think about what the best for her and her children would be now. She had been praying about the whole situation and hoped something was about to come to light.

All day long she kept thinking about Sally and Pastor Adams and her confession last night, assuming it had gone ahead. These situations were so horrible. People always ended up getting hurt.

"How is Sally going to cope with Dan?" Lisa thought to herself. "She'll have to come down a peg or two!" Lisa decided that whatever was happening, she wasn't going to waste her time thinking about them. She was going to take the bull by its horns and not be blown around in the wind by other people's decisions. She decided she would keep an eye open for a cheaper property, pray and move on with her life.

It had been a few days since she'd had any real God-incidences happen. She had heard someone call it that, rather than co-incidences and liked the term, even though up until a week or so ago she had never really seen anything happen, either God-incidences or co-incidences.

Although a part of her now feared that any plan God had for her life was scuppered, she also had a deep sense that God was truly walking by her side, watching, guiding, keeping her on the right path. She felt like she was being trained up for something. For what, she had no idea but whatever it was, it was going to change her life and now more than ever she believed Charles too was a significant part of the picture.

Whenever she and Charles were apart, she found herself thinking about him. She wished she could keep him in her pocket and take him around with her. Then she could bring him out when she needed his advice or to talk things through with him, which very recently was most of the time.

She was clearing her desk and putting all her papers in the neat folder system she had at home, thinking about her 'pocket

Charles's when she heard that now familiar soft voice whisper in her ear,

"Lisa, that's why I am here!"
She fell to her knees and wept. It was so true! God was still with her! Right there and then! She suddenly realized that He was there with her all the time. That soft, quiet, yet incredibly strong voice was God inside her. It was the Holy Spirit in her. The pocket Charles she had imagined being with her was really just a joke and God knew that. The truth was that she had the creator of the entire universe with her twenty-four seven; someone who loved every fibre in her; who had made her; who knew every little thing about her and who lived inside her.

"Father, thank you! Thank you for Your mercy" she cried. "I love you too!"
The funny thing was, hearing His voice so clearly like that was more powerful and meaningful than all the miraculous happenings that could ever take place. She knew that she wasn't alone and that if she did go off track at all, He would gently guide her back. That was the most reassuring and comforting thought in the world. The things that had happened and that were to come would have blown her mind a few weeks prior but now she was starting to feel equipped to handle almost anything that could be thrown at her, realising that the only confidence that she needed was confidence in the love and power of God! She felt relaxed in the fact that He was there and would intervene whenever it was necessary. All she had to do was to be available, have faith in Him and be obedient.

These days, when she read her bible, things were so different than ever before. She could recognize the God that was talking to her, the God of the Bible, loved her so much that He took the
time to speak to her! He felt so real now and it truly amazed her that it was Him, the same God, way back then guiding Abraham, Moses, David and all those bible heroes she had grown up with in her bible

studies were walking with her, holding her hand and guiding her steps. It felt incredible.

Lisa picked her bible feeling compelled to read some of the Gospels. She laughed at the story of the disciples being afraid when they saw Jesus walking on the water. She imagined a boat full of grown men all screaming and flipping out! As she read the events of the crucifixion, it made her weep. The pages of the Bible were now filled with real life situations and not just stories as she used to think. She saw the disciples and other men and woman of God as her friends.

Reading helped her to really get to know the nature of the one who had made her and loved her beyond measure, the one whom she would spend eternity with.

She closed the bible but the feeling that God had something more to show her stayed with her. She went to the kitchen to make herself a cup of coffee. She noticed a newspaper on the side. She sat down at the table and flicked through the pages as she drank her coffee. In the middle of the newspaper was a pull-out section with properties for sale. She thought she'd have a look due to the recent situation.

She was glancing through the pages when the phone rang. She picked the phone up with a cheery,

"Hello?" It was Pastor Adams. As soon as she recognized his voice on the telephone, shock hit her. All her troubles with Dan and Sally had slipped her mind for a while, as she had been engaging with her maker. She realized that maybe she shouldn't have sounded so happy.

"Is that Lisa?" asked the pastor.

"Hello Pastor," Lisa replied in a more serious tone. "How can I help you?" Pastor continued,

"Would it be okay for me to call round to see you sometime this afternoon, say two o'clock?"

This time, even though Lisa had the upper hand, she knew that he must be really hurting right now and despite the way he had treated her on other occasions she still felt sorry for the man. No one should have to go through what he must be going through now she thought. Although she felt sympathetic towards him she knew that she must maintain her position. She responded,

"Well, I have to go out in a few minutes, but I'll be back around three-thirty, so if you could make it around four, that would work for me."

"I have a meeting at four o'clock myself with Governor Philips," he explained. "So that's out of the question. Can't you change your plans?" Lisa could not believe the audacity of this man. She knew that 'meeting' was another word for a round of golf! He had totally tried to put her and her walk with God down the other day and now he had the nerve to try and make her adjust her schedule. She was having none of it. Her feelings of sympathy were interrupted by feelings of annoyance as the true colours of this so-called Pastor revealed themselves again. She took a deep breath and said,

"If you want to see me today, I can fit you in at four. You'll just have to rearrange your 'meeting' or come and see me another day, although my schedule is looking very full. I may be able to squeeze you in next Monday." There was an obvious pause on the other end of the line. Then the pastor responded with,

"Very well, I'll see you at four." With that she put the phone down. Her hands were shaking as she sat back down at the table to finish her coffee and her brief look at the local properties that were for sale or rent. As she started to calm down, she turned to the last page of the newspaper supplement and to her astonishment one of the ads had a red circle around it.

"How strange!" she thought to herself. The paper looked very new. Who could have read it before her? It could have only been either Dan or Sophie. There was no way the boys would have done that, but just to make sure, she called the boys in to the kitchen and asked them if they had been drawing in the newspaper. Even as she was speaking, she realized what a stupid question she was asking them. As if they could have done that! But she had started asking them, so she thought she'd finish, so as not to look silly in front of them. They stood there looking so cute and innocent, and a little bit confused. She sent them back in the lounge. Of course, it wasn't them.

Then she looked at the date on the paper. It was last night's free paper! Dan had left at three and it wasn't delivered until around six o'clock, so if it was anyone it had to be Sophie. It was a possibility, but to be honest, a very remote one. She looked at the paper again and the house with the mystery circle around it. There was something about the house that caused her to look at the description and the details of the sale. It was a run-down old farmhouse up in the mountains and outside of the town. She calculated that it must be about twenty to twenty-five miles out of town to the east away from the coast. One of the features of the sale was that it had one hundred and twenty-five acres included in the sale, with the option to buy another three hundred and fifty acres.

As she read that, her head dismissed it immediately but something in her heart told her to make an enquiry about it.

"That's crazy!" she said to herself. "What would I do with all that land? Just look at the state of the place as well!"

Suddenly, right out of the blue, she heard the soft voice in her head that she knew was God's say,

"It's yours, Lisa! Now go and get it!"

"What? Why?" she shouted, causing the boys to run in and stare at her. She sent them back into the lounge and carried on her conversation with God.

"I can't afford it!" she stated firmly. Quite why she had said that she had no idea, because it didn't have a price on it. It just read POA.

Why she was questioning what she knew to be God's voice

she didn't know, but she did. It looked very expensive even though it was run down, and she was needing to cut back on her expenses not increase them. Also, what would a girl like her do with a farm! She argued with
herself, remembering what she had read in the bible earlier. She knew that God didn't make mistakes and so then came phase two of the battle, she did what so many people do: she questioned whether she was hearing God or not. Was this voice just her own thoughts?

There was only one thing for it. She had to put it to the test. Remarkably, she felt that she actually heard God laugh, but regardless of all the miracles she had witnessed over the past days it just showed her humanity. She heard a voice say,

"And you laughed at the disciples?"
That really hit her hard. It was so true. She had, minutes before, laughed herself at the disciples' lack of faith. How they saw Jesus perform great miracles and then within hours questioned Him. He had just fed five thousand people with a small boy's lunch and they were all crossing the lake. They were hungry and realized they hadn't brought enough food and wondered where it was going to come from. They were human just the same as she was.

God said it was hers and she was going to find out for sure but before she made any enquiry, she was going to just check that Sophie hadn't circled the house for herself. She sent Sophie a text asking her the question. It came back immediately saying she hadn't even read the paper last night.

It was God - it had to be! What was her problem? Now she felt as faithless as the disciples, but at least she knew she was in good company. She decided to bite the bullet and make a call to the estate agent. Lisa dialled the number on the advert and waited for an answer.

"This is nuts," she thought to herself. "How am I going to be able to afford a house of any description? Never mind a farm with hundreds of acres! And why would I want a farm anyway? Oh well, here goes. If God wants me to have a farm then so be it. Who am I to argue? Have faith, Lisa!"

A young lady politely answered the phone and Lisa gave the details of the property she was enquiring about.

"Can you hold the line, please?" asked the woman and she was put on hold. An annoying tune played as she waited impatiently, drumming her fingers on the telephone table. Just as she was starting to get into the music, she was interrupted.

"Mrs Jeffreys?" asked a more senior lady. "Sorry to keep you waiting, we've just been checking on the details for you." Lisa was positive she hadn't given her name, but then maybe her mind was playing tricks on her.

"Mrs Jeffreys?" the lady continued. "This property has been on the market for over two years now and we haven't had a single enquiry. You are the first person to even call us about it. It's been most peculiar. I have been to the property myself and can tell you that the location is spectacular. When we took on this listing we felt sure it would be a quick sale, but no one seems interested at all. Very strange. Would you like a viewing?"
Lisa replied inquisitively,

"So just how much is the asking price?" Lisa explained her circumstances to the agent. A picture of Peter the disciple, almost drowning, flashed in front of her eyes.

"Well, Mrs Jeffreys," the estate agent went on, sounding almost ashamed that she couldn't answer Lisa's simple question. "This is a most unusual sale, in that we have no price and all the owner told us was that it was negotiable. We have been told to inform him when we have an interested party and then he will see if you're suitable." The lady seemed quite embarrassed about the terms of the sale but went on to say, "Shall we arrange a viewing and take it from there?"
Lisa finally realised that if God wanted this to happen it would.

"Yes, okay then," she replied boldly. "Why not?"

Chapter 9

The Pastor's True Colours

The appointment was made. She had arranged to see the farm on the following Monday morning, which was in two days' time. She could hardly wait.

Even though owning a farm was the last thing that Lisa had ever expected to do, she was now starting to look forward to viewing what God had told her was already hers. Every time she thought about the impracticalities of living twenty-five miles outside of the Hightown area, not to mention the financial burden it would be to her even if she was able to get a mortgage for it, she just thought about the disciples and their lack of faith even when they personally witnessed many miracles. She thought about the Israelites losing their faith in Moses even though he was the vessel through which God was able to part the Red Sea along with many other monumental miracles.

Then she would also look at the reality God had been to her in the last couple of weeks; how she had been given so many messages and how she had been able to single-handedly fight off and disarm three muggers. God was obviously in control here, she just needed to be obedient and stop doubting. Allowing herself to do that was still a battle, but she knew that with God anything was possible.

***

Lisa was shopping for groceries with the boys when she noticed the time. It was half-past three and Pastor Adams was due to be at her house in half an hour. She was not looking forward to this meeting with Pastor at all and she decided that she was going to turn up at the house right on four o'clock.

She sent Charles a text message to keep him informed of things to which he replied and said he would be praying for her; that he would have loved to be giving her his support but obviously couldn't be there in person. It just wouldn't look good if she was there with any man. It was nice to feel that he was there for her too.

Her main ally, of course, was God and He would be the one to make things happen. She trusted in him implicitly. She knew he would give her the words to say and the courage to say them and the wisdom to be quiet if necessary.

When she arrived home, Pastor's Mercedes was in front of her house. She pulled past it and onto her driveway. As she opened the front door and let the boys in, she could see Pastor getting out of his car. She told the boys to go and play upstairs and left the front door open for Pastor to come in.

"Father, help me now. Give me the love I need to defeat this man!" she prayed. Why those words she didn't know. There was a rat-a-tat-tat on the open front door.

"Come in, Pastor!" Lisa shouted from the kitchen and Pastor Adams came in. Lisa had decided that she wasn't going to start the discussion or say anything. She was just going to answer any questions he may have and get rid of him as quickly as she could.

Pastor did his usual politically correct greeting and complimented her home by calling it 'cosy', which Lisa knew meant small, in his eyes.

"Coffee?" she asked him.

"Oh yes please, Lisa. With cream?" he replied.

"Oh, I'm sorry I'm fresh out of cream, is milk okay?" Lisa said with some pleasure. To this he responded,

"No, I'll take it black."

It felt like he even wanted the upper hand in his choice of coffee. This was not going to be easy. He was a hard core, arrogant man who in Lisa's opinion was about to be brought down a peg or two.

"Lisa, let's not beat around the bush," Pastor interjected. "I'm sure this won't be news to you, but your husband has committed adultery with my Sally and has convinced her to leave me and my ministry and live with him and his sinful life."
Lisa gave him a wry smile and said,

"Well, Pastor, that is news to me! I heard she did all the chasing, but whatever you say. I know they are living together, yes."

The next ten minutes were all about what this was going to do to him and the fact that it could ruin him financially.

"I'm sure you'll cope, Pastor," Lisa responded encouragingly, trying to remember to show some empathy towards him. Big man or not he must be hurting.

He began to get angry towards Lisa's encouraging words.

"It's people like you, that do this to people like us!" he ranted. "There is no way my Sally would have done this to me. It's his doing, all of it! But she'll come running back to me when they run out of money - I know her! I just want you to know, Lisa, that I intend to fight this all the way and I will have my revenge. I have the best lawyers in the country and they tell me that they can take everything you have, because not only have you ruined my marriage but possibly my Church and therefore my livelihood!"

"How can you blame me, Pastor?" said Lisa calmly. He was turning red with rage and shouted right into her face,

"Because you should have kept your man satisfied, my dear! Haven't you read your bible? It says what will happen if you don't satisfy one another. It says he will stray. Don't you know?"
Quite how he managed to blame her was beyond Lisa, but he certainly was trying to intimidate her, that was for sure. She calmly

replied,

"All I can say, my loving Pastor, is that God will be my vindicator, He will be my judge!" She wasn't going to lose it as he was. She truly had God on her side and she needed Him. A fortnight ago she would have called the Police on this guy!

"Can't you remember my dream, Pastor? The sheep being devoured by the wolf? God told me something was going to happen, and you ignored my words and chose to put me down instead!" Suddenly he broke down and began crying like a baby.

"I know you are right, Lisa! I'm so sorry for being such a big fool! Will you please forgive me?" This haughty man suddenly looked so broken, almost childlike as he stood in the middle of the kitchen with his face in his hands.

"Yes, of course I will, Pastor, of course I will," replied Lisa, putting her hand on the shoulder of the sobbing 'man of God'. He turned and hugged Lisa in return and squeezed her tightly, too tightly. Within a flash, right out of the blue, Pastor Adams pulled Lisa's head back by her hair and tried to kiss her passionately. She shouted and tried to fight him off, but he was a big man and could easily over power her. He was shouting back at her, telling her it was God's plan for them to be together, and how he had always thought she was sexy. They wrestled in the kitchen as he tried to kiss her. Lisa screamed as he forced his advances on her.

Suddenly, a deep voice shouted from the front door,

"Get off her! Leave her alone!" It was a Policeman, who just happened to be passing the house when he heard Lisa's screams. He pulled the 'messed-up' man off Lisa and pushed him against the wall, turned him around and put his hand up behind his back. Adams shouted at the Policeman, telling him to take it easy but in one swift movement he was in cuffs and being dragged out of the house. He forced Adams onto his face on the front lawn for all the neighbours to see and read him his rights. Lisa sat down at the kitchen table, completely unharmed but visibly shaken.

107

The policeman called for assistance and within minutes a car with two more officers arrived. They bundled Adams into the car and took him away. The policeman came into the house to check on Lisa and took a statement from her.

The boys had come downstairs to see what all the noise was about. They were playing on the stairs with their Dad's old 'ghetto' blaster when all the fighting broke out. They were a little scared at first but when they saw the policeman it became much more fun, just like TV. Lisa explained to the officer what had happened, as well as everything that had gone on with Dan and Sally, which she felt was the reason for Adams' strange behaviour.

"The man is obviously completely messed up!" she said to the officer, who was taking notes.

Suddenly, they heard screams coming from the old stereo the boys had been playing with. Lisa got up and rushed over to them. She recognised the sound of her own screams and the terrifying voice of Adams shouting at her. Somehow the boys had managed to record the whole thing, by complete accident, on tape. How there had even been a tape in the thing was miraculous as far as Lisa was concerned, but there was, and they had somehow captured it all, from Adams blaming Lisa for Dan and Sally's affair right up to the police arriving. She gave it as evidence to the policeman who took it, along with her statement. The policeman thanked her for her co-operation and after Lisa assured him that she was fine, he left the house. She was badly shaken by it all, but she knew she would get over it soon enough.

She immediately phoned Charles. She really needed to see Charles. She asked him if he could meet up with her after he'd finished work.

"Of course," said Charles. "Are you okay?" He could tell by the tone of her voice that something was wrong. She said she'd explain everything later when they met up. What she needed right

108

now was a hug, a coffee and some way of venting. Charles was always good for that. He unknowingly helped her to be herself. Fortunately, Sophie was able to come around almost immediately. She had heard about the incident at Lisa's house, well at least that the police were involved in something, and wanted to help out where she could. She was such a great help and considering she was still only seventeen she had a very wise head on her shoulders. Lisa really found a connection with Sophie and had started to feel that they would be together for a long time in some capacity or other.

When Lisa arrived at the coffee shop on the High street, she pulled into the car park and was immediately followed in by Charles. She parked and ran over to his car, hugged him, sobbing on his shoulder.

"Hey, Lisa! Hey, it'll be okay," said Charles compassionately, drying her tears with his finger.

"Come on, let's go in and have a coffee and relax for a while. I think we've both got things to talk about."

They were lucky in that they were able to get a sofa seat and sat facing each other, in a little private area in the corner of the shop and there Lisa filled Charles in on the terrible meeting she'd had with Adams. Charles was amazed, shocked and angered by the words coming from Lisa's mouth. He could hardly believe his ears.

"Goodness me, Lisa, that's awful. And he calls himself a man of God!" Charles sympathized and held her hand. It felt cold. He massaged her hands in his. She was noticeably trembling as she relayed the gruesome story.

"Are you sure you're okay? There are people who can help with this type of thing you know!" he said in a concerned manner.

"No honestly, I'll be fine. I don't want to talk to anyone but you and God right now. I don't feel I can trust anyone!" Charles agreed and continued to rub her hands with his.

"Lisa? I have something to tell you too." said Charles

seriously. He paused and then said, "They're letting me go at work."

"No! Not you!" Lisa replied sympathetically. "Why?" Charles continued.

"They said that things have gone from bad to worse at the plant here and they can either transfer me to another plant on the east coast about three hundred miles away, or I can find another job, but they agreed to pay me up until the end of my contract, which would mean full pay for the next eleven months, which is a generous offer." Lisa shook her head.

"What are you going to do?" she asked.

"Well," replied Charles, pausing again while looking into Lisa's concerned but still overwhelmingly beautiful brown eyes. "Ordinarily I would have no problem in making this kind of decision; I would have no hesitation in taking the transfer. It's a very well-paid job that I really enjoy, but…." Charles paused again and squeezed Lisa's hand. "…. I can't leave you!"

There was silence for a few moments then Lisa burst into tears and hugged Charles tightly and sobbed in his ear,

"Thank you, Charles! Thank you so much!"

"Not a problem, Lisa," said Charles as they unravelled and looked at each other. "You mean the world to me, Lisa."
Lisa hung her head. She wanted to say something back but now wasn't the time. They hugged again, both sobbing now. Charles put his strong hands on her shoulders and looked her in the eyes.

"And also," Charles carried on, "There is no way God would let me go!" They smiled at each other, relaxed into their seats and both took a drink of their coffee.

Lisa's cappuccino left foam on her top lip. They both laughed hysterically, which caused people to look over, but they didn't care. Charles took a napkin and wiped Lisa's lip and gazed into her eyes.

"Thank you for this, Lisa," Charles said lovingly, to which Lisa replied,

"But I've not done anything. It's you I have to thank, Charles."

Lisa suddenly realized she hadn't told him about the farm, the house she'd seen in the paper that she was viewing on Monday. With all the talk of the pastor molesting her and Charles losing his job, it had completely slipped her mind.

"Oh, my goodness, Charles!" Lisa gasped, holding her hand to her mouth. Charles eagerly waited for Lisa to carry on. She said, "There's something else that I have to tell you."

"Oh no! I'm sure I can take any more!" he said jokingly. "But go on, tell!"

As Lisa told Charles excitedly all about the property being ringed in red in the newspaper and the voice saying it was hers to have and the fact that no-one had even enquired about it, he sat listening intently with his fingertips over his lip, shaking his head in amazement.

"That's amazing! How great is our God!" Charles went on emphatically. "Lisa, this has to be Him, it has to be! I have never really thought it necessary to tell you Lisa, with everything that has been going on, but as a youth I spent eighteen months working on a farm and really loved it. I never pursued it as a profession because I got my degree in engineering and knew I was to go in that direction, but wow that's amazing!" Lisa chuckled,

"I can't imagine you in dungarees, Charles!"
They both laughed out loud again causing people to turn and look and some people near to them actually got up and left.

"If only they knew!" whispered Lisa.

"I know," said Charles. "They'd be joining in the celebrations with us!"

They talked for what must have been a couple of hours and found that the more they talked things through, the more things made sense. God was totally in control and their faith was getting stronger and stronger. Lisa felt genuinely happy, which was incredible in itself, considering the day she'd had.

They both agreed that they needed to forgive Adams; he was a man under intense stress and pressure and not everyone knows the comfort of a saviour in their lives even though they may be labelled a pastor. They also agreed not to call him by his title anymore.

One thing they had both found interesting was that Adams had overpowered her in her kitchen. God hadn't given her the strength to overcome the man, the way He did with the muggers in the park, but he still took complete care of her by having the policeman walk by at that precise moment. They determined from this that God didn't want her to think that he had given her any super powers or anything but it was entirely Him working through her. Lisa admitted to Charles that when it was all happening she wondered, for a split second before the policeman arrived, where God was. This again, gave them more reasons to proclaim how great God is and how He is truly in control of everything in their lives.

As they were chattering away, in awe of the greatness of their maker, Lisa's mobile phone rang. She answered it quickly as it would rarely ring unless it was Sophie. It wasn't. It was a Policeman from Hightown asking Lisa if she could just pop down to the station.

"Now?" she asked, and the reply was an affirmative. Lisa said she'd pay for the coffees as Charles was now unemployed, but as usual Charles insisted that he should pay, then they both left the building. Lisa felt nervous and uncomfortable at the thought of going to the police station at night, so Charles said he would drive her there and go in with her even if he had to wait for her in the reception.

"Come in, Mrs Jeffreys," said an officer coming out of an office at the station. "This shouldn't take too long." Lisa got up and

112

followed the officer, leaving Charles sat at the near end of a long line of chairs in the waiting room. She went into a little office and the lady officer told her to take a seat. The officer asked if Lisa was okay after the incident to which she confirmed her wellbeing.

"We need to know what you want to do regarding Adams," the officer asked. "Do you wish to press charges or not? We need to know how you feel about the whole matter because we know you attend his church and know him personally. I will inform you though, that Adams has admitted guilt over the said incident but has claimed to you provoked him and came on to him. He said that you had made it clear to him on several occasions that you 'liked' him and would often flirt with him."

As Lisa listened she felt her own jaw dropping.

"What?" she exclaimed. "That man is amazing! What a liar! How can he call himself a man of God?" The officer calmed Lisa down and asked again if she wanted to press charges.

"Look," said Lisa with great authority. "I want this noted by you, please! What that man has said is a complete fabrication. I completely deny everything that he has said. You have the tape and my statement. You can surely tell what he is like? That is what happened." she continued. "I have never flirted with that man. I am a married woman and even though my husband has left me for Mrs Adams, there is no way I would do anything to dishonour my God and the vows I made to Dan when I got married. In fact, if you want a character reference to agree with what I am saying, there is a gentleman outside in the waiting room, who drove me here, who will vouch for me. No, I do not wish to press charges, but under the condition that Adams refutes those words and denies all his accusations. If he wishes to continue with his lies, I will press charges and you can tell him from me that I will see him in court and watch him squirm under oath!" She sighed and took a breath.

"That's all we need to know, Mrs Jeffreys. We'll be in

touch," replied the officer and showed Lisa to the door. She stormed out of the office and didn't even wait for Charles. She just walked out

of the station and onto the street. Charles followed her,

"Are you okay?" He asked. "What happened in there?"

"Just take me back, Charles," Lisa replied. "I'll explain on the way." They got in his car and drove away.

Charles was as angry as Lisa as she explained what that man had said.

"It's hard to believe who he really is! How could he make such accusations?" said Charles emphatically. "What a disgrace for a so-called man of the cloth!"

She explained how she'd left it with the police and Charles agreed that it was the right thing to do. At least her name would be cleared.

"God will deal with him, Charles, in a way that will be right. I have to leave it to Him now."

They got to the coffee shop and Lisa thanked Charles. They said they would see each other over the weekend sometime and talk some more. Lisa got out of his car, gave Charles a little wave and went to her own car and drove home.

When she arrived home, she thanked Sophie for her usual reliability and saw her out of the door and home. Lisa closed the door behind her and went into the lounge and flopped in her couch.

"Life has never been this eventful!" she thought to herself and laughed, remembering people from her past telling her how boring it must be to be a Christian.

Chapter 10

The Name Above All Names

On the one hand, it seemed strange not going to church on Sunday, but in some way, Lisa also felt a sense of relief. She put it down to the whole hypocrisy of Mr Adams. She wanted to be obedient to God in everything she did but hadn't felt right about going to church at all this week.

She brushed it aside and thought she'd spend this Sunday with the boys who hadn't even surfaced from out of bed yet and it was now 9:30am. So, she decided not to wake them but to use the time she had and get some cleaning done around the house.
She was cleaning the shower in her bathroom with the shower head and some new spray cleaner she wanted to try.

"Hmm pretty good!" she said to herself and stepped back to admire her handywork. She just noticed how much she had steamed up the bathroom, when something caught her eye. There was writing on the main mirror under her lamp. At first, she thought the boys had been doodling or something, but then realized it wasn't them when she read,

'Read, Pray, Obey'.

Even though she had now seen many messages from Him in different forms, it never ceased to completely amaze her and take her by surprise. Under normal circumstances this may have even scared her but instead, she felt comforted and knew that God was speaking to her.

"I am! Erm, I will, thank you!" she said apologetically,

stuttering a little as she realized she almost sounded a little stern with Him. She looked again at the mirror. It had changed. This time it read,

'Stay close!'

"Yes, Father," she replied. "I will."

There was no way she was going to clean the mirror, so she left the bathroom and went to sit on her bed to pray. She asked God if he needed to speak to her and as soon as she uttered the words, that familiar soft voice spoke. He said,

"Lisa, I need you to pray so I can speak to you. When I created Adam, I gave man authority on Earth, so I need you to pray to allow me to do what I need to do. I cannot go back on my word, my child."

"Yes Father," Lisa replied, almost gasping for air, flabbergasted that she was conversing with Him in such a way.

"I need to teach you my ways." God continued. "I need you to know who I am. I need you to know my Name and much more."

"Yes Father," Lisa repeated not knowing what else to say. He carried on,

"Stay close, my sweet child, stay close." Lisa replied,

"I will, my Lord, I will!" Her eyes opened, as if they had a mind of their own. She was on her knees on the floor and she hadn't noticed herself move from the bed.

The house was silent. Completely silent.

She knelt in the peace with her head bowed thinking about what God had been saying. 'What did he mean by, "I need you to know my name"?' she thought to herself. 'But your name is God isn't it?'

She heard the boys moving in their room. God must have kept them quiet for a reason that morning. They bounded into her room screaming,

"Mummy!" and flinging their arms around their kneeling mother. The peace was certainly broken.

They all had their breakfast and went out in the car. Lisa took her bible with her and everywhere they went she kept taking a look through the pages, trying to discover things about God that could help her find out more about Him.

They went to the park but today the boys had to swing by themselves; mummy was reading. Not that it bothered them, they were happy just to be out of the house and playing. When they had lunch at the burger house; mummy was reading. In fact, everywhere they went, mummy was reading but it was still a great day for the boys, they had fun and did a few things that mummy never noticed.

For Lisa though, it was getting more and more frustrating. Nowhere, could she find anything about his name other than God and Lord. Although she did notice that sometimes Lord was written in capital letters. She asked God himself for help but at that time she heard nothing. One thing she did find out though, was that it says in 2 Timothy that we are called to study. Was God telling her to study? Did he want her to search for these answers rather than just give them to her? It certainly seemed like it.

When they got home the boys went off to play and Lisa started up her computer. She wondered if any theologians could throw any light on the subject.

She made herself a coffee and sat down in her little study room. She bowed her head and asked God to reveal to her his name. What was she to call Him?

She opened up a search engine and typed in the words, "what is the name of God?" She was quite shocked at the result. There was so much information on something that she had no idea about. Which should she read? Again, she asked God and was immediately drawn to a website. She clicked on the link and sat there reading.

She was there for over an hour. She found out something that totally shocked her, if what they were saying was true. On this

117

website, the people were stating that the name of God had been removed from scriptures and replaced with the words 'the LORD', written in capital letters. She opened her bible in the Old Testament to check again and sure enough, there it was many times. The website went on to say that His name had been removed nearly seven thousand times because apparently the rabbis at a certain time, many years before Christ, had decided his name was too holy to be spoken. The word LORD had replaced His name, YHWH, commonly known as the 'Tetragrammaton'.

"Not so common!" Lisa thought, as she had never heard of it, but carried on reading. She was advised to read the 'preface' of her bible and sure enough, it was confirmed there too, only not in so much detail. Why had she never seen this before and why was this been so subtly hidden?

Apparently, no-one was totally certain of the exact pronunciation of YHWH, but it was more than likely to be Yahweh or Yahuweh. The term 'Jehovah' had come from this, which she had heard because of a certain religion, but this website was saying that this was an error.

"So," she said to herself with a smile feeling that she had actually achieved something. "Your name is Yahweh!"

"And yours is Lisa!" a voice said in her head.

"Amen!" she replied laughing. "Amen!"

She had actually achieved something that God had told her to search for and she was delighted. Admittedly she had been aided by the internet, which would become an amazing help to her in the weeks that followed. The years of study people had done was readily available at the click of a mouse. All she had to do was to ask the Holy Spirit for discernment, to eliminate what was fact over somebody's opinion.

That Sunday she learned that so many of the names of the people in biblical times had Yahweh's name within their own name.

People like Isaiah, whose name was really Isayah, contained His name, as with Jeremiah and anyone with 'iah' in their name. 'Yah' had been replaced with 'iah' so many times it was astonishing. She discovered that even the name of Our Saviour Jesus had been changed. He would have been called Yahshua or Y'shua for short, when he was walking the earth, meaning 'Yahweh saves' as, she discovered, it says in the bible where the angel appeared to Joseph. She found the notes of the Bible said that Jesus was the English translation of 'Iesous' which was Greek for Yahshua. The truth was that our saviour's precious name had been altered through the centuries by different translations and transliterations, from Aramaic to Greek to Latin and then to English to arrive at Jesus. A name that

she discovered did not even exist at the time of Christ! Mary would have called him Yahshua and so would everyone who knew him at the time. If we simply wanted to translate His name to English, then we would use the name Joshua!

"What was going on here?" she wondered. She began to realise just why God had wanted her to study. Now she was a woman on a mission! A quest for the truth! She felt like a female Indiana Jones, searching and digging, uncovering hidden treasures. When she read her bible now, things somehow started to be a lot more personal. From now on she would try to read the name 'the LORD' as Yahweh. She found the Scriptures came alive and when reading the Psalms, she felt closer to how David must have truly felt about his God.

This alone was true revelation to Lisa and her relationship with her heavenly Father, from this point on, really accelerated and grew deeper and deeper by the minute.

She was feeling on top of the world. Most people, looking in from the outside, would have thought that everything was going wrong for Lisa; her husband had left her which meant she was going to have to move to a new house and relocate; she had little or no income coming in other than what Dan would pay her; she had just been attacked physically and verbally by her pastor, who now had accused her of being a 'tramp'. Through all this, however, she was building a deeply meaningful relationship with her maker, her heavenly Father, Yahweh.

She sent a text message to Charles to check he was going to go with her to see the farm in the mountains, which when she thought about it, excited her spirit.

"I wouldn't miss it for the world!" was the message that returned and with that, Lisa settled the boys in bed and tried to get some sleep knowing that she had some big days ahead of her.

As she lay in bed, thinking about all the things that she had been learning that day, she felt amazed and quite privileged to have discovered so much.

"This must be really important to Him!' she thought as she snuggled up to her duvet. "I would hate it if people called me by another name that wasn't mine!" She prayed,

"Father, thank you for revealing what you have today. Speak to me in my dreams, help me to see the truth behind all this, in Jesus… erm Yahshua's name, Amen."

As Lisa woke early the next morning she rolled over and stretched. She turned her head to check her alarm clock.

"Oh, my word!" she exclaimed, jumping up immediately. "Boys! Hurry up and get dressed! We're late!" It was 8:45 and Charles was picking them up at 9:00. Normally she didn't need an alarm clock, she was always up early.

"I must have been in a deep sleep!" she thought to herself as she looked at herself in the mirror as she hurriedly ran her straighteners through her hair. It was right then that she remembered what had happened. She had been dreaming. As she recalled her dream it all came flooding back.

In her dream, she was a bride about to get married, only she

120

couldn't because for some strange reason she didn't know the name of her husband. There was a book on a table within which she knew his name was written, but there was a man dressed in a suit there, who had his hand over the pages of the book, so that she couldn't see. The groom was standing at the altar, waiting to get married and she, the bride, was talking with this man in the suit. She remembered

that this man had a mobile phone and a big shiny watch and his hands we covered in jewellery. He was talking about everything he could apart from the wedding, totally distracting her. Meanwhile, the groom continued to wait. At one point in the dream, she actually danced with this other man, while the groom looked on.

She was pulled away from the replay of her dream by a loud 'ding dong'!

"Aarrgghh Charles!" she exclaimed, putting on her dressing gown and then running down the stairs. She opened the door to Charles and ran back upstairs shouting,

"Make yourself at home."

She was ready in ten minutes which was a record for her and ran back downstairs. She stopped in her tracks at the lounge door. Charles was in the lounge with the boys and they were bouncing all over him. It was a sight she had been longing to see for years now; something Dan had never done with them. She didn't want to interrupt them, but time was pressing on.

"Hey you lot!" Lisa laughed. "Come on! we're late and I'm waiting to go!" They all laughed, left the house and got into Charles's shiny, silver BMW. It had a lovely clean, warm, leathery smell inside. Lisa found it hard to keep the smile off her face as they drove down the road.

"Life is great! God is good! Yahweh is amazing!" she thought to herself and sat back in her seat for their drive into the mountains.

They were to meet Mrs McLean, the estate agent, at the

entrance to the farm because apparently, it had a long driveway and the house couldn't be seen from the road. The 'sat-nav' was telling them that they were a just few miles from their destination, so everybody in the car was looking out for the estate agents red Peugeot car.

The scenery was incredible with mountain views, pine forests, streams and rivers. God's creation seemed to be everywhere around them. It was almost overwhelming; so much of it and the amazing thing to them all was that they hadn't seen another car in ten minutes. They were all gasping at the wonderful landscape when they came across the red Peugeot. They were only a few minutes late, which was amazing in itself, considering all the 'oohs' and 'ahhs' that had been going on in the car and how late they were when they started out.

Mrs McLean was already standing outside her car enjoying the panoramic views and the beautiful weather. Everybody greeted each other warmly with smiles and laughter, pleased and relieved to see one another. Jenny McLean got back in her car and shouted,

"Follow me!"

The two cars set off slowly down the driveway towards the property. The air was thick with anticipation. The boys couldn't contain themselves and were literally bouncing with excitement. Two minutes down the driveway, the house still wasn't visible. The location, however, was incredible. They drove into what was almost like a hidden valley with far outstretching views. It was amazing to think that this was only half an hour or so from the busyness of the towns around Hightown.

They went over the brow of a hill and suddenly, there in front of them was a wooden sign which read, 'The Ark'. Just seeing the sign made Lisa gasp but before she could say anything there it was; a huge, beautiful old colonial style farmhouse with a wonderful porch wrapped all around it. Surrounding the house were various outbuildings and lots of small paddocks and corrals. It was like something off an old TV show. Almost like 'The Waltons' but grander in its day by far. It was a little run down now. It certainly needed some TLC, but it was truly breath-taking.

They all got out of the car and just gasped open mouthed at the beauty and wonder of this place.

"Welcome to The Ark" said Jenny with a smile.

Lisa slowly turned right around trying to take it all in but still thinking to herself that there would be no way that they would be able to afford it, but she was just going to enjoy it for now and have a nice day out. As she was turning around, admiring the vistas, a picture flashed into her mind of Yahshua Jesus sleeping on a boat in a storm. It took her by surprise, but it went as quickly as it came.

Jenny led them towards the front door explaining on the way that the boundary to the property was right from the entrance where they met and that it was all included in the sale, but there was more available if they wished.

Charles stood on the deck, looking out at the view, with his hands on his hips. He thought to himself,

"Why does this place look so familiar!" Nothing came to mind, so he brushed his thoughts off and continued listening to Jenny's sales banter. The boys were positively springing up and down by this time and wanted to run around rather than go and look inside the house, but Lisa insisted that they stayed with her and Charles.

The inside of the house was fantastic. All original features and in much better condition than it looked outside. Lisa loved it and the more she saw of it, the more she fell in love. Charles was being more serious, looking at problems around the place that needed to be fixed but underneath his professional looking seriousness, he was bubbling over too. It was certainly way bigger than Lisa needed right now but there was just something about this place that couldn't be explained but she knew that it would be a wonderful place to live and a great place for the boys to grow up at.

"So," asked Lisa tentatively. "When the owner says it's negotiable, has he given you any idea of roughly how much he wants? Not that it matters, because I'm sure we can't afford it, but I'm just curious." The picture of a boat in a storm flashed on and off in her mind again; the same scene as before, only this time the disciples were trying to wake Jesus up. Jenny replied with a smile on her face,

"I don't have any idea of the price, Mrs Jeffreys, all old Mr Carter wants is for the right person to take this place on. He says he will know if it's the right person when they see his conditions of sale."

"What are they then?" asked Lisa curiously. Jenny paused and then went on to say,

"You have to answer three questions correctly and then I will be able to get the price for you."

"Oh, my word," said Lisa despairingly. "What sort of questions? I've never been very good at quizzes!"

"Well if you're interested in living here, I have to ask you the questions in this envelope." Jenny waved a simple brown envelope at them. She said,

"Let's sit out on the deck and enjoy the views, shall we?" Charles and Lisa followed Jenny smiling at each other.

"What do you think, Charles?" asked Lisa, to which he replied,

"Whatever you think is right, Lisa. Go for it!" The boys played on a grassy area in front of the porch as they all sat at a picnic table on the deck.

"There's a lot more to see, Mrs Jeffreys, if you wish to do this after you've looked around?" said Jenny with her finger under the flap, about to open the envelope.

"Let's just get it over and done with, so I know if I can have

124

it or not!" Lisa replied impatiently.

"Okay then, here we go!" As she opened the envelope Jenny said to Lisa and Charles. "You know, we have never been able to understand how no-one has even enquired about this place. It's quite spooky, really." She smiled and unfolded the piece of paper. Lisa and Charles sat leaning forward waiting intently. Jenny cleared her throat,

"Okay then… question one: do you love this place?"

Lisa looked at Charles and laughed.

"I adore it! Don't you Charles?"

"I do!" replied Charles, sounding like he was marrying the place.

"Good! Correct answer!" replied the quiz master with a broad grin on her face. "Question Two," Jenny began again. Lisa shuffled on her seat, now feeling a little more confident.

"Will you agree to use this land for the purpose God has intended for it and only use it to grow produce and rear animals?"

Lisa thought a little and looked at Charles for reassurance. He nodded. Lisa said,

"I agree!"

"Correct answer!" chuckled Jenny. She carried on. "In that case, you have also just agreed not to build or develop any part of the property to sell, but you may build for the use of guest accommodation."

"Great!" admitted Lisa. Charles nodded again and smiled with excitement and anticipation of question three.

"And finally, question three," said Jenny with a slight puzzled expression as she read the final question.

"This may be slightly harder. Anyway, here goes… What do the letters Y A F M P T Y H B L T B mean?"

As Jenny was halfway through the acronym of those so, so

125

familiar letters, Lisa almost fell off her chair with astonishment. She let out a little squeak of excitement. Charles gasped,

"No way! Are you serious?"

Charles and Lisa looked and laughed at each other in utter bewilderment, completely lost for words. Another picture came into her mind. Yahshua Jesus was standing up in the boat, on a calm sea, laughing at the disciples. Again, it disappeared as quickly as it came. Jenny said in a concerned voice,

"I'm sorry, would you like me to read the letters to you again, I think they stand for something." Lisa cut her off and said,

"No, no Jenny, it's fine! We just didn't know anyone else knew those letters and what they mean. They mean…." Lisa paused, knowing that Yahweh was fully involved in this. She almost couldn't believe what she had been asked and what she was about to say. She continued. "…. They mean, 'You are far more powerful than you have been led to believe.'"

Chapter 11

Old Mr Carter

The rest of The Ark was fabulous. Jenny looked after the boys as Charles and Lisa looked around what seemed like every inch of the grounds around the house and outbuildings. There was a guest house with two bedrooms in addition to the main house and a building called the bunkhouse which was exactly that; a house full of bunk beds.

Of course, there was a lot they couldn't really see as it would have taken them the best part of a week to see all of the land. The big question as to what they would ever do with such a place and the slightly smaller but more obvious question of how much 'Old Mr Carter' was going to ask for The Ark were both going to be left to Yahweh now.

Lisa was excited. This had to be a God thing. No-one else could have done that. The messages, the acronym, the coffee shop rest room door and now question three of the qualification for this awesome property. Even with her small amount of faith, she deep inside knew that this place was to be somehow put in her hands by Yahweh. This had to be his will.

None of them wanted to leave. Both Lisa and Charles felt very comfortable up there on the mountain. The boys just loved the space. It felt like they could run forever and still be in their back garden. Charles was full of enthusiasm, planning how this could be part of his future as well as Lisa's and above all hoping that Lisa was going to be a large part of his future too. He'd mentioned the other day to Lisa about his farming experience in his younger years and now having lost his position at work, he had no real reason to stay in Hightown and he'd also said that he didn't want to leave the area because of her, but nothing was said between them about their future and whether they had one together. One thing was for certain though, he loved everything about her and being in her company was the best place to be in the world. To be with Lisa at the Ark and carve out whatever future God had for them both would be paradise for him. He just wasn't certain if Lisa felt the same way.

It was late afternoon when they decided that they had better head off home. Jenny had been there for hours with them too, although it was her job to sell this place and she would be making a good commission; that they were sure of.

They all got in their cars. Lisa said goodbye to what she knew was going to be her new home and they followed Jenny back down the drive the way they had come in.

"What a place!" Lisa said with total excitement. "But what would we do with all that land? Would we have to farm it?" she asked. Charles replied,

"I know God wants us to have it that's for sure, well you anyway. So, we should just accept what he's got for us because it's going to be good!"

Lisa could sense the uncertainty of his involvement, in his tone of voice and dearly wanted to say something. She wanted him with her all the way. She always felt safe whenever he was around and hoped it was right with Yahweh for them to be together at the Ark. Dan had always been a stumbling block for Lisa but now he had resolved that problem. She truly hoped Dan was going to be happy and had indeed, asked God to bless him. She couldn't tell Charles about the way she felt, by no means. But she knew it was right to include him, at least in the plans for 'The Ark'.

"What do you mean, 'well you anyway'? I hope, Charles Michaels, that you're not getting cold feet and trying to back out of

128

this?" She knew he didn't mean it that way, but it was easier for her to say it like that. She went on. "You're in this as deep as I am surely?"

"Oh, I didn't mean it like that, Lisa," said Charles apologetically. "I want this as much as you do, I just didn't know if you had included me in your plans!"

"Oh Charles!" responded Lisa. "I know Yahweh has brought us together for this very purpose. I couldn't do this without you!"

"Great!" said Charles. "That's a deal then." He paused. "Who is Yahweh?"

Lisa took great comfort in the fact that Charles hadn't heard the name Yahweh before. She felt slightly less stupid about being a Christian for as many years as she could remember and not knowing the name of her God.

"Can we go for a bite to eat somewhere first," pleaded Lisa. "And I promise on the way back I will tell all."

"More secrets?" laughed Charles. Lisa playfully slapped Charles on the shoulder. They laughed, and Charles pulled into the car park of a family pub with an indoor play area.

"Is this okay?" he asked knowingly. The boys were already springing up and down with excitement.

"That'll do fine!" smiled Lisa. "Just fine, Mr Michaels!"

The journey home was none stop conversation; Lisa telling Charles about her findings concerning God's name and Charles firing back questions. He took it on board like a dry sponge in a bath. He said it 'filled in holes' he'd had for years and questions that somehow were never answered.

She told him about the dream of the groom waiting to get married. They both agreed it was Yahshua and the Church, the second coming of the Christ, and the smartly dressed man hiding the name of the groom from the bride was Satan in the world, deceiving the Church.

"You see, there is power in the name, Charles!" Lisa said emphatically. "Satan does not want the church to realize the power that it has!"

"It makes sense, Lisa," Charles added. "Think about the messages you've been getting." It was all starting to come together for the first time and was extremely exciting for both of them. She told Charles about the conversation with Yahweh and what he had asked her to study.

"I feel there is a whole lot more, Charles. Satan has taken the power from the Church and we've not even noticed it going. It has been taken right from under our noses but over such a long period of time that no-one has seen it leaving.

"We have to get it back! We have to get back to the truth!" Charles agreed and said,

"When you took on those muggers in the park, what was the first thing you did?" Lisa replied,

"I disarmed the guy!"

"Exactly!" said Charles. "You took away the very thing that could do you harm - the weapon! That is what Satan has done. He's removed the weapon. He's disarmed the Church!"

"Wow," said Lisa thinking hard about what they were saying. "Can you answer this for me then, Charles?" He laughed,

"I'll try!" Lisa went on,

"In my dream, what stopped the groom marrying the bride? Can't you marry someone if you don't know their name?"

"Not legally," replied Charles, putting his lawyer hat on. "If someone has a pseudonym it wouldn't go on their marriage certificate. The certificate has to have their real name on it unless it had been changed by deed poll. The marriage wouldn't be valid."

Nothing was said for the next few minutes as they deliberated on what their conversation meant. As they approached Hightown, Charles broke the silence.

"We need to pray, Lisa. This is huge!"

Lisa agreed. She looked in the back of the car at the pair of sleeping boys. It had been a great day. She was feeling kind of tired too and longed to put her feet up on her couch. She imagined the time that she would be able to do that at The Ark with Charles and sighed contently.

They pulled up outside Lisa's house and Charles turned the engine off.

"I'm going to call Jenny in the morning to find the outcome of our test and see where we go from there," Lisa said and asked. "Can we meet up sometime tomorrow? We need to start to plan things, if that's alright with you."

"Of course," replied Charles. "I have some idea's too that I would like to share with you. Shall I come early?"

"Yes," Lisa smiled. "That would be lovely, come about eight and I'll make you breakfast. How do you like your eggs?"
Charles laughed and said.

"I'll let you decide!"
They hugged, and Lisa got out of the car. She opened the back door and woke the boys, who both stretched and yawned and reluctantly got out of their comfortable back seat and stepped out onto the drive way. Charles reversed down the drive and they all waved after him.

They went into the house and all went off to bed. Lisa took her notebook and jotted down all of the day's events. She smiled as she read little bits from previous occasions, feeling that one day she would be able to share an incredible story.

The following morning, Lisa left the boys to sleep in a little and got on with some chores around the house before Charles arrived. She put some coffee on and at 8:00am on the dot as usual, the doorbell rang. She opened the door and there stood Charles, looking as fresh as ever. This man was obviously a morning person! Lisa was always a 'somewhere in the middle' person when it came to mornings, but today she felt really good and excited about the day ahead.

She made hers and Charles's eggs 'sunny side up' to suit the mood they both seemed to be in. They sat down together and ate for the first time in Lisa's house.

Being with Charles felt so right to Lisa. For the very first time she allowed herself to imagine a future with Charles. She didn't allow herself to process that thought too far though because technically she was still married. She hadn't heard anymore from Dan about the divorce and knew she would have to chase him up on the subject before seeing her solicitor about the whole issue. She was going to make this happen, even if Dan hadn't been completely to blame for their lack of interest in each other, he certainly was to blame for his affair and subsequent departure from his home and his family.

"What time does Jenny open her office, Lisa?" asked Charles wiping his mouth with a napkin.

"It should be any-time now, I'll give her a call," said Lisa nervously putting her fingers to her mouth, mimicking biting her nails to show just how nervous she was.

"Yeah, go for it," replied Charles supportively. "I'm here for you." She got up to go to the phone looking at Charles all the way. He smiled at her and gestured to her to get on with it.

"Would you like me to call?" Charles said, laughing at Lisa's hesitant manner.

"No way!" said Lisa and picked the phone up and dialled Jenny's number.

In a way, Charles wished he had called because for the next few minutes he was completely in the dark making his anticipation all the harder to bear and by the look on Lisa's face and tone something had happened. He was trying to get the gist of the conversation by reading Lisa's facial expressions. She was listening hard and frowning when she heard that Jenny had seen Mr Carter last night when she got back from showing the property. He was in hospital being treated for some long-term illness. Jenny said that when she gave Mr Carter your answers he was absolutely delighted. This made Lisa's persona completely change with a broad smile which in turn relieved Charles, especially when Lisa said,

"Oh great!" Then Jenny said that after he had told her how much he wanted for the property he signed power of attorney over to her to allow her to complete the sale on his behalf, which made Lisa frown again.

"He just has one more request for you Lisa," said Jenny. "And what's that?" replied a desperately inquisitive Lisa, Charles hanging on every word and expression. Jenny continued,

"He wants to meet you. Nothing more."

"Okay, no problem!" confirmed Lisa.

"Good!" said Jenny. "So… I can give you the price now we've done all that."

Lisa was desperate to know. This, initially, for her, could have been their stumbling block but now all she wanted was to see how God was going to make this happen. It was going to have to take a miracle.

"So," said Jenny tentatively. "For the whole estate, including all outbuildings and one hundred and twenty-five acres… there is no charge!"

"What!" exclaimed Lisa. Charles was now worried looking at Lisa's concerned expression, thinking that the price that Jenny had given her must have been way more than they could manage.

"Could you repeat that please, Jenny?" asked Lisa trying to act calm and collected on the outside, while on the inside she wanted to explode with joy! Jenny repeated,

"No charge, Lisa! He just wants you to pay our fees."

"So how much would they be?" asked Lisa, playing it cool again. Jenny replied,

"I haven't worked it all out yet, but it won't be any more than five thousand pounds!"

133

"What? No way! Really?" shouted an excited Lisa, not able to contain herself now; Charles did not know what to make of it all.

"Oh, my goodness!" shrieked Lisa. "Can we come straight away?"

"Of course!" said Jenny. "And would you like me to take you to see Mr Carter?"

"If that's okay with you? Yes please! We'll be right over!" She put the phone down slowly and thoughtfully.

"Well, well? What did she say?" begged Charles chomping at the bit with excitement.

"Oh Charles," she said looking saddened. "We won't be able to afford it!" She looked at Charles's change in expression from excited anticipation to despair, then said, "Not this week anyway!"

"What?" screamed Charles. "How much? Tell me!" Lisa paused. Her face changed from sad to a huge grin and shouted,

"It's free! It's free! We just have to pay the agents fee and at the most it'll be £5000!"

"No way! You're kidding!" Charles shouted back at her and they both jumped up and down in the kitchen like a couple of kids on the playground. They couldn't believe what was happening. There were screams of "Praise God!" and "HalleluYah!" ringing all over the house.

The boys came running downstairs wondering what was happening. Lisa explained to them that they were going to live at the house with all the land and then there were four of them jumping up and down.

"You see, Charles? Faith works if you work it! Let's go!" cried Lisa. "We have to go and visit Mr Carter in hospital with Jenny. Charles, would you look after the boys for me when we get there?"
He replied,

"No problem at all!"

134

Lisa got the boys ready and they all jumped in Charles car and headed off for Jenny McLean's office in Big Town.

There were similar celebrations at the office when they got there. Jenny jumped in Charles's car with them and they all took off for the hospital. It was so noisy in the car with everybody almost shouting for joy. In fact, the bewildered boys were the quietest of them all, just staring at the excited grown-ups.

***

At the hospital reception Jenny told the nurse who they were and they both headed off for his ward. Charles went off with the boys and took them to the children's play area. On the way to the
ward, Jenny said that they had told her that Mr Carter had taken a turn for the worst and that they mustn't cause him any stress.

When they got to Mr Carter's bed he was almost asleep. Jenny spoke to him gently in his ear and he opened his eyes instantly.

"I've been waiting for you for a long time, Lisa," Mr Carter said shakily. "Thank you for coming and thank you for your obedience!"

"Thank you, Mr Carter, for your great gift to me, and your obedience too!" replied Lisa in a soft gentle voice. "I will take great care of The Ark and it will be used every day in Yahweh's service."

"Oh, you know His name too!" said Old Mr Carter. "I have chosen well." He smiled at Lisa and closed his tired eyes for a moment. He opened them again and reached for Lisa's hand. His hand was quite cold to the touch. He leaned towards Lisa and said in a frail but firm voice,

"Lisa, I want you to have all the land, no charge, just do with it as He directs you. May Yahweh bless you and keep you, make his face shine upon you all the days of your life. You have a big job ahead, my dear. Be bold, be strong and know that he is with you. I have to go now, sweetheart, I'll see you later."

135

He closed his eyes and Lisa felt his hand go limp in hers. The heart monitor next to him bleeped a single tone. A nurse came in casually and said,

"Has he gone? We thought he would. He said he was just waiting for someone. It must have been you, my dear."

Lisa and Jenny were speechless. Tears streamed down Lisa's face as though a long-standing friend had just passed. She placed his hand across his chest and took hers away. She had never seen anyone die before, but it was one of the most reassuring experiences she had ever witnessed. Mr Carter had gone to be with Yahweh, of that there was no doubt.

When they got downstairs and saw Charles and the boys, Lisa ran to them all. She hugged Charles and whispered in his ear what had just happened, not wanting to disturb the boys.

"It was amazing, Charles. He had been waiting for me to come!"

They all got back in the car a little more subdued than when they arrived, which wasn't surprising due to what they had just witnessed.

"Our God is amazing," Lisa said as they drove out of the hospital grounds. Everybody agreed.

At Jenny's office, Lisa signed the relevant paperwork and Jenny handed over the keys.

"Wow! As easy as that?" said a surprised Lisa. "Do I own it now?"

"You certainly do!" replied Jenny. "But if you could see to my bill when it arrives, I would be very grateful." Lisa smiled and nodded, holding back the tears almost unable to say anything. With her lip quivering she said,

"Yes of course, send it to The Ark." She got back in the car to Charles and the boys and shook the keys at him.

"It's ours, Charles, it's ours!"

Charles drove them back to Lisa's house and asked if it was possible for him to take her out one night before they moved as there was so much that he wanted to say to her but didn't have the time right then. She agreed, thanked and hugged Charles and took the boys into the house. She closed the door behind her. The boys ran off upstairs to play and Lisa wandered into the lounge and flopped onto her wonderful couch again.

It was becoming a regular occurrence that she was always exhausted and exhilarated when she came into the house these days. She reached into her pocket and pulled out the keys to her new home. She looked at them and smiled to herself and thanked Yahweh for taking such great care of them all.

For some reason she knew that there was going to be difficult times ahead in the not-too distant future but with God, with Yahweh by her side, she also knew that they would have victory. Whatever He needed her to do, she now knew that she was able to handle it.

"What a great God you are! Thank you, Father!" She closed her eyes feeling very satisfied and very comfortable at the thought of the new life of adventure ahead of her that God had prepared.

Chapter 12

The Invitation

When Lisa woke she knew she had work to do. There was a whole lot of cleaning up to do in Hightown before she could move to The Ark and moving to The Ark was urgent. She lay for a moment on her side staring at a bunch of keys on her bedside cabinet. She had to get out there. She didn't know quite why it was so urgent, but she had a gut feeling it was.

She needed to pray and put together a plan of action; she needed help, that was for sure. Yahweh had brought her to the point of readiness, where she was prepared to do anything for Him, but exactly what she had to do she didn't know, other than it was going to involve Charles and The Ark.

She got up and dressed and spent the following half hour in prayer. She felt Yahweh urging her to 'stay close' once again. It seemed imperative that she did. Again, she didn't have a clue why, she just knew she needed to do it. That morning Yahweh told her to be a 'watchman' and be vigilant and stay on guard, to look out for attacks from the Enemy.

He gave her a scripture to read: Genesis 39. It was the story of Potiphar's wife and how Joseph was imprisoned for allegedly trying to abuse her when in fact, she was the one who asked Joseph to go to bed with her. Several things went through her mind when she read the passage. Had she been the one that caused the pastor to be arrested? Was she to blame?

"You're Joseph!" came the voice. "Not Potiphar's wife!" She

then realized what God was saying to her and why she needed to stay close to Him and not to trust her own thoughts. She felt God saying to her that the Enemy will often attack a person's conscious mind and in certain circumstances it was important for her to check what her mind is saying. She thanked Yahweh and went downstairs to make some breakfast for herself and the little ones.

Lisa's desire to get things moving was strong. They needed to leave Hightown as soon as possible. She decided she would give Dan a call to find out what was happening with him and Sally and what he wanted to do regarding the house and their subsequent divorce.

She called his mobile. It rang for a while and then Dan answered laughing; obviously in someone else's company. The whole tone of his voice was different. He seemed to be very happy and actually quite civil.

"Sally must be doing him some good." she thought to herself. It made a change to have a proper conversation with him. Dan explained that Sally had asked Christopher to move out now. He was going to have the beach house and they were going to move into the house on Lake View estate. Dan was really pleased to tell Lisa that he had quit his job at the store too, which was great for him so he could spend more time with Sally.

"Good for you!" said Lisa almost sarcastically, while having to make a conscious decision to remove the question, 'why wasn't he like this when he was here?' from her mind. She chose instead to remind herself that they were never meant to be together in the first place. This was a closed door in her life. She could thank God with all her heart that He had brought something beautiful out of it all: her two little boys. So, she was not for a moment going to fall into the trap of regret, she was going to stay focused on the future and instead of being angry with Dan she tried her best to be pleased for him. Apparently, he had seen his solicitor and was paying for a quickie divorce if that was alright with her and that if she agreed he would give her all the equity from the house if she needed to sell up and buy a cheaper place.

"Thank you," she said, not willing to say a word about The Ark to him. Keeping quiet about it all was definitely wise when it came to Dan. She figured the less of a stir she made, the better.

"And yes, that's fine about the divorce. I assume you'll sort out the child maintenance too?" she asked.

"Yes of course," replied Dan. "I wouldn't want you and my angels going short, would I?" The conversation was obviously being overheard; he would never speak of the boys as his 'angels'.
For once Dan seemed to have things in hand. In Lisa's eyes that was yet another miracle, but at least she could relax regarding the whole situation with him and Sally. She called Charles to tell him and asked him if he would like to come over to the house as they had some planning to do. That's what she told him anyway; the reality was that she missed him whenever he wasn't there.

When Charles came around, Lisa was at the kitchen table with her notebook and a calculator. She was trying to work out how much money they would have to move out to the Ark.

"That's what I have been wanting to do with you, Lisa!" laughed Charles. "It's been on my mind now for days!"

"Let's do it then!" replied Lisa excitedly. "And we can go out later and just relax rather than figuring things out all the time." They both agreed that was a great idea and got down to work. Lisa rang her mortgage lender to find out what was still owed on her house and Charles called Jenny to see if she would handle the sale of Lisa's house for her. Jenny agreed and said she'd call round that afternoon to value the house.

"Right, what's next?" said Lisa excitedly to which Charles replied, "Well, there's the question of my house."
Lisa responded,

"What about it?" This was the question that Charles had

been wanting to directly ask Lisa for days now. He knew Lisa wanted him to be part of the 'goings on' at The Ark, whatever they would be, but he didn't quite know what her plans were. He wanted to be with her twenty-four seven and ultimately marry her and settle down with her and the boys.

"Well do I keep it and commute to The Ark daily or do I sell it and move in somewhere at The Ark with you and the boys?" He blurted.

It was the question Lisa had hoped he was going to ask her but she always tried to avoid it somehow. Lisa stared at Charles. Her eyes instantly filled up. She wiped a tear trickling down her face and said, clearing her throat,

"What would you like to do, Charles?"
Charles thought to himself, 'Here goes! The time is now!' He replied to Lisa's question calmly and slowly.

"I want to live with you. I am in love with you." Lisa kept quiet, staring intently at Charles. He continued clearing his throat now, holding back the tears himself, "I have been since the first time I laid eyes on you!"

'I've done it now,' he thought to himself, followed by a million questions in a split second. 'Oh, my word, I hope I haven't blown it! What if it's too soon? She's still sorting her divorce out! Oh no! What have I done? You fool! Why couldn't you wait?'

Lisa stretched her arms out across the table to take hold of his hands. She couldn't believe it. She knew he really liked her, but she wasn't quite expecting this. She squeezed his hands and said,

"And I love you too, Mr Michaels, I love you!" She hadn't really wanted to admit all this to him right now, but it just seemed so right and as a child of Yahweh she allowed her feelings to direct her for once.

They got up from the table and hugged each other. Charles looked Lisa in the eyes and went to kiss her. This time she kissed him back. It was beautiful. Lisa looked at him with her big brown eyes and a huge smile broke out on her face.

"So, to answer your question, Mr Michaels," Lisa said, holding back the tears. "It would be fantastic if you would come and live at The Ark with us, truly, although you'll have to have your own place there. I want to do things right with God and I feel that it is important that we don't do anything outside of marriage." Charles replied,

"Lisa, I wouldn't want it any other way. Everything we do has to be centred around Him!"

"Then it's a 'yes' from me, Mr Michaels!" Lisa said with a huge grin on her face.

They hugged and laughed out loud together, and did their happy dance, dancing round and around in circles. The boys ran in from the lounge and joined in the celebrations even though they had no idea what they were actually celebrating. When the jollity calmed down, the boys slipped back into the lounge and Charles and Lisa sat back down at the table and continued with their work together.

They spent the next few hours calculating just how much they had between them. Now that it had been decided that Charles would be living at The Ark with Lisa it meant that he too, could sell his house and put the money into refurbishment or some other capital expense.

Lisa was overjoyed to discover that his house was unencumbered, so whatever it was valued at they could put in the 'kitty'. They reckoned if they sold both cars and bought a four by four of some description they would also end up better off. They could get an accurate calculation when Jenny had looked at both properties they had for sale.

Just as they were discussing the matter the doorbell rang and there stood Jenny. She surveyed Lisa's property and agreed to go and see Charles's straight after. Everybody including the boys got in Charles's car and they all went to look at his house. They met Mrs Brown, the housekeeper, who Lisa once suspected was Charles's wife, when she answered the phone. Of course, Charles reminded her of that and got a slap for being cheeky and making fun of Lisa.

It was a very grand home for a manager at a food plant, but Charles explained that his last house was particularly lovely and had been left to him by his late grandparents, who had been very wealthy. He said it had been a real struggle to come to terms with selling his grandparents' place as he'd remembered it so fondly as a child, but God had different ideas than him staying loyal to a house. Looking back now he could see exactly why it all happened the way it did. Now if the house in Hightown sold for its true value he would have half a million pounds in the bank from his sale alone.

They all went back to Lisa's house and Jenny said her goodbyes and that she would draw up a sales campaign to get both houses sold as quick as possible.

Charles and Lisa sat back down at the kitchen table and got the calculator out again. With the money from Charles's savings and the equity from both homes, assuming they sold for market value, was over £600,000. It seemed like a huge amount of money to Lisa but they both had a gut feeling that it was going to be used very quickly. She said reassuringly,

"Whatever we get Charles will be a plus. Yahweh will look after us and that's for certain!"

It was the night of the bible class and Lisa had decided that she was going to go and show her face to tell all her friends there that she was leaving town and so leaving the bible class. She was dreading going after what had happened with Adams, although she felt fairly certain that the gossip wouldn't have got as far as the people there, not yet anyway. Charles was going to arrive late again as it wouldn't look at all good if they arrived together.

She was just about to leave for bible class, when she realised that she hadn't even had chance to open her mail today. There were the usual bills but there was one letter in a white envelope with unusual franking. It was from the church. She opened it. It was from Pastor Adams. With a concerned expression on her face she started to read the letter.

"Charles!" she shouted. "Come and look at this!" Charles was in the lounge play fighting with the boys as he was going to babysit until Sophie arrived. He came into the kitchen looking all dishevelled and worn out.

"Look at this!" Lisa said, handing the letter for Charles to read. Adams had invited her to church the following evening to a special service to explain to the congregation what had happened and a chance for him to clear things up with her.

"Is that an attempt at an apology?" Lisa asked Charles.

"I've no idea! I'll have a good read of it while I'm waiting for Sophie, you had better get off, if you're walking. You don't want to be late now do you?" They chuckled, and Charles gave Lisa a peck on the cheek.

"I'll be along soon." he said reassuringly, and Lisa left. She arrived at Tom and Jan's house and just as she was walking up the path she heard a soft voice in her head say,

"Lisa, I am with you!"

"Thank you, Father." she replied and rang the doorbell. It opened. It was Jan.

"Yes Lisa, can I help you?" Jan said sternly.

"I am here for the bible class and I wanted to...." replied Lisa only to be abruptly interrupted by Jan.

"I don't think it's a good idea that you come here anymore, young lady! Not with what you've done to our Pastor! Go away, Lisa! You're not welcome here anymore!"

Lisa tried to interject but it was no good; she was pushed back and the door was shut firmly in her face. Lisa rang the doorbell again determined to at least say something in her defence.

144

"Go away!" Jan shouted from the other side of the door. "Just go away!"

With that Lisa turned around and walked back down the path. She looked across at the window to see a number of faces she recognized looking out at her, obviously wondering what all the shouting was about. More people knew about this than she had imagined. Well if they didn't they surely would now.

She took her mobile phone out of her bag and called Charles. He answered,

"Hey Lisa! I'm just about to leave. Are you okay?" She replied,

"I'm fine, but just stay there, Charles, I'm on my way back!" Charles heard the key in the door and Lisa walked in.

"What has happened?" he asked anxiously. Lisa explained everything to Charles, who was getting angrier the more she explained,

"Listen don't worry about it Charles," Lisa went on. "We'll be moved soon. The thing I'm more concerned about is tomorrow night. Do I or we go, or do we just ignore it?"

"I'm not sure," replied Charles. "But I could go for you anyway, they can't suspect me of anything." They laughed together.

"Lisa!" came a voice out of the living room. "I know that this is not my business, but I've overheard a few things. I don't understand fully what is going on, but I know you guys, I know you and I want to support you. So, if you do go, I want to go too!"

"Aww thank you, Sophie," said Lisa walking over to her.

"Charles, come on in, we should talk to Sophie for a while."

They sat in the lounge with Sophie; the boys glued to the TV and explained what had gone on, with Dan and The Ark and the incident with Chris Adams. They explained in lesser detail how God had been interacting with them both. To anyone outside of the situation, it would seem like they were crazy!

145

"So, Can I come with you guys?" asked Sophie excitedly. Lisa and Charles looked at each other surprised. She continued, "Not just to your meeting but to The Ark. I'm eighteen in a month. I have almost finished at College now, all I have to do is revise and take my final exams in two months' time! Then I've done. Oh, please say yes! I can do lots of jobs for you and help out with the boys and…"

"Okay! okay! We'll think about it!" interrupted Lisa, laughing at the speed she could talk without even taking a breath. "But you must talk to your parents about it"

"Yay!" screamed Sophie. They all laughed together and talked about The Ark and all the work that did need doing there.

"Shall we all go up on Friday?" Charles suggested. "We'll get this church thing out of the way tomorrow and then go up for the weekend. We can take some cleaning things with us and make a bit of a start."

Everybody agreed unanimously and even the boys had pulled themselves away from the TV and were bouncing up and down with enthusiasm. Lisa had a feeling that Sophie was going to be more involved in The Ark than just helping out. She felt Yahweh had a real key role for her there.

After they had chatted for a while, Sophie put the boys to bed. When she came back down stairs, Lisa suggested that she should go home and check with her parents that it would be okay for the weekend.

Sophie thanked Lisa, gave her a hug and left, skipping down the drive. Lisa watched her home as usual and when she was safely at home, closed the door.

"You know he's invited you and the boys, tomorrow?" said Charles, back on the subject of the church. "It feels kind of strange that he would want to apologize, especially after what he must have told people," Charles continued thoughtfully. "Or maybe it's his way of clearing it all up in front of the church. Maybe he's said too much to too many people and it's easier to do as an assembly. What do you think, Lisa?" She replied,

"I don't know what to think, especially after tonight! Will you pray, Charles? I will too of course, and we'll talk tomorrow about the whole thing. One thing's for certain, worrying won't help. Let's bring Yahweh into the situation!" They smiled and hugged, "Now, would you like a coffee, Mr Michaels?" Charles replied,

"Good idea Mrs Michaels, erm, Jeffreys, I mean, sorry!" Lisa looked at him shocked with her mouth wide open. Charles laughed. Lisa slapped him on the arm and giggled,

"That's a bit presumptuous, Mr Michaels!" and went off into the kitchen to make some drinks.

They spent the rest of the evening just talking. It was nice to have some time alone to find out more about each other. They reminisced about their childhoods and told each other all the secrets they could that no-one else knew.

It was getting late and Charles being the gentleman that he is, got up to go and said,

"It's been really great, Lisa, thank you." Lisa said nothing in response. She just smiled. She longed for the day when they would be together permanently, and Charles wouldn't have to go home but for now this was how it was, and she would have to deal with it.

Charles kissed Lisa on the cheek at the door and left for home. Lisa closed the door behind him and sighed longingly.

"What a man!" she said and smiled to herself, in a satisfied way. She was truly happy; her life was really coming together. She locked up and put the dishwasher on and went up to bed. She thought to herself, 'Yahweh is good, that's for sure.'

She sat up in bed and thought she'd pray but before she could say a word, Yahweh spoke to her.

"They intend to humiliate you and your family, Lisa! Just as they did to me when I came to Earth. They want to see you squirm!" Lisa replied,

"But why?" Yahweh didn't give an answer but said, "Go anyway! Be strong! I am with you!" Lisa replied, "Thank you Father I will. Bless you!"

Chapter 13

Behold, The Woman

She felt that no sooner had she closed her eyes when the light coming through her curtains woke her up. It was morning.

"What?" she exclaimed as she sat up in bed. She didn't even remember going to sleep, but according to her clock she certainly had. She didn't feel tired, in fact, quite the opposite; she felt refreshed and ready to spring out of bed and get on with the day. Something had happened to her again while she'd been sleeping.

The things Yahweh had said to her last night about how He was treated when He was on earth were forefront on her mind. She had a connection with Him in a way that she had never felt before. She thought about Yahshua, his trial and crucifixion; it made her weep but at the same time she found herself in full understanding of why he was willing to go through what he did. She suddenly knew that she had to go through something bad to achieve something that would ultimately bless them all. What, she had no idea, but she had built such a trust and faith in Yahweh that she didn't really care. She knew that it was part of His plan and whatever He wanted her to do, she would do. As well as seeing His will fulfilled, she knew that she would benefit greatly too.

Her phone rang and disturbed her thinking. It was Jenny.

"Hi Jenny! How are you?" Lisa responded. Jenny replied,

"I'm good thank you, Lisa, very good. I have a lady in the office who is possibly interested in your house and wants to come and view."

"Goodness me!" replied Lisa. "That was quick!"

"I know, and a cash buyer too!" chuckled Jenny. "Would it be possible for me to bring her around tomorrow afternoon?" Lisa thought for a second then said,

"Oh Jenny, I'm going up to The Ark for the weekend with Charles and another friend, but if you could show her around, I would be fine with that."

"No problem," said Jenny. "I'll sort it." She hung up and Lisa jumped out of bed. Now she had tidying to do as well.

Lisa asked Charles if he would come around to the house to help and within minutes he was there. She filled him in on the news about her house and what Yahweh had said about church meeting.

"You're a brave woman, Lisa," said Charles. "I know plenty of men who would sit that one out, particularly knowing what was going to happen!"

"I know, Charles," replied Lisa. "But I have to do this! Trust me, if there was any way Yahweh could do this without me being there, I would not go."

Charles held her hand to comfort her. He told her that he would sit slightly away from her but keep his eye on her constantly. They decided to invite Sophie as well. She was determined to go anyway, and it would be great for them all to show some kind of solidarity.

"It would be nice to have someone to sit with too, other than the boys!" Lisa remarked. So, it was all agreed that they would get there at exactly 7:30pm to avoid people being able to ask any questions or make any comments. She called Sophie and it was all arranged.

After lunch, Charles was handed a pair of rubber gloves and told to clean the bathrooms. Although Charles was a man who liked his home to be kept clean, he usually had his cleaner do most of it. Even so, he took the gloves and spray-cleaner and did as he was told. No breaks were allowed until the job was finished. Charles was once caught trying to sneak a quick cup of coffee only to be reprimanded and sent off with a duster and spray polish to another area of the house. It was great fun having to be subservient to Lisa, unlike his usual position as a manager was all about handing out orders and delegating jobs for other people.

The exhausted pair finished at pretty much the same time and sat down together for a coffee.
Charles asked Lisa if she had any thoughts on what they were going to do with the Ark, as a whole and what they were going to do with all the land that came with it. Lisa replied,

"I'm not sure really, but I know Yahweh will tell us in good time. We just need to stay close to Him."
Just then she heard the voice again in her head say,

"Why do you think it's been called 'The Ark'?"
She put her cup down hard on the table, slightly spilling some coffee.

"Are you okay?" asked Charles noticing the shocked expression on her face.

"I'm fine," answered a bewildered Lisa. "Yahweh just asked me something."

"What did He say?" demanded Charles.
Lisa replied, "He said, 'Why do we think it's called The Ark?'" They looked at each other, trying to figure it out.

"Well," started Charles. "The Ark was built to ensure the survival of man and all the species of animals from the flood that God himself sent to wipe out the wicked. Agreed?" Lisa nodded. Charles carried on. "Assuming it's Noah's Ark that we are referring to and not the Ark of the Covenant!" Lisa, with her head in her hands just lifted her eyes to look at Charles, then said,

"Yes! That's right! And the Ark of the Covenant contained the presence of God himself!" They stared at each other some more.

151

"Let's check the dictionary!" Lisa shouted, startling Charles and jumped up to go to her bookcase. She picked out a book and started to flick through the pages.

"Aardvark, Antelope, here it is, Ark!" She read out the three definitions of the word. "One: also called Noah's Ark: the large boat built by Noah in which he saved himself, his family, and a pair of every kind of creature during the Flood. Genesis 6–9. Two," she announced. "Also called 'Ark of the Covenant': a chest or box containing the two stone tablets inscribed with the ten commandments, carried by the Israelites in their wanderings in the desert after the Exodus: the most sacred object of the tabernacle and the Temple in Jerusalem, where it was kept in the holy of holies." They looked at each other again, looking for any clues. Lisa continued. "Three: a place of protection or security; refuge; asylum." She looked up at Charles. "Is that it? A place of refuge?" she asked. Charles replied,

"It could well be, Lisa, it could well be!"

Sophie came right on time as usual and they all got in Lisa's car to go, apart from Charles who drove his own car. They met at the entrance and all went in the sanctuary together and found some seats near to the back. The worship band had already started, and everybody was jumping around all happy and clapping. No-one said a word to Lisa directly although one or two people who recognized Sophie from school said 'Hi' to her.

The worship ended, and Adams got up on stage to a rapturous reception. Everyone seemed particularly excited to see him. He thanked everyone for their warm hand and started to talk about him and Sally and 'as they all knew' the fact that she had been attacked by the Enemy and had been convinced to leave him.

He then told everyone about a dream he'd had where there were sheep riding a train in pairs, who were suddenly attacked by wolves. Lisa couldn't believe her ears. She couldn't even look at

Charles. She hung her head. She could have felt angry but instead she felt sadness and compassion for this little man on the stage. He told the story of the dream exactly as Lisa had told him.

Everybody was in awe of the amazing prophet on stage. Applause erupted all around the Sanctuary and people stood to acknowledge this 'great' man. Lisa felt ready to walk out but she remained seated.

The applause died down after Adams had sufficiently taken the credit and shouted,

"Is Lisa Jeffreys in the auditorium?" This was it. She felt power surge through her body and she stood up involuntarily. She shouted back,

"Yes, I am here!" in a powerful voice.

"Would you come to the stage please?" Adams asked, and she began the walk to the front. The room went silent. You could have heard the proverbial pin drop.

"Bring your children, Lisa!" he shouted, and Lisa took them by the hand and walked down with them. They went up the steps onto the stage and as they did she heard Yahweh whisper in her ear,

"I am with you, my child." It brought a smile to her face.

"Hello, Mr Adams!" she said, looking him directly in his eyes.

"And this," the pastor shouted to the congregation, "Is one of those wolves and her offspring! I wanted you all to take a good look at this woman because she should be an example to you of exactly what not to become!"

He proceeded to humiliate Lisa and the boys publicly over the next few minutes. Charles couldn't stand it any longer and stood up and shouted,

"You are a liar, Adams! You know you're the one that attacked Lisa! Your wife left you!" Suddenly two large security men got hold of Charles and dragged him out.

Sophie then stood up too cried out,

"You're a dirty, cheating liar! No wonder your wife left you!" along with a few other choice words too, until she too was removed by some other men. The congregation moaned at Charles and Sophie and applauded the men who took them out.

Throughout the pandemonium in the congregation Lisa kept calm and silent, remembering what Yahweh had said about Yahshua's accusation and how he'd stood there quiet, not saying a word.

The Pastor's accusing words had simply bounced off her and hadn't troubled her at all. She looked down at her boys, who smiled back at her.

"Have you finished?" she said to Adams when he stopped. He said,

"Yes, I have! Now go and be out of here!"
Lisa calmly walked down the steps and made her way out of the sanctuary. She walked past Tom and Jan Phillips on the way out, who couldn't even meet her gaze. Other faces she recognised seemed to completely shun her.

She pushed open the doors of the sanctuary and walked through only to find a brawl going on in the foyer. Charles was wrestling with two large security men, who had pinned him to the floor. His uncle Sam was trying to pull them off him but had two other men pulling him away at the same time and Sophie was kicking whoever she could.

Lisa, with a small boy on each hand, walked straight through them all and shouted,

"Back off!" in a voice that would have scared a giant, and the men amazingly did. They stood up and quickly moved away to the wall.

"Come on Sophie, Charles, let's get out of here." Charles got up off the floor, took Sophie by the hand and followed Lisa out of the church.

"We'll meet back at my house!" she shouted to Charles who

was already climbing in his car.

Sam came running out of the church towards Charles's car, shouting,

"Can I come with you?" He got into Charles's car and they followed Lisa, Sophie and the boys back to the house. They all climbed out of the cars and went inside. Sophie dashed upstairs to get the boys off to bed and Lisa welcomed Sam into her home. She took Charles into the kitchen to clean him up a little, after being mauled by the security guards. Sophie came back into the kitchen just as Charles winced out loud when Lisa wiped the graze on his cheek with antiseptic.

"Big baby!" mocked Sam unsympathetically.

"I thought you were awesome, Charles! My hero!" responded Lisa, defending her champion.

"And you Sophie! And thank you too, Sam!"
They all laughed together as they reflected on the evening they had just been subjected to.

"And wow, you were scary, Lisa!" remarked Charles. "Where did all that come from? You terrified me!"

"And me!" echoed Sophie.

"Me too!" said Sam and they all laughed again.

"And did you see those guards stand to attention?" continued Charles. "They sure knew who was boss!"
When the laughing died down, Lisa asked Charles if he would take Sam into the lounge and bring him up to speed with everything that had happened, and she went with Sophie into the kitchen to make some hot drinks and snacks for everyone.
Sophie stood alongside Lisa, cuddled her arm and said,

"They were horrible to you, Lisa. How can those people call themselves Christians?"
Lisa replied sympathetically,

"I know what it looks like, Sophie but don't be too hard on them, it's the shepherd that's the problem there, not the sheep."

"You're such a nice person, Lisa," said Sophie looking at her admiringly. "After all they did to you tonight and you still see the good in them!"

"We have to forgive people, Sophie, no matter how painful it may be, or else God won't forgive us for the things we do wrong and that's more important than we know," replied Lisa smiling. "He is with us, Sophie!"

Sam sat in the lounge with Charles, amazed at what he was hearing. Unlike his nephew, Sam never had very much in the way of money and success, but he was an honest man who certainly wasn't afraid of hard work. He believed his calling in life was to encourage and serve others and that's what he did, always with a smile and a good word.

Lisa and Sophie took the refreshments into the lounge and sat down to listen to what Charles was saying to Sam.

"Well," said Sam. "If there is room for a small one up there in the mountains, I'd love to join you on this adventure."

"What a great idea!" said Lisa. "What do you think, Charles?"

"I agree," said Charles. "If we are to make The Ark a place to protect Yahweh's people, I think that Uncle Sam would be a valuable addition to the team."

"That's a deal then," said Lisa with a smile. "As long as you stop calling him Uncle Sam! It sounds like a recruitment campaign for the army!"

Everybody was really pleased with the outcome of that evening, even though it had been quite an ordeal for everyone concerned. Lisa invited Sam to go with the rest of them to the Ark over the weekend, which he gracefully accepted saying that he couldn't wait to see the place.

"Just bring a duster with you, Sam," Lisa laughed. "It's been a while since it had a spring clean."

They arranged to meet in the morning at 8:00 am at Lisa's

house. Sam joked that he needed his 'beauty sleep', so Charles said goodnight to everyone and took Sam home. For the next hour Sophie helped Lisa to tidy up the house before she too confessed that she was tired and needed to sleep.

"Thank you again, Sophie!" shouted Lisa as Sophie left. "See you in the morning!" She watched her cross the road and go into her home two houses down. She closed the door and locked it behind her.

"Another crazy wonderful day!" she said to herself and went to bed. She heard the words,

"Well done!" as her head hit the pillow. She smiled and whispered,

"Thanks to you, my Yahweh." She turned out the light and slept like a log.

It was amazing to see everybody so enthusiastic. Sophie arrived fifteen minutes early and Charles arrived with Sam at precisely eight o'clock.

Lisa had the boys ready with their overnight bags and the car was loaded with a wide variety of cleaning products, cloths and utensils. It felt like they were about to embark on a two week camping trip rather than a weekend at a house in the mountains. Food supplies, laptops and mobile phones were packed, everything was ready to go. There was a real buzz with everybody and a feeling that something really special and significant was about to happen.

The two cars took off the estate agents where Lisa had to drop off her spare keys with Jenny.

When they got there, Jenny seemed very excited about their move to The Ark. She asked Lisa,

"I know this may sound a bit cheeky and if you don't agree just say so and I won't be offended but would it be okay, if I could come over at the weekend and bring my husband, Ben?"
Lisa replied,

"Yes of course! And anyone else you know who want to

157

help clean up! Just bring a sleeping bag or something; we might have to rough it a little, although I did see a pile of mattresses there in the old bunkhouse." They laughed, and Lisa turned to leave the shop. As she opened the door she shouted back to Jenny,

"Oh, and Sell that house for me, too!" Jenny gave her a thumbs-up and a broad smile and Lisa left to re-join the troops in the car park.

They finally set off for The Ark.

It was another beautiful day and the sun was warm already, which was lovely for a March morning. Charles led the way with Sam sat in the passenger seat and the rest of his car was packed with his things. Lisa and Sophie followed, trying to guess why Charles's car was so full.

"There's more in there than just cleaning chemicals!" laughed Sophie.

"Yes," replied Lisa. "I think Charles has forgotten that there is already a kitchen sink there."

They giggled like a couple of school girls.

"Let's hope there is water too," laughed Sophie.

The journey seemed a lot quicker this time and soon they found themselves ascending the mountain. It was steep for the cars, which was why they had decided to get themselves a Land Rover or something with four-wheel drive. Charles and Lisa had both agreed it could be real 'fun' up there in winter especially in the snow but for now, they could all enjoy the beautiful scenery and look forward to a glorious summer up there.

Within no time at all, they were pulling into the entrance and driving down the beautiful winding lane, through the valley and down to the house. There were trees all around and it looked so amazing with the morning sun glistening through the leaves of the silver birch.

"Wow!" shouted Sophie as they went over the brow of the hill to see The Ark, slightly below, in all its glory. It looked more beautiful now than the first time they saw it as the drive swooped down to the house.

The cars pulled up outside and they all jumped out with total excitement. The boys were jumping up and down with joy but not as high as everybody else. Elation was all around. Lisa and Charles hugged each other and danced around.

"Charles?" Lisa said when they finally stopped. "You know, great things are going to happen here."

"I know, Lisa," He replied. "You can really feel that Yahweh is here."

They all went in the main house and decided that it was best to tackle that first and at least get the house liveable. Everybody set to the task, even the boys. The dust was flying, cobwebs were coming down, windows were letting light in for the first time in what must have been ages. It was great fun as well as being hard work.

Sam was keen to paint the outside of the house, but everybody convinced him that it was a later job when everybody had moved in, but it was really encouraging to see everyone's enthusiasm to get the place back to how it would have looked in its glory days.

It was soon obvious that they would need to build a fire or get the power on so that they could eat and drink.

Lisa decided that she was going to clear the fireplace in the main room and Charles was going to sort out the water and electricity.

The transformation of the fireplace was almost miraculous, going from a dingy, dusty old thing to a beautiful centrepiece of the room. It looked wonderful now that she had brushed it all down and removed the soot from the inside of the fire surround. As she was sweeping the outside of the chimney breast she noticed that a few stones on the side near the wall were a little loose.

"This is a job for you, Sam!" she shouted.
Sam shouted back,

"I'll be with you in a minute, Lisa!" Just then the lights came on and everybody cheered. Lisa shouted over them all,

"Well done Charles!" It felt great to have little bit of civilization and now at least they could have coffee, with the emergency spring water she had bought, just in case they couldn't get the water on for any reason.

Sophie brought the coffee maker in from the car and in no time at all they could smell the wonderful aroma of fresh coffee circulating through the house.

Suddenly there was a large thump, followed by more cheers from the kitchen. Lisa ran through to see what was going on. The commotion was about a thick, brown, sludgy liquid that was coming out of the tap. The more it flowed the thinner the sludge got and within a few minutes it was running with clear fresh water from their very own mountain spring up in the hills.

Things were really happening fast, and The Ark was soon going to be liveable. If they could light a fire in the hearth they would be warm enough to get through the night.

They discovered that the whole house was heated by a back boiler at the rear of the fireplace, so Sam's fixing of the loose stones on the chimney breast was very important. Charles brought in a small bag of mortar which he had found in one of the outbuildings and Sam removed the loose stones and cleaned them up so that he could put them back in. He was just clearing out the hole in the chimney breast when he noticed that something was inside the hole.

"Hey, Lisa!" he shouted. "Come and look at this!"

What Sam had discovered was a small recess in the fireplace going into the wall itself. It turned out that the chimney breast wasn't damaged at all. The loose stones were just covering up something that was hidden in there. He shone his torch in the hole for Lisa to see. Something was definitely in there; it looked like a box of some description. Sam dragged it out with a struggle. It was about six inches wide and about eighteen inches long and covered in dust and cobwebs. It was made of solid wood and felt quite heavy. As it came into the light they could see that the box had carvings all over it. Sam placed it on the floor in front of the fireplace. Lisa took her duster and started to clean it up. It had carvings of what looked like angels on it. Certainly, some creatures with wings and it had an inscription of some kind all the way around the top of the box. The lid was hinged but had a small padlock on it. As she cleaned the box she could start to make out some of the letters. She gasped and stepped back.

"Charles! Everybody! Come here quickly!" she shouted. "Look at this!" Everybody gathered around. "Look." She pointed with her finger at the inscription around the edge of the lid. It read in beautifully carved words:

YOU ARE far more POWERFUL than you have been led to BELIEVE, with the words YOU, ARE, POWERFUL and BELIEVE in capital letters.

The room was silent. For a moment, everybody stared in amazement. It was a first for Sam and Sophie. They had heard about the messages that both Charles and Lisa had witnessed but seeing for themselves felt incredible. Lisa said to them all,

"Before we attempt to open this I feel we need to pray." They all got on their knees, closed their eyes and bowed their heads.

"Father," Lisa prayed. "We thank you for this place. We thank you for bringing us all together to serve you. We thank you for this box and whatever it contains. I know this is significant to this place in some way and I praise you for it. We thank Old Mr Carter for his obedience too and we will work hard to continue the work that he has passed on to us all. We receive the 'baton' from him and we will run, my Yahweh and see this through to the end. In Yahshua's name, Amen."

"Amen!" echoed the rest of them and they all stared at the box.

161

Suddenly Lisa remembered the bunch of keys. There was a little key on it. She took the bunch out of her coat pocket and tried the key in the padlock. It fitted. It opened.

Lisa lifted the lid and looked in. Inside was a scroll of paper with a ribbon around it. She took it out and held it in her hands. They all looked over her shoulder. She pulled the bow on the ribbon and the scroll relaxed and opened. It was a very old piece of paper, that was for sure. On it, written in ink, were words in some Eastern language and maps of the Estate.

"I wonder what it says?" said Lisa.

"I don't know," replied Charles. "It looks something like Hebrew!" They looked at all the maps and drawings for a short while and then Lisa rolled it back up and placed it in the box.

"We need to get someone who can speak Hebrew as fast as we can. Does anyone know anybody that does?" asked Lisa. They shook their heads. Nobody did.

"Well, Yahweh will provide!" continued Lisa. "You wait and see!"

Chapter 14

The Scroll

It was awe-inspiring to look at all of the drawings and maps on the scroll. Whoever had drawn them was a real artist; the detail was just beautiful, but they needed a translator as soon as possible; everybody was desperate to know what it read.

In the meantime, everybody agreed to get on with putting things straight around the house. Lisa continued cleaning the fireplace as she was sure they would need the fire lit in the evening and overnight. Sophie and the boys collected kindling for the fire and Charles and Sam carried the mattresses from the bunkhouse up to the house. It was fast becoming quite a real-life adventure and everybody felt like their work had real purpose. The back barn, amazingly, was full of dry, chopped logs. Someone had spent a lot of time preparing fuel for the place. Old Mr Carter must have worked very hard making sure it would last a long time. One thing was for certain, they had enough timber for years to come; there was over sixty acres of fir trees in the woods.

Charles lit the fire and they all cheered as the smoke wound its way up the chimney and out of the pot. Now they had heat as well as water and electricity.

"By the way, Charles," Lisa laughed. "What did you bring in your car? Me and Sophie were trying to guess why it was so full."

"You may laugh now but you'll thank me later," replied Charles with a sheepish laugh. "You'll see!"

Bit by bit, throughout that afternoon, he brought various things in from his car. He had brought a small table, with a lamp and odd pieces of furniture including an inflatable sofa and chairs - even a small Television. When the boys saw the TV, they jumped for joy but were bitterly disappointed when they discovered that there was no satellite dish. Not knowing what to expect, Charles had even bought an old rabbit antenna and as it turned out it was a good job that he did.

As it started to become dusk, everyone was getting tired. Lisa and Sophie fixed up some food while Sam and Charles attempted to get the TV working. It made Sophie and Lisa laugh as they could hear the cheers and boos as they found a signal and within seconds lost it. It was hugely entertaining for the boys, even better than watching the TV itself.

They all had a great evening sitting around the fire chatting and laughing at all the incidents that had gone on over the previous weeks. Sam had endless stories of things that he had done in his life and it was great to hear. Lisa looked over at Charles many times during the jollities. It was so good to see this man laugh and enjoy himself. Even though they'd had fun with each other over the time they had known one another, there had also been a lot of heartache. He seemed so free and happy. She thanked God for bringing him into her life. What Lisa didn't realize was that Charles was looking at Lisa too, thinking the very same things. One time he turned to look at Lisa and she was already looking at him. They looked at each other for a moment and smiled contently. Life was great and getting better.

Lisa put the boys to bed in their sleeping bags in their new bedroom that they had chosen earlier with her. They had their teddies and toys and Lisa was going to sleep with them for a night or two. She read them a story, settled them down to sleep, then wandered down the stairs and joined the others back in the lounge.

One by one they left the conversation and said goodnight to each other. It had been a long, hard but satisfying day.

The scroll box took pride of place on the table in front of

164

the fireplace, full of mystery and truth. Charles noticed as he drifted off to sleep that the box seemed to have a presence of its own; he could almost imagine what it would have felt like to have been in the company of the Ark of the Covenant; powerful and holy.

Lisa lay there staring into the silent darkness, asking questions in her head even though she was exhausted. Who had written the scroll? Why was it written in Hebrew? What was written in Hebrew? Where could they find somebody who could read the scroll and translate it for them?

Eventually the questions and trying to figure out the answers to the questions sent her into a deep sleep.

Charles woke first and made a pot of coffee for everyone. He took his cup out on the porch and sat and looked out over the tremendous views. The sky was so clear that morning that it was possible to see Hightown and even Tolchester on the horizon. He thought about the life that he had living in the town and working at the plant, compared with how it was now turning out up there in the mountains, serving Yahweh.

As he thought about the box and the scroll inside he heard a voice in his head say,

"The man who speaks Hebrew is coming today!" Charles jumped up, spilling his coffee as he did, just as Lisa came out with her coffee to join him.

"Whoa! Are you okay, Charles?" she said, laughing at his misdemeanour and handing him her drink. "Here, have a fresh one."

"It's okay, Lisa!" said Charles excitedly. "Don't worry! Yahweh has just told me that the man who can translate the scroll for us is coming here today!"

"Oh wow, amazing!" smiled Lisa. "You see? I told you he wouldn't let us down."

They were just trying to figure out who was coming that day, when a car pulled up on the driveway.

165

"Jenny!" they both shouted together.

"And her husband!" smiled Lisa knowingly.

Charles smiled back at her and said, "And I bet you a hundred quid he can speak Hebrew." Lisa laughed.

"Charles! I didn't think you were a gambling man." They chuckled as the couple got out of their car.

"Don't say anything!" Lisa whispered to Charles. "Let's watch Yahweh in action." Charles winked at her and they walked down the path to greet their friends.

"Jenny!" Lisa shouted. "Great to see you again."

Jenny threw her arms around Lisa and Charles and introduced her husband to them both.

"Charles, Lisa, this is my husband, Ben." They shook hands with Ben and walked back towards the house. Ben said politely,

"It's an amazing place you have here, guys. Jenny has told me the whole story; it's exciting stuff!"

"It is indeed." said Charles. "I hope you've both brought your overalls." They all laughed. Jenny responded,

"We sure have! And our sleeping bags!"

"Let's have a coffee first though," said Lisa and led up the steps to the front door. Charles and Ben sat on the porch and the girls fixed the drinks.

"Wow," said Jenny. "It looks so different already. You did a great job yesterday."

"Thank you," Lisa replied. "How did you get on yesterday with our prospective buyer?"

"Well," said Jenny. "It's kind of unbelievable really, but then I guess not for you guys."

"What do you mean?" laughed Lisa.

Jenny went on.

"Let's take the drinks out and I'll tell you both."

They went out on the porch to see that Sophie and Sam had joined them. Lisa introduced everyone and said,

"Come on then Jenny tell us all what has happened with the house, we're all friends here."

"Well," said Jenny. "I've been an estate agent now for over six years and I've never seen anything like it before. I mean first of all with Old Mr Carter and now this!" Everyone sat on the edge of their seats, listening intently. She continued, "I took the lady to view the house yesterday and she was very taken with it. So much so that she wants to buy the house immediately. She has cash and she has offered ten thousand pounds over the asking price if you can move out in a week! I said I was seeing you this weekend and would ask you if that was convenient."

Lisa was jumping up and down on the spot almost squeaking with excitement. She asked,

"So, it's sold?"

"Totally," replied Jenny. "In fact, I have a fifty-thousand-pound cheque in my safe at the office as a deposit."

"That's incredible! Oh, thank you, my God, thank you!" exclaimed Lisa, still bouncing. They finished drinking their coffees and Charles gave Ben the grand tour. Lisa showed Jenny what they'd
done so far and picked some jobs for her to do.

Still nobody had said anything to Ben about the box but Lisa deliberately prepared lunch for everyone around the table in the main family room. Everyone took a plate from the table.
Ben took the bait.

"Wow! Is that a Capsa? Where did you come across that?"

"What's a Capsa?" said Charles, encouraging him to carry on.

"It's an ancient box that they used to store scrolls in." He explained that he lectured on ancient history at the university in Tolchester and he was very passionate about anything old.
Jenny joked,

"Yeah, that was why he married me!" Everybody laughed.

"Can I have a closer look?" asked Ben.

"Oh of course you can Ben, help yourself," said Lisa. "We have the key somewhere. There's just some old papers inside with a foreign language on that none of us can read." She opened the box for Ben and the look that came on Ben's face you would have thought it was his birthday. Ben gasped with excitement as he unrolled the scroll.

"This is Hebrew, guys. It's very old but it's my native tongue."

"We knew that, Ben," said Lisa. "We just wanted to see God at work." Lisa and Charles smiled at Ben and explained what had happened last night and that morning before they arrived. Ben smiled and said,

"Yes, I can easily translate this for you, it will be my pleasure! You see I am not only a Jew, but I am also a Messianic Jew!"

"A what?" asked Sophie. Ben continued with a smile,

"A Messianic Jew. In other words, I am a Jew who believes in the fact that the Messiah has already come in the form of Yahshua Ha Mashiach, or who you know as Jesus Christ."
Lisa interrupted,

"Oh, we know Him as Yahshua, too, Ben. Our God's real name we know to be Yahweh!" Ben was surprised.

"Most Christians don't know the name of their God," he said. "And even when they do, most refuse to use it for some reason! HalleluYah!"

They all sat around Ben as he opened the scroll and carefully put a weight on either end to stop it rolling back together.

"It reads," he began, "To my children, who have received my Name, this is my will on Earth. Follow carefully the instructions laid before you." As Ben read on it was as though Yahweh himself was talking to them personally. Lisa looked around at the others as she listened. They were all listening intently, not wanting to miss a single word. Ben described the work they were to do there at The Ark in preparation for a huge event that was to occur. Again, Lisa looked at everyone listening. She noticed an almost supernatural calmness about everyone. Normally she would have expected a completely different response from anyone who had just been given a vast amount of work to do, without a glimpse of any remuneration.

There were no details of this 'event', apart from its consequences; apparently this was still to come, but there was great detail of the tasks that needed to be done. They were going to have to farm the land in certain parts of the estate and create a refuge for people, believers and non-believers alike, as a shelter from this event, which to the world would look like a natural disaster, although, as the scroll was describing, it was part of the plan God had revealed to John in the book of Revelation.

Survivors from the impending disaster would need to come to the Ark to rehabilitate, to get their lives together and learn about their future. The leader of the group was to put in place a plan to get as many people together as possible and to warn them of the times ahead from that moment on until the day when it would happen. The Ark literally would be a modern-day Noah's Ark. Ben finished reading with the words,

"Stay strong, have faith. I am with you always. You are far more powerful than you have been led to believe. I love you." It was signed at the bottom. pp Thomas Carter.

There was silence in the room. They all looked at each other in turn. Finally, Lisa spoke in a quiet tone,

"Wow, so this is it then!" She felt guided as she spoke out with an authority that none of the others had heard before. She said, "It's decision time, guys. If you're in with me here, then say. If you're not, then I'm afraid it's time to leave!"

One by one they all committed to give their time and effort

to the works ahead, even Jenny and Ben, who Lisa had really only just met and had no idea of their level of faith. They all had lots of work to do and no idea of the time frame to do it in. They would all have to be totally reliant on Yahweh and His instruction.

Great times were ahead, of that they were certain. There was an excitement in the midst of the conversations. Questions were being tossed around like, how do you think it's going to happen and who's going to do what jobs and many more.

Charles stood up and cleared his throat to get everyone's attention. He started,

"It feels to me that it's no accident that we are here right now, together, with all the skills we each have. I feel we should pool our resources of skills that we have, together and start to plan ahead. I also am suggesting that Lisa be our leader and that she has the final say in matters of importance, purely because of the anointing given to her from Yahweh."

They all laughed and joked about their skills and what they could do to progress the plan and finally came up with all their subsequent jobs: Lisa was in overall control and was to head up the outreach to bring people in; Sam was in charge of all building works and general maintenance; Charles was going to organize all aspects of farming and food production; Ben was going to put together plans for schooling and education; Sophie was going to be in charge of all younger children and their guidance; and Jenny would first of all finish selling Lisa and Charles's houses, then she would take charge of the treasury and all purchases.

It was amazing how they were all so skilled at their respective jobs. Everything seemed to be covered and as new people came in they would join certain teams or have their own particular area dependent on their abilities, but for now, it was agreed they should all muck in and finish cleaning up. They all set to and got busy. Beds were going to be needed very soon so Charles and Sam set off to solve the sleeping arrangements. Charles teased Sam because he was in charge of building and so he should make the beds. Sam fired back at him that whoever made the beds got to sleep in them. They all had mattresses so a temporary frame for everyone would be all that was needed and as people's furniture arrived from their homes the beds they made could be used in the bunkhouses for emergency accommodation.

Lisa called a removal company to box and pack her things at her home in Hightown as it needed to be clear in a week for her 'angel' buyer. The company agreed to do a special deal for her and for Charles's house too.

Later on, that afternoon, Jenny and Ben approached Lisa with a question that brought a smile to Lisa's face. They had been talking all morning together as they were cleaning one of the outhouses.

"Of course, you can! I was going to ask you if you would but didn't quite know how to approach the subject with you. I prayed but had no answer. I guess Yahweh spoke to you guys directly." They laughed and hugged each other. Jenny and Ben had asked Lisa if they could live at The Ark permanently. They agreed to sell their home and pool the money with Lisa and Charles.

"I'll put it on the market tomorrow when I pop back to the office," Jenny informed her enthusiastically. "It should sell very quickly!"

It was then that it hit Lisa like a brick and it must have shown clearly on her face. She felt as though the blood had drained from her body. Until then she hadn't even thought about it.

"Is that okay?" asked Jenny, noticing the concerned look on Lisa's face. With urgency Lisa cried,

"Where's Charles? We need to speak. I can't do it, Jenny! I just can't do it!"

Chapter 15

They Came from Afar

Jenny and Ben followed Lisa outside as she ran to find Charles.

"What's wrong, Lisa?" asked Jenny. Lisa replied,

"I'm sorry, Jenny, I'll explain in a minute. Charles! Charles! Where are you?" Charles and Sam came running out of one of the barns.

"What's the matter, Lisa?" shouted Charles, running towards her. They all congregated in the middle of the yard, in the glorious sunshine.

"Can I have a word with you all?" said Lisa, breathing heavily. "We have to talk!" They walked back to the porch and sat around the table and Lisa started to tell everyone her concerns.

"We cannot sell these houses of ours!" she began. Everyone looked at each other in surprise.

"Why Lisa, what's the problem?" asked Jenny with a concerned expression on her face. Lisa continued,

"It's like this, Jenny. We all heard Ben when he was reading the scroll earlier. There is going to be some catastrophic event that will happen probably sooner than we all think, which is the reason why we are all here together. We are being called to prepare this place to rescue people and bring them from all the surrounding towns and cities and wherever else. For me, the last thing that I can do is to warn someone of impending doom and then sell them a house in that area and they ultimately die!" Everyone looked at each other again.

"My goodness!" said Charles. "You're right!"
Everybody was stunned. Of course, Lisa was right and they all knew
it.

"But what are we going to do without money?" asked Sam.

"Yes, we need money to buy all the equipment and
machinery, so we can survive here!" Charles pointed out.

"I know! I know!" admitted Lisa, her head hung low. There
was a small silence, then Lisa lifted her head and looked them all in
the eyes and said, "But I know my God is faithful and He will not
let us down! He is in control here!"

They all agreed and threw different ideas around for the next
few minutes but they all agreed that they would need to look at
different ways to raise capital. Suddenly Jenny spoke up.

"What do you all think I should do? I mean I sell houses for
a living!"

"Well we're all in this boat or should I say, this Ark,
together," said Lisa sympathetically with a smile. They all laughed at
her pun.

"But Lisa," continued Jenny with a straight face, interrupting
the laughter. "Don't you think that your 'angel' buyer, as we've
called her, is a provision from God? I mean houses just don't sell
like that. At least I've never seen it." There was silence as everybody
thought about the sense that Jenny was talking. Lisa just stared at
Jenny.

"I don't have an answer, Jenny." confessed Lisa. "But I
know
Yahweh will have!" It was true; they'd all rejoiced at the seeming
miracle of the house selling so quickly and easily. As far as Lisa
was concerned, there was only one answer.

"Thank you all for your input. I'm going to go and pray
about this right now," she said. "Can we meet back here in, say, half
an hour?" With that she walked down the steps of the porch and
wandered up the hill at the back of the house. Everyone went back

173

to their jobs feeling a little bewildered and confused, questioning in their own minds the discussions they'd been having over the last hour.

Meanwhile, Lisa was walking and talking to Yahweh, trying to find a secluded spot where she could get close to him.

"Here's fine, Lisa," she heard from a voice in her mind, so she sat down right where she was. "Trust me, Lisa," the voice said. "You are right. I didn't have anything to do with your buyer. Someone else did. Be careful and stay close. If you're unsure, check. I am here for you. You don't need any more money. I will provide for you. Meet at eight o'clock and you will start to see who I really am." She replied with some frustration,

"I know who you are! You are Yahweh, my everything! The creator of all! Without you there is nothing! I know that, but how do we buy all the things we need to complete this task if we don't have money? And what's going to happen at eight o'clock? Is this really you speaking?"

There was only silence. Apart from the cry of a hawk over the trees there was nothing to be heard. Lisa sighed, almost annoyed. She needed to reflect and look back at everything that had happened. She wandered back down the hill towards the house. She could see everyone busy at work as she strolled down the path and it made her smile.

"What a great bunch of people!" she thought to herself. "Thank you and forgive me for doubting you, Yahweh." She heard the word "Believe" disappear into the ether, which gave her 'Goosebumps' all over her body.

The sun was shining with a light breeze and the views were just incredible as she made her way down to the main yard in front of the house. It felt just great to be alive. Everyone gathered on the porch again and Lisa, smiling like the Cheshire Cat, told everyone what God had said. Nobody could guess what was going to happen at eight o'clock, but it was certainly exciting. Lisa spoke out,

"I know we are all used to depending on money and have become totally reliant on it, but Yahweh wants us to rely on him in the same way and more. We cannot be a part of the world anymore as we have known it. The lifestyles that we are all so used to are about to come to an abrupt end!" Everyone still had many questions, but they also had a lot of faith. After all that was why they were there.

It was now seven o'clock and Lisa was pacing around with excitement not knowing what to do with herself. Jenny was helping her in the kitchen to prepare the food for their meal and had to agree that she felt the same way.

"How amazing this is, Lisa?" Jenny confessed. "I would never have believed that Ben and myself would be doing this." Ben walked in. "Me neither!" he agreed. "But I know it's right. I'm so excited!" They all hugged.

Charles walked in from the lounge to see the group hug.

"Can I join in or is this for the select few?"

"The more the merrier," Jenny replied. They all laughed. Sam came next followed by Sophie with the boys to join the party and the jollities. Everybody seemed so happy.

The men brought a large table in from one of the buildings and placed the chairs around it in the dining area. The aroma of the food being prepared in the kitchen was wafting through and the girls were setting the table. It felt like a real occasion to be celebrated and nobody really knew why.

At 7:30 the meal was served, and the party began. They had roast lamb with all the trimmings. The grape juice flowed but no alcohol. People there were high on life and not substances. Lots of joy, laughter and extreme anticipation.

What was going to happen at eight o'clock nobody knew but Lisa was amazed at the people around her and their surety that something was going to happen. God was real in these people's daily lives, not like the people she had known in the past who just went to church on a Sunday and then got on with their lives and never involved or acknowledged Him in anything.

They ate their meal and chatted amongst themselves, laughing and praising God and each other for their blessings. Lisa, as their leader, wondered what she should do, as it approached eight o'clock but decided to let Yahweh take control and just wait.

At one minute to eight, according to Charles's watch, the most expensive and therefore, according to everyone else, probably the most accurate, they became quiet. It fell silent. Not a sound could be heard as they anticipated whatever was going to happen. Just as Charles was about to say that it was time, there was a loud knock on the door. Everybody jumped in their seats. Charles got up to answer the door, slightly annoyed at whoever it was choosing such an inconvenient time. Everybody just sat wondering who it could possibly be.

Someone suggested it may be a neighbour, even though they didn't have any for a good few miles.

Charles walked towards the door and opened it. He looked out and stepped through the opening of the door and closed it behind him. Everyone inside was listening intently as they could hear Charles chatting with whoever it was. After a minute or so, Lisa couldn't stand it any longer and got up to check it out for herself. The rest just sat there with an intensity that could be felt physically.

Who was it outside? They all looked at each other not knowing whether to laugh or cry.

Lisa timidly opened the door a few inches to see Charles on the porch with four men. He was talking to one of them while the three others stood around him. They looked intimidating but at the same time non-threatening and even though they seemed quite serious in their discussion, it seemed none-the-less friendly. Lisa stuck her head out to get a better look at what was going on. The men seemed very official in some strange way but casually dressed. They all seemed very clean but at the same time rough and unshaven.

She plucked up some courage and opened the door just enough to get out but not enough for the others to see. She interrupted their conversation and said,

"Charles? Are you okay? Who are these gentlemen?" Charles replied,

"Hey Lisa, these men have been walking for days and need shelter. They are willing to help with our work here for food and lodging." There was something different about these guys, that was for sure. She couldn't quite put her finger on what it was but for some reason she knew that they were okay. Normally she would be so wary of letting any stranger into her home, never mind four freakishly tall wanderers. Charles continued,

"They say they can put their hands to anything and we do need the help, Lisa."

"Oh totally!" Lisa replied. "Come on in and meet everyone!" Lisa opened the door to find Ben, Jenny, Sam and Sophie right behind it, with only the boys still sat at the table.
Lisa named everyone in turn, then said to the men,

"Sorry I didn't catch your names?" One by one they spoke, all with the same strange accent. They were obviously foreign but from where she couldn't tell.

"I'm Eli," said the one who had done the talking up to now.

"I'm Jonah," said another.

"I'm Joshua," said the third.

"And I'm Noah," said the last.

"Of course, you are. Welcome to the Ark," said Lisa, smiling. They all went inside, and Sam pulled more chairs around the table.

"Come and sit down for a while. Sophie, would you fix these gentlemen something to eat?" They sat down at the table and everyone else gathered around them, fascinated by them.

"So where are you guys from?" asked Charles. "I don't

177

recognize your accents."

"We're from Damascus in Syria," said Eli.

"Well, recently anyway," Noah continued, "We move about quite a lot, so I guess we sound kind of strange." Everybody agreed and laughed. Sophie and Jenny walked in with plates of food and put them down on the table.

"Right, come on everyone!" said Lisa authoritatively. "Our guests don't need an audience while they eat!" So, they all went to sit down at the table on the porch while the four men ate their supper.

"Who do you think they are?"

"Do you think God sent them?"

"It was exactly eight o'clock!"

"What strange accents they have!"

"How did they end up here?"

"It can't be just coincidence, can it?"

Questions and statements were being bandied about on the porch like a steely in a pinball machine. Charles spoke up.

"I'll put them to work tomorrow and see if they can cope with anything. Then we'll know whether they are from Yahweh or not." He grinned.

"Be kind to them, Charles!" Lisa laughed in return. "I know God told me clearly eight o'clock and indeed, it was exactly eight when they turned up."

The door opened from inside the house; it was Eli, who seemed to be their spokesperson.

"Where shall we sleep tonight? If we can put our bags somewhere that would be great," he said. Sam piped up.

"I'll take you down to the bunkhouse whenever you're ready, you'll just have to mind the piles of rubbish in there, we haven't quite finished tidying yet."

"Oh, don't worry," said Eli. "We'll do that. It can be our first job!" The four followed Sam down to the bunkhouse with their rucksacks. Jenny came running out of the kitchen exclaiming,

"Wow, you should see this. Not only did they eat all their food up they washed their pots and everyone else's! Just how long were we talking out here?" They all agreed it couldn't have been more than fifteen minutes but, in the end, they put it down to the fact that they must have been extremely hungry and very appreciative of our hospitality.

"At least we can be sure that they aren't going to be a burden to us!" said Lisa.

"That's for sure," said Jenny. "I could do with a few of these guys at my house!" They all laughed, and Charles broke out the grape juice again. They sat at the table looking over the glorious view in front of them on that beautiful evening. They could see Sam walking back up to the house from the bunkhouse looking slightly bewildered. When he reached the others, he said in a quiet voice,

"They must have been tired. As soon as I showed them their beds they got in their sleeping bags and went straight to sleep. I also noticed that not one of them has a watch." Lisa replied,

"That must be a lovely way to live, to not be restricted by time." Charles remarked with a smile,

"I'd be tired too, if I'd just walked from Damascus." They all chuckled and sipped their drinks and watched the sun go down with an incredible sunset.

"Yahweh is great indeed!" said Sam to a unanimous "Amen!" from everyone.

The following morning everyone got on with their jobs while Charles and Sam took their four new guests for a guided tour of the estate. He explained to them that the upper fields were going to be sown with various crops this year to provide food for them all and the surplus would give an extra income. He explained that they were going to purchase all the necessary equipment with the money from the sale of their houses, but that idea had taken a turn now, so they would be hiring the tractors and implements they needed this year and hopefully buy them after a harvest. In all they had over three hundred acres that needed to be ploughed, cultivated and sown.

"It's a lot of work for any ardent farmer, let alone a bunch of amateurs," thought Charles.

"What about all the broken-down equipment in the bottom sheds? Can't we fix them?" asked Jonah; it was the first time they had heard him speak.

"Well," said Charles. "None of us are motor mechanics or welders here, so we figured it was a 'no go' area. Can you help? It would be great if you can, because we need to get on with it all."

"Leave it to us!" said Eli. "Let's fix what we can and then we can hire anything else that we don't have." It was agreed, and they continued their tour.

As they wandered back to the farm, Sam whispered to Charles,

"Most of that stuff is rubbish, Charles. I've been through it all. The tractor needs new parts and it would be cheaper to buy a new plough than to try and fix that old rusty thing! We haven't got much time to waste on that stuff we need to get on and sow the land." Charles replied,

"I know, Sam, we'll give them a week then we'll hire it in."

Lisa's furniture was due to arrive after lunch, which was a great relief to her as she would be able to sit and sleep more comfortably. She figured that if everyone brought their own belongings to the Ark, they'd all have more than enough, and it would be only the bunkhouse that they would need to make beds for.

The house was looking very clean on the inside now and would look great properly furnished. She was going to ask Eli and company to fix things up outside and do some landscaping too. Jenny was helping Lisa to sort out a strategy for bringing new people to The Ark, while Ben was brushing out the barn which was to be the classroom. Sophie was doing her usual wonders with the boys. She had now become their full-time nanny and tutor all rolled into one and was thoroughly enjoying herself in the process. Child care was definitely her thing.

Lisa rang the bell for lunch and everyone descended on the house. Sam went to tell Eli and the gang, who were working on the equipment, that the lunch bell had rang as there was no way that they could have heard it over all the banging and clattering that was going on the barn.

"We'll skip lunch today, Sam. Too much to do in here," shouted Eli in his broken accent over all the racket; he laughed.

"Isn't lunch for wimps anyway?" Sam laughed, turned around and walked out, still a little bothered that they we even contemplating fixing any of the junk in there.

"They're certainly very busy in there, Charles!" Sam said as they walked up to the house together. "I just hope it's not all in vain!"

"Not if Yahweh builds it!" replied Charles.

"Very profound!" laughed Sam. "Don't get all religious on me."

Just as they approached the house they saw a large truck coming over the hill, down the drive towards them. It was Lisa's furniture.

"Oh well!" laughed Sam. "Lunch is for wimps anyway!" They directed the truck back to the steps of the house and the driver jumped out.

"I know you!" shouted Sam. The driver replied, "Sam Smythe? Is that you?" It was one of Sam's friends and co-workers at the Church, Jim Wilson.

"What are you doing delivering furniture?" asked Sam.

"It's my new job!" explained Jim. "I had to leave when you disappeared. You're not very popular down there, you know. The whole place was in turmoil and the stuff they were saying about you. I had to go." Charles left Sam to talk and grabbed a quick bite to eat.

They started to unload the truck. It seemed strange for Lisa to see her furniture being carried into her new home. It felt like it all belonged at The Ark. Everyone grabbed boxes and all that they could to help. When the last chair was unloaded Jim got ready to leave. Lisa signed a document of satisfaction and he jumped in the cab. Charles had arranged for Jim to collect his belongings from his house too, so it wouldn't be the last time they would see him. They waved as he made his way up the drive and out of sight.

"What a nice guy he is!" said Sam. "A good and loyal friend." Sam told Lisa what had been going on down at the Church. He also informed her that there were more people than she would think who were actually on her side. Jim had told Sam that some people were appalled at the way she had been treated.

"Maybe even a couple of hundred people!" Sam exclaimed.

Suddenly, they were interrupted by a loud bang and huge black cloud of smoke came billowing out from the equipment barn followed by the revving of a large diesel engine.

"No way," shouted Sam. "It can't be!" The next thing was the double doors of the barn were swung open, followed by the grinding and clunking of a gearbox and out came a very dirty faced Joshua wearing a huge grin, driving the old international tractor. The three others came out of the barn running after Joshua cheering and laughing.

"How on earth have they done that?" shouted Sam as he ran down the yard towards them.

They passed Sam on the way up to the house and stopped in front to show off their success. Not only was the tractor running but they had cleaned it all up too. It looked fantastic.

Out of breath, Sam came back up to the house and said,

"How have you done that?"

Eli replied, "Unless Yahweh builds the house, the builders labour in

182

vain. Unless Yahweh watches over the city, the guards stand watch in vain. Psalm 127:1, Sam," Everyone laughed and cheered. Charles shouted,

"Who cares how they've done it! They have done and that's all that counts! HalleluYah! Praise Yahweh! He builds this house!"

Chapter 16

The Belt of Orion

The house looked very different by the end of day two and looked much more like a home. The boys were thrilled at having their own bedroom furniture back and more importantly the return of their toys.

That evening they had a meeting to discuss where they go next and the plans for the days ahead. Lisa was delighted to hear what Sam had said about people from the church being on her side. Maybe they should be the folk that she should approach first with God's message.

It was agreed that Jenny should go with Lisa for a while as back up and support. It was also agreed that when Jenny had any enquiries for a house purchase the prospective buyer should be warned of the troubles that were coming. The message was finally going to start to get out.

It was fantastic for Lisa to get into her own bed. It felt really cosy and comfortable and when she rolled over and switched off the lamp on her night stand she quickly drifted into a deep sleep.

The next thing, she found herself standing at the window of the lounge, looking up at the night sky. She was staring at Orion's Belt. It started to noticeably move closer as though she was slowly zooming in with a camera.

Suddenly, the three stars of Orion's belt exploded before her eyes and there was a huge flash. Everything was so bright that she had to hide behind her couch. When the brightness subsided a little she got out from behind the couch and went outside to see what

184

was happening. She looked up at the sky. It was like a piece of cloth, torn in two, and between the two veils of sky were the sun and moon side by side, day and night together. She knew that Yahshua was coming! She quickly gathered her children and friends together. It was time. Meteors were hitting the earth. Pieces of the exploding stars were crashing down causing great tsunamis around the world. At the same time, the land was breaking up and earthquakes demolished cities all over the globe. Lisa took her 'family' up a hill and they all sat there calmly, safely waiting for their Saviour.

Lisa woke with a jolt. For a moment she felt as though she was still in the dream. As she sat up in bed, she started to come around and realized that she had just been given a vision. She had to tell everyone. She looked over at her clock. It was still only five thirty in the morning, so she reached for her bible and her journal. As she wrote down the details of the dream she asked Yahweh for help and heard,

"Amos, 5:8." Quickly she turned to Amos and read:

"He who made the Pleiades and Orion, and turns deep darkness into the morning and darkens the day into night, who calls for the waters of the sea and pours them out on the surface of the earth, Yahweh is his name."

"So, is this it, Father?" she asked. "Is this the end?"
A voice said,

"The time for my Son to return is soon. Be prepared, stay close to Me and do all that I tell you. I am with you always."

Lisa jumped out of bed.

"Five-thirty or not, they need to hear this!" She woke everyone in the house and asked Ben if he'd get Sam and Charles and the four visitors from the bunkhouse and she would put some coffee on.

Ben ran into the bunkhouse shouting,

"Charles! Sam! Wake up! Come up to the house now!

185

Yahweh has given Lisa a vision! Where are the other guys?"

"I've no idea," said Charles sleepily. "But I'll find them. You go on up, Sam." Charles threw some clothes on and went out to find them. He didn't have to look far. They were just where he thought they would be; in the equipment barn. He opened the door to the barn. The sight before him stunned him for a moment. Before him, lined up in a row were all the pieces of equipment that they had but now in great condition, looking in perfect working order.

"Erm, guys? Wow! Can you come up to the house? How did you...? Anyway, Lisa needs to talk to you."

"No problem," shouted Eli. "I hope you approve of our work Charles?" Stunned, Charles didn't reply, he just stood there staring at all the farm implements they now possessed.

"Are you coming too, Charles?" said Eli as they left the barn.

"Er, yes! I'm coming now!" Charles backed out of the barn still staring at the sight before his eyes and closed the door behind him.

When they reached the house, they could smell the coffee from the door. They walked through the open door and closed it behind them. Sam was already sitting, talking to Ben with cup in hand.

Lisa beckoned them to sit down and Jenny poured them some coffee. Lisa began.

"Yahweh has spoken and given me a vision. The time is soon, and we need to be prepared!" She told them of the vision she had and the way the earth was hit by the meteors.

"We are up here in the mountains for a reason and we will be safe here, but all those who stay in the towns and cities will be destroyed. We need to get this message to all that we possibly can. They are God's children and He loves them."

"Amen," said Eli, Jonah, Joshua and Noah in a spooky

186

unison and the rest agreed too.

"What I need to do now," continued Lisa, "Is to fast and pray to get Yahweh's strategy, to get our message across without people dismissing us as crazy and thinking that we are just some religious cult! I think that Jim showing up yesterday was by no means a coincidence. The church has to be the place to start."

"We will help you, Lisa," said Eli. "That's why we're here!" Lisa smiled and said,

"Thank you, Eli but haven't you got enough to do with Charles?" He replied,

"We have indeed but talking to people about Yahweh is what we do best! We can put our hands to anything but some things we excel at!"

"Well, you're certainly excelling at restoring farm equipment, because I've never seen anything like what you boys have achieved down there!" exclaimed Charles. "It's breath-taking!"

"Thank you, Charles, but that is something we are relatively new at," explained Eli, smiling, "We must be just naturals, I guess."

"You can say that again," laughed Charles. "The seed wheat and fertilizer are arriving tomorrow, and we need to get it all sown as soon as we can." Eli responded,

"Leave that to us, Charles. We will deal with that."

"I believe you will, Eli," said Charles. "I believe you will."

Everyone left the house and continued with their jobs. Lisa asked Charles if he could help her in the kitchen for a while. When they were alone she took hold of his hands, looked him in his eyes and said,

"I had a letter yesterday from Dan's lawyer about the divorce, it's all going through." Charles nodded understandingly. Lisa continued. "He has taken full responsibility and has admitted adultery and says that if I sign immediately it could be all over legally in about six weeks." She paused and said, "I just wanted you to know that I have repented, for marrying the man that God told me

187

not to marry and for how that ended up leading to divorce. I hate divorce; Yahweh hates divorce. It really hurts all involved. I know that Yahweh used it all for good and blessed me with two very good and precious little boys, but I should never have married Dan. I should have waited for you, Charles. My mistakes made things so complicated when they should have been simple. I've had to repent of meeting with you before I was divorced, even though I should have met you before I was married! How I wish I'd followed Him closely all of my life"

Charles's eyes filled with tears. He replied,

"Lisa, you are such an amazing woman. I hate divorce too. Yahweh told me that we should be together. The truth is, you were always mine and I was always yours, we just lost our way. But we love a merciful and forgiving God. I want to be with you with all my heart, forever, and when this is all over, Yahweh willing, He will help us to make things right and we will be together." Lisa smiled; Charles continued, "Until then, I won't touch you or kiss you or even hold your hand romantically. I respect and love you and Yahweh too much to potentially mess this up through lack of patience." Lisa replied,

"You're so perfect Charles. I love you too."

"I have to go," said Charles as he let go of Lisa's hands and backed out of the kitchen.

"There is much to do!" He smiled at her and closed the door behind him. Lisa hugged herself and smiled and she spun around in complete joy.

"Thank you, Father!" she said with a broad grin on her face. "Thank you!"

***

Sam and Charles looked in amazement at the machinery that they now had in the barn.

"So, what else do we need to sow the wheat?" Sam

188

questioned. Charles replied,

"Well we have the tractor, a plough, various harrows to break down the soil, a seed drill and chain harrows to cover the seed. I think that's it."

"Yes, Charles," said Jonah. "That is enough to do the job. Good eh?"

"Fantastic, Jonah," Charles replied. "And all down to you guys. You are miracle workers, you really are." Sam agreed and said,

"Shall we take the plough up to the top fields and make a start? We can at least mark the fields out."

"Don't worry Sam, we have it covered," said Joshua.

"Yes, leave it to us now," said Noah. Eli added,

"We'll take the seed up with the quad bike and trailer when it arrives, and, in the meantime, we'll make a start with the ploughing. Don't look so worried, Charles, it's in safe hands. You and Sam can get on with other jobs around here."

"Well if you're sure," said Charles. "We have got plenty to do around here." They were interrupted by the 'whoosh' of air brakes. Sam and Charles went out of the barn to find the seed wheat and fertilizer had arrived. They explained to the driver where to unload and watched Jonah and the gang driving off with the tractor and plough.

"They make me nervous," said Charles. Sam laughed,

"Yeah, me too. We have to get this right."

Charles wrote a cheque to the driver for the seed and bade him goodbye after warning him about the impending meteor storm which would mostly hit Hightown. He took it very well considering this guy wasn't a Christian, which they assumed according to the pictures splattered all over the inside of his cab. He said that he knew where they lived and if it was okay with them he would come up to The Ark when he saw it on the news. He too would hopefully be back with more seed too, so they could try again then. At least they had 'sown seeds' in his mind.

"Shall we fix up the hen house, Sam?" asked Charles.
Sam replied with a cheeky grin,

"That sounds like a 'fowl' idea to me, but okay."

Plans had been made for all manner of livestock to abide at
The Ark and in pairs too. They were going to need to be completely
self-sufficient up there in the mountains; they had no idea
how long for, either. What Yahweh meant by soon was only his
business. The money they had, needed to be used very sparingly for
the same reasons.

Lisa and Jenny agreed that they would go down to the
Church in Hightown the following day as it had been advertised as
an open day there and there was sure to be a good crowd of people
throughout the day. Lisa was very nervous about it but knew that
God would give her the finer words to say when she needed to say
them. They had made a bunch of simple flyers with contact details
on for people to take home and maybe, just maybe they could get
through to one or two people.

Sam and Charles chuckled as they watched Eli and Co.
going to and fro with the equipment.

"They sure are an amazing bunch. We are so lucky to have
them with us," said Sam.

"There's no luck needed when Yahweh is on your side,"
added Charles. "I'm just so relieved He chose us."
They were soon ready for the hens, so Charles called the suppliers
and they were on their way.

"Fresh eggs soon, Sam!" laughed Charles.

"Yes," said Sam. "And Chicken dinners!" They both
stopped in their tracks. They suddenly realized that when their
animals arrived, at some point they were going to have to slaughter
them. Neither Sam or Charles had ever killed anything before and
both of them said that they wouldn't do it.

"Maybe we should just eat eggs and vegetables," said Sam.

"Yes," agreed Charles. "And we can get fish from the lake too!" They high-fived each other and got on with their jobs. They both knew that at some point animals may need to be slaughtered but they'd meet that problem when it arose.

***

Ben's classroom was now complete with its one desktop computer and home-made chalk board, but it would suffice. His next task was to prepare another outbuilding to make a small home for him and Jenny. It was right next to the school which they joked was very convenient for work. It had an open fireplace and would be pretty much open plan too with one main room and a bedroom with an adjoining wash-room. It would be simple but sufficient for their needs. Both him and Jenny knew what they were doing and were looking forward to making the 'shed' as homely as possible. They too had some money saved and planned to spend a little on their new abode.

When Lisa rang the bell for supper time that evening everybody was ready for it, apart from the four farmers who still hadn't returned from the fields. Charles suspected that they wouldn't
either, at least not while they had light.

The rest of them ate well that night although Lisa explained that their supplies were running low. Ben volunteered to do some shopping with Sophie and the boys as one of their lessons. They had the best school ever.

Everybody was woken in the morning by the sound of the horn of a pick-up truck. The hens had arrived.

Lisa and Jenny got ready to leave for the church open day and Ben prepared a list of everything they were going to need from the grocery store and Sophie got the boys dressed and ready for their adventure to the shops.

The hens looked great in their custom-built house. They had

fresh straw in their beds and everything they needed to produce lots of wonderful, tasty eggs. It felt great to start to produce at The Ark. Things were starting to take shape.

Within minutes of the chicken farmer leaving with a flyer and a warning of the vision, Charles's furniture arrived. Charles and Sam unloaded the furniture truck with Jim.

Lisa 'tooted' the horn as her and Jenny took off up the drive, leaving The Ark for the first time since they had all arrived.

"She seems really nice," said Jim.

"Who? Lisa?" replied Charles, picking a chair from the back of the truck. Jim added,

"Yeah, not at all like everyone has described her at that church."

"She'll have fun there today," said Charles. "I hope they'll be okay."

"God will be with them, Charles," said Jim. "You know something," he said. "I really admire you lot up here. I told Connie all about you when I got home. She's really tired of town life and won't go to that church anymore after the way they treated Lisa."

"Well why don't you come and live here?" Charles said taking hold of the opportunity to say something.

"Yeah!" agreed Sam. "You could even bring your RV and live in that if you didn't want to stay in the house." Jim replied,

"I know Connie would in a shot, but I'm a working man and it's too far to drive to work every day from here."

"You wouldn't need to." said Charles. "There's enough work to do here for an army! You get all your food provided and a lot of fun too." Sam added,

"Plus, the fact that you get to survive the storms that are coming!" Jim hadn't heard anything, of course, of the devastation that was ahead. Charles and Sam explained everything right there and then. Jim couldn't believe his ears.

"And when's this going to take place?" he said.

"That we don't know." Sam explained. "All we have been told is that it's soon, but that could be a month or a year, we just don't know. We're just being obedient. It's not a bad place to hang out though while we wait is it?" Charles concluded, "Look Jim, go home and speak to Connie and get back to us. You're always welcome here. We'd love you to be here with us."

They finished unloading the truck and Jim drove home, promising to be back in touch as soon as he spoke to his wife. The house was now completely full of furniture. Charles had a large four-bedroomed house in Hightown, so now they had a real surplus. They had no idea where to put it all, so they decided to wait until the girls got back from town. When Ben got his there too they would have enough to start a furniture store.

***

Jenny and Lisa arrived at the Church. The car park was completely full, and Jenny had to park on the overspill. They both wore white t-shirts, so they could be noticed and more importantly people would realise that they were together, part of 'Team Ark'.

Lisa was hoping that some people who weren't against her would recognize her and come and say hello, rather than her having to stand on a soap box shouting that the "End is nigh!" And that was exactly what happened.

They were just milling around in the grounds of the church where there were stands and balloons and music playing. Lisa said hello to lots of people who she recognized and eventually one couple responded,

"Hello and, how are you?" Lisa introduced Jenny to them and started explaining where she had been and what she had been doing since that traumatic day in church. Miraculously, they stood there listening. Then another couple, who Lisa had been quite friendly with at the bible class at Tom and Jan's house, joined them and pretty soon there was quite a little group of people around them, just how Lisa had envisioned. She spoke with great authority and sense combined with a taste of humour. She was really winning them over.

The people asked questions about what had really happened with Pastor Adams, why she had moved to the mountains and what they were doing up there. Jenny put the flyers into people's hands and asked them to give her or Lisa a call. It all seemed to be going really well; Jenny had handed out at least twenty flyers to people who seemed genuinely interested and intrigued.

When they heard about The Ark and old Mr Carter there was a real positive reaction from the steadily growing group of onlookers. What Lisa and Jenny hadn't realized was that Tom Philips had spotted them and had disappeared inside to Church to find Christopher Adams. Mr Adams had still been at the church, amazingly, since his arrest and had carried on being Pastor there, still advising people and preaching on Sunday mornings.

When he heard that Lisa Jeffreys was outside in the grounds he was totally overcome with rage on the inside, but he kept his cool outwardly.

"Thank you, Tom," he said quietly and walked to his office. He burst out a few minutes later and headed straight for the front doors. He went outside and looked around, his head turning like a radar tower, searching for Lisa.

The group around Lisa and Jenny was becoming quite loud with laughter and gasps of amazement as Lisa told stories and answered the people's questions. Adams soon spotted them and made his way over to the group surrounding Lisa and Jenny.

Suddenly he shouted out,

"If you listen to this harlot, you'll go to hell like she will! Don't believe her lies! Get out of here, Lisa Jeffreys! You are not welcome here! Go and take your friend with you! Leave my people alone!" Lisa replied,

"Aren't they God's people, Mr Adams? These people just

want to know the truth! Don't they deserve that? Will you tell them, or shall I explain what you are really like?"

Suddenly, from his inside pocket he produced a hand gun and pointed it at Lisa. The crowd gasped and screamed and dispersed in every direction. It was pandemonium.

"Don't be stupid, Adams!" cried Jenny.

"Don't worry Jenny," Lisa reassured her. "There are bigger people in control here! Don't be frightened of this little man!"

"Shut it, Jeffreys!" Adams screamed and shook the gun in her face. "Get out of here or I'll use this!" More screams rang out as people ran for cover.

All of a sudden, four tall men dressed in long black coats stepped out from the crowd and stood between Adams and Lisa like four sentries' shoulder to shoulder. It was Eli and the gang.

"Oh! So, you brought your body guards with you did you, Jeffreys? Move you lot or you'll get it too!" screamed Adams, holding the gun in both hands, aiming at Eli.

"Put the gun down, Mr Adams. Now!" Eli's voice boomed in Adams face, so loud you could almost see Adams hair blow with the force. It visibly shook Adams, but he shouted back, filled with rage,

"Nobody tells me what to do!"

and he pulled the trigger. Click! went the gun without going off. He pulled the trigger again. Click! Nothing happened. Then repeatedly, click, click, click, click! He shook it and shouted,

"What's up with this stupid thing?"

Eli grabbed his wrist and took the gun calmly out of his hand and pointed it to the sky and shot the six rounds into the air. People's screams and the gunshots echoed around the church grounds. Police sirens could be heard in the distance. Eli threw the gun down and grabbed Adams by the collar and pulled him up to his face, lifting him off the ground. Eli grimaced through his teeth.

"Live by the gun, Die by the gun!" Eli threw Adams to the

195

ground and disappeared into the crowd with Jonah, Joshua and Noah close behind.

The Police pulled into the car park with all their blues and twos. Two cars screeched to a halt and several officers came over to where Adams was still sitting on the floor, shaken by what he had just done and witnessed. They questioned a few people who were around, including Lisa and Jenny then they took Adams, put him in the car and disappeared as quickly as they had arrived.

A Policewoman took Lisa's address and told her that they would need to take a statement from her but would come to her house to do it. Interestingly enough Christopher Adams' 'people' weren't quite as faithful to him as he expected. All the people who were questioned pointed to him as the assailant.

Jenny handed a few more flyers out on the way to the car and they left. What had just happened was truly supernatural. She and Jenny both now realized for sure that Eli and the boys were a lot more than just handy wanderers;
They truly were sent by God.

Chapter 17

The Angels of God

By the time Lisa and Jenny had reached The Ark, a police car had caught up with them. The girls hadn't said much to one another; they were still in shock. They all pulled up at the house together and got out of their cars. Ben, Sophie and the boys came to the porch to greet them wondering why they had been escorted by a police car. Jenny briefly explained as they walked up the steps to the front door. Lisa showed the police women into the lounge only to turn around immediately due to the fact that it was completely packed with furniture. Lisa smiled,

"Shall we sit here?" They sat on the porch in the end as it was the only place that was free to sit. Charles and Sam came hurrying up the yard to the house to see what a police car was doing in front of the house.

"Don't worry, Charles," shouted Lisa, noticing Charles and Sam on their way up to them. "You guys carry on, everything is fine. I'll explain to you later." Sam and Charles stopped in their tracks, turned around and went back to work.

"It seems Mr Adams doesn't like you, Mrs Jeffreys." said Officer Jones, with a sarcastic smile on her face. Lisa replied,

"Don't I know it, and all I did was be married to the guy who ran off with his wife!" They made a subdued laugh and took down Lisa's account of the event. Fortunately, the police knew all about Adams and his antics from the last time he was arrested.

When they had finished with Lisa, they took a statement from Jenny. After they had taken down both their accounts of the events, the other Policewoman, Officer Scholmann, asked them why they had gone to the church in the first place. When Lisa explained what God had been telling them, Scholmann sat back in her chair and folded her arms. She said to Lisa, firmly,

"So, you're telling me that God has told you that we are going to be hit by meteorites which will cause a tidal wave that will wipe out the entire coastal town area?"

"More than that," replied Lisa. "It will happen all over the world."

"I'm not going to write any of this down, Mrs Jeffreys, because nobody down at the station will believe this and in any case, it doesn't have any bearing on why Adams would pull a gun on you. You could have been telling your friends down there that Aliens were coming to kill us for all I care, but I would keep quiet about this if you talk to any other police officers; they'll think you are nuts!"

"But we have to tell people!" replied Lisa. "That's what God wants us to do. Should the police all die?" Scholmann responded,

"In the line of duty, yes!" Lisa persisted. "Well, I'm telling you as friends, then."

"That's fine then," said Officer Scholmann. "Thank you for the warning." They all smiled at each other. Solution found. Through all this, Officer Jones sat quietly, just listening. Papers were put together, pens put away, notebooks closed. They stood up and said their goodbyes. It was recommended to Lisa that she shouldn't leave the country to which she agreed, and they got in their car and drove back up the drive, over the hill, out of sight and back to the world.

"Wow, what a day," Jenny remarked. Lisa sighed and said,

"I know, Jenny, but we have to be strong. We have to be obedient. But well done today, you were amazing!"

"Oh, thank you," said Jenny. "You were fantastic too!"

Lisa was just making her way down the steps to see Charles, when

she heard a tractor and saw
Eli and company driving down the back lane from the upper
meadows with the plough on the
back. She turned and looked at Jenny with her mouth wide open.

"It can't be," said Jenny.

"But it is," answered Lisa. They could see all four of them
jump off the tractor by the implement shed and dust themselves off.
No long black coats, just the old, dirty clothes that they
had been working in. Lisa and Jenny looked at each other, then
looked at the men, then at each other again and shook their heads in
amazement. Who were these people? They had to find out.
Lisa ran down to the barn where Charles and Sam were. She almost
leapt into Charles's arms and hugged him.

"Hey Sam," she said from over Charles's shoulder.

"Hey Lisa," replied Sam. "Have you had a good day?"
Charles put her down and they walked back up towards the house.

"Coffee anyone?" shouted Jenny from the porch.

"All round, I think," Lisa shouted back. "I'll get the 'fab'
four!" and she turned back to walk down to the shed. Charles and
Sam carried on up the house. Lisa walked into the barn where they
were cleaning the plough and said,

"Hey guys! Come on up to the house, the coffee is brewing!
You must have had a busy day."

"You wouldn't believe," said Eli, smiling.

"Oh, I think I just might," Lisa laughed and they all walked
out of the barn and up to the house.

Coffee was on the table when they got there, and everybody
sat down on the porch and steps. Lisa spoke up,

"Can I have a word with everyone? I think it's easier if I do
this while we're all together." Everybody fixed their eyes on her. She
continued boldly. "Today, we have seen the reality
of Yahweh." She paused, finding it hard to find the words. "When
we waited, anticipating something to dramatically happen the other

night at eight o'clock, I don't know about you guys but I was a little disappointed when all that happened was that four wanderers turned up to help us with our jobs. However," she said looking at Eli and the crew, "You have been amazing with your work. We have been shocked at the speed and efficiency that you can work and we all respect that so much because the last thing we have in our hands is plenty of time. So, thank you Eli, Jonah, Joshua and Noah. I can accept that you can repair tractors that need new parts and implements that were corroded and all rusted up, suddenly looking like brand new. I can accept you working all night without a break and accomplishing great things physically," she paused again, then said. "But guys, you have to explain to us how you did what you did today. We are all true believers of the one true living God. We are all his children and have seen many miracles, so please do not feel that we can't handle the truth. If it is possible for you to do so, please tell us." She sat down. Eli stood up.

"Thank you, Lisa," he said. "Thank you all for your hospitality to all of us." He, too paused, searching for words. He made a funny little guttural sound, almost bird-like, as if he was speaking in tongues at mega-high speed, then continued.

"We are from Yahweh, the most high Elohim, Creator of all things. He sent us to help you in all ways until His return. So, if it is alright with you, we'd like to stay here until that time. Like you, we have no idea when that will be, so please don't ask us. We don't know. When the time is right, and everything is complete it will happen. Yahweh's time is always perfect. We are what you guys would call 'Angels' or what we would call...." he made some kind of noise, which was obviously their language, which to a human was totally unrepeatable. A strange sound, impossible to say or write down. "…. But you can call me Eli." Nobody laughed or made any kind of expression. Everybody was silent, completely transfixed by what he was saying. It was incredible, totally unreal but totally real.

200

He continued. "We can do things here, that you cannot; it's easy for us. What you do not yet know is that all the fields are ploughed and cultivated. All the wheat has been sown and the other fields are now only waiting for the appropriate seed. We have done this in less than a day, which to you would be impossible but for us is easy. Please just trust us when we say we can do something. We can hear your thoughts and know what you are going to say in advance but don't even think about that, we would ask you to just treat us as men and nothing more. What happened today was as simple as this. We heard your anguish when that man held a gun to you. We were in the fields

but as…." he said that word again, "We are able to move within your time and space and can appear anywhere we need to at the blink of an eye. Please, do not be afraid. We are here to help, to take care of you if necessary and to give you messages if need be. Again, thank you for your hospitality, you too are Angels in our eyes. If any of you have questions just ask, but the sooner you accept us for who we are, the easier it will be for us to interact with you guys and not make other people, who join us here, frightened."

With that he sat down and sipped his coffee. Lisa had a million questions in her head, never mind a few. So did all the others but Eli sat down and there was silence. A strange but comfortable silence, as though God was allowing them to take this all in and accept it without the need for questions. Sophie piped up,

"Does anybody fancy a burger from Burger Express? It's our nearest fast food store." It was the most ridiculous thing to say after what they'd all just heard but everybody agreed and they all got up and went off to get ready to go out.

"We'll meet at the front of the house in half an hour," shouted Lisa and went upstairs with the boys.

They took three cars and drove to the outskirts of Hightown, some fifteen minutes away, to the nearest Burger

Express.

They all had a great time, well deserved by all, especially after the day's events.

When they were all suitably fed and watered they left for home. They still had a lot to do that evening as the main house was now packed with all of Charles's furniture.

When they got back they sorted out what was going in the main house, what Jenny and Ben could use and whatever else needed to go wherever. The rest was put in storage in one of the dry barns. At about ten o'clock they all sat down in the lounge of the main house around the log fire to relax.

Charles had a huge selection of films, so Sophie chose one and they all sat down together to watch. About half way through the film, they were interrupted by a car's headlights shining through into the lounge.

"Who can that be now?" Charles sighed, getting up to go and see.

"I hope it's not the police again," shouted Lisa.

"No, it's not," Charles shouted back. "Sam, come here! You're not going to believe this!" Sam jumped up and went over to Charles.

"Well I'll be…." Sam said in astonishment. It was not a car at all. It was an RV! It was Jim and Connie. Sam ran out to greet them and Charles, briefly explained to Lisa and the rest, who Jim and Connie were and what had happened that morning that they had forgotten to tell with everything else that had happened during the day.

Sam brought them up to the house and burst into the lounge with a huge smile on his face and introduced them to everyone. Jim spoke up.

"I just couldn't keep her away. When I told Connie what you had said this morning, she started to pack and said that if I wasn't going, she was going to come on her own. So, we're here guys. I hope it's okay."

"Of course it is!" shouted Lisa and everybody jumped up out of their chairs and went over to hug Jim and Connie. It seemed like the perfect end to an incredible day. Not only would Jim and Connie be great friends for Sam, but they were obviously very trusting people, another couple giving their lives in the service of their Saviour and Creator.

The TV was switched off and they all sat down to talk. They didn't bombard their new friends with what had happened that day, that would have been too much for any human being, but they just talked about Jim and Connie and how great God was and what he was doing in all their lives.

They were having church. Sam and Charles showed Jim where to park the RV and everybody made their way to their respective sleeping facilities. Whether it had really sunk in to everybody or not, who could say, but no-one had even mentioned an Angel or anything since Eli had spoken. Even so, as everyone lay in their beds going through the day in their own mind, questions were being thought of and asked.

Jim and Connie, who were none the wiser about the whole incident, slept soundly.

As Lisa got undressed and climbed into bed, she thought to herself, 'I wonder what miracles tomorrow will bring?' It was exciting. She could remember what it felt like as a child on Christmas morning and now her life felt like that every day.

She snuggled down and thanked Yahweh for the day. She thanked Him for protecting her and Jenny, for sending the Angels to help and look after them, for bringing everyone together and now for Jim and Connie Wilson. She asked Yahweh to cultivate the hearts of the people they had spoken to that day and gave Him authority to intervene in their lives.

"Make it happen, Father!" she prayed and felt a warm tear fall down her cheek. She felt so fulfilled. So empowered. She was more powerful than she had ever believed but only because of Him, only because of Jesus The Messiah, Yahshua Ha Mashiach. She knew that she was only a servant and it was only through Him that she could do great things. She thanked Him ahead of time for any dreams He would wish to give her that night and for anything He wanted to say to her. Then she sat up and threw the bed covers to one side and jumped out. She had forgotten to go and see the boys. Sophie had looked after them so dearly recently but with all the busyness of the recent events it felt like she had slightly neglected them. She went into their room next door and looked at their sweet little faces lying there sound asleep, journeying through their dreams.

"Take care of my dear little ones, Father," she prayed. "Feed them, teach them, inspire them, bless them." She touched both their faces and smiled. They were so precious. "Thank you, Father, for choosing us, our family, thank you!"

She went back into her own room and looked out of the window. There was still some activity outside. She could see the lights on in Jim's RV and Eli and the others were up to something. She didn't want to even think what. Then, she noticed Charles writing something in a book, sitting on the little decking of the bunkhouse. She picked up her phone and sent him a message. She typed,

"What are you writing about?" To which Charles replied,

"Oh, you're spying on me now huh? ;-)" He looked up at the

window where Lisa was standing and beckoned her to come outside, so she put on her dressing gown and walked downstairs and outside into the warm evening air.

"I know it's late, Lisa," apologised Charles. "But I have something to tell you and ask you."

"Go ahead," Lisa replied, smiling curiously. Charles continued,

"I've been keeping a journal. I am writing down everything, and I mean everything, that's been going on; from your dreams to the things that are happening every day and I was going to ask you if you would do the same." Lisa laughed and said,

"This is so strange, I feel like I've either dreamed about this very moment or we've had this exact conversation before! Anyway, it's funny that you should say that I should keep a journal because I have been since before I met you. I think that one day we will have some amazing stories to share with people." Charles responded,

"You're on the right track with 'stories' but it's more than that. I am going to write a book." He smiled. "And I'm going to call it 'The Ark'. And you are going to be the leading lady." He interjected, "If that's alright with you?" Lisa replied with a grin on her face,

"Well, as long as it's put in the Christian fiction section because no one will ever believe this!" They both laughed.

"Well, I've already been in bed once so I'm going back there! Goodnight Charles," said Lisa and she turned to go back to the house.

"Sweet dreams and thank you," replied Charles.

"You too," Lisa responded and walked up to the house. She went back upstairs and looked out of the window again to see Charles still writing in his journal.

"Dear Charles," she thought to herself. "Thank you for him, Father. I know he will be a good husband to me and a great daddy to the boys. A great example to us all. Bless him, Father, bless him." She closed her curtains and got back into bed. This time when her head hit the pillow she went out like a light and into the world of dreams, where so many men and women of God had been given life-changing, world-changing messages and visions. Where adventures begin, and batteries are recharged in the life of this woman of Yahweh, a child of the living God.

Chapter 18

The Ark on Air

Since they had decided that their homes couldn't be sold, the only capital that they had was people's savings and unearned incomes. It was pretty obvious to all concerned that they were going to need to create income at the Ark until such a time when they could be totally self-sufficient. Up to now all they were producing was eggs, which Sam proudly delivered the first of to the house, but the twenty hens and one cockerel (called Solomon) that they owned wouldn't feed them all.

The fields were being sown with various crops which would produce towards the end of the summer but even then, they would need some equipment to reduce the crop to a usable state to make flour and other commodities. They were growing barley, soya, maize and oilseed as well as their wheat crops.

Some areas around the house were being cultivated to produce herbs and specialized vegetables, while the ground to the east of the estate was being plated with root crops - potatoes, carrots and turnips. All the pastures on the west side were being kept for grazing animals. They had decided that milk was essential, so some cows were needed; sheep for wool and meat and some horses were going to be purchased to create immediate income in the form of organized trekking, taking groups out riding on the estate. With the incredible views and beautiful woods and streams it was certain to be a winner if they marketed it correctly. Plus, it would mean that they could warn more people of the troubles ahead and invite them to live there at the mountainside paradise.

Charles, Sam and Jim had been busy visiting neighbouring farms to buy livestock which had been reasonably successful as they were now waiting for their first delivery of twenty-five ewes, already in lamb and due to give birth at any time. They were very expensive, but everybody agreed that time was something that they didn't have and the needed to produce quickly. Three cows were due to arrive, too, so things at The Ark were happening but it always seemed too slow. They had also managed to save four old mares from slaughter. Charles was certain they would have another foal yet and be fine for pony trekking anyway.

Due to their supernatural success, Eli and company were in charge of all the sowing of crops. They were always very humble concerning their achievements, which never ceased to amaze everyone else, although Charles's calendar for planting was now very different to his first model that he set out for the crops. They would get jobs done in a day that would take normal people a few weeks.

Eli spoke to Lisa about the importance of prayer. He said it was important to give Yahweh worship, to pray continually and fully trust in Him for provision. From that day, daily prayer sessions were organized, and the group would pray for all the crops, the fruit trees and the livestock to produce supernaturally and yield abundantly. It was certainly working too. By harvest time they would certainly have a lot of produce and would need a complete storage system for it all.

When the first lambs were born, there was great celebration. It felt fantastic to have the flock growing although Charles had looked at these cute little woolly animals and wondered how on earth they were ever going to kill them. He hoped that maybe Eli or one of the others could do it. One thing was certain: they would need a small abattoir and refrigeration for storage.

Now Jim and Connie had arrived there was fourteen of them up at The Ark and according to Jenny there would soon be many more. It would be okay during the summer months because at worst people could stay in tents, but obviously as winter approached that would be impossible.

More accommodation would need to be put up. Yahweh had already given them the answer and all they need to do was to follow the guidelines that were written on the scroll. On the drawings there were ten bunkhouses which would allow for five hundred people to be accommodated plus the house and the other buildings.

They were going to need lumber to build the bunkhouses, plus the food storage and manufacturing buildings. Fortunately, they had nearly one hundred acres of woodland, of which sixty acres pine trees and another forty acres of deciduous trees, which would be great for furniture. They had all the tools to do the job; chainsaws, hand saws, hammers, planes and chisels and would pretty much only need nails and glazing for the windows. The workshop already had a bench saw large enough to handle the job of sawing trunks into planks.

The neighbouring farmer had a huge old tractor that was suitable for lugging timber and he had agreed to loan it to them on condition they kept him supplied with logs for his wood burning stove. Sam joked that the Angels could probably manage on their own anyway.

There certainly was a lot of work needing to be done and as usual not enough time or help. This didn't really bother anyone at all though because they all knew that with God's help the job would get done.

They had decided that they should produce their own energy at The Ark. They were going to have solar panels fitted wherever possible and generate electricity through wind turbines. It was going to cost around £25,000 to set up but they could pay overtime and it would be an incredibly valuable resource to have. Not using the national grid was essential as it was sure to go down with the storms that were coming. What wasn't clear to anyone was how long they were going to need to survive before Yahshua came. They guessed there would be no need to worry after that.

For now, though, they had electricity, diesel and gas so they devised a plan to prioritise the use of energy which started with the building of bunkhouses and extra buildings.

They marked out the bases and started to get all the footings dug. Sam, Charles and Jim left the digging to Eli and Company while they concentrated on a drainage system for the compost toilets they were going to use, which would deal with the majority of waste produced by five hundred men, women and children.

Lisa and Jenny were taking calls from people who had read the flyers and were enquiring about The Ark and all that it was about. Some calls, as expected, were actually very short and sweet with people saying that they would wait to see what happened but they had about twenty five positive enquiries, which felt like a huge success. The phone rang again, and Jenny answered.

"Oh hello," she replied to the caller. "Yes, that's right." Jenny listened intently which got Lisa's attention. "Yes," Jenny went on. "You should speak to Lisa really, I'll just get her for you, hold on."

Jenny put her hand over the mouth piece of the phone and whispered, "It's Sharon Long from Wales Radio, she wants to talk to you with the view to an interview!" she mouthed. "Big station, could be huge!" Lisa took the phone from Jenny.

"Hello, Lisa Jeffreys speaking." Jenny watched her closely as Lisa nodded and agreed. "Yes, that would be great," she said. "Or you can come here and see what we're doing up in the mountains." Lisa smiled and then laughed. "Yes, that will be fine, look forward to seeing you. No problem. Bye!" And she put the phone down.

"What did she say?" asked Jenny immediately. Lisa replied,

"They are coming on Friday to interview us, in three days'

209

time."

"Wahey!" shrieked Jenny and they ran outside to tell the others. "We're going on the radio!" they shouted in unison. Jenny role played, in her best radio voice,

"Lisa Jeffreys, live on Wales Today!" Everybody was excited, even though they all knew that they could come out of this really successfully or they could be just as easily branded a cult, but they knew this would have to happen sometime. After the celebrations they went back up to the house to see who was next to call the Ark.

It was now possible to see where all the bunkhouses were going to be, and they looked fantastic. A little holiday-campish, maybe, but still fantastic. The footings were all dug, and the drains were marked out; it was happening much quicker than expected. There would be a communal wash-room with showers and toilets, kitchen and utility room with each bunkhouse enabling each one to function separately.

"Isn't it great working with Angels?" laughed Sam. "You don't even have to tell them what to do, you just think it and it's done!" Jim and Charles laughed with him. He sent Ben a text message to order the concrete lorry. Ben was now in charge of ordering supplies for building and farming projects, as his teaching job hadn't really begun yet as he only had the boys to teach at the moment.

A few minutes later Lisa and Jenny ran out of the house, shrieking again. Everybody ran to meet them again to see what all the commotion was about this time. It was great news.

"We have our first recruit!" cried Lisa, so excited that they could hardly make out what she was saying.

"Yeah," said Jenny. "And she's got two kids, eleven and fifteen." A single mum and her two children, who used to attend the church in Hightown, were on their way up to The Ark to live with them all.

"Great news, Lisa and Jenny. Well done," said Charles. "The first of many! HalleluYah!" They all cheered. Ben was really pleased because he would now have to start taking his teaching sessions more seriously, albeit with small numbers of different aged children.

It was agreed by everyone that women and children could stay in the house for a while until the bunkhouses were finished and men in the one bunkhouse they had, apart from Jenny and Ben who had their own 'little house' and Jim and Connie who were in their RV.

***

"Right come on then, Men and Angels, let's head off to the woods!" shouted Charles and they took off with the big tractor and a long trailer to fell and bring back trees. Lisa, Jenny and Connie went back up to the house.

Connie was starting to put in place the beginnings of the food production. She was quite an expert in the kitchen, so she was beginning by simply making bread for their own consumption and jams and cakes to be able to sell, with their own label containing a short message and phone numbers. It was to be simply called Ark Foods. They would have a stand at the local farmers' market, which was in two weeks, so she had to get busy. She was secretly hoping to have some help from this single mum who was about to arrive.

Ben, Sophie and the boys were now cleaning out the small annex of the school room, which would suffice as a school office and crèche.

The Ark was becoming a massive hive of activity. What money they did have was spent on capital purchases such as equipment for food production, farm equipment including Silo's for storage, the deposit for the energy system and building materials of all sorts of shapes and sizes. It seemed everything had been covered; all they needed now was the manpower to make all this happen. Bit by bit, it was all coming together.

211

Carol arrived that afternoon with John, aged eleven and Chloe, aged fifteen. Lisa took some time away from phone calls to give them the guided tour of The Ark and show them their rooms in the house. She was delighted that Carol and her children settled down so quickly. Within an hour of arriving at The Ark, Carol came to her to ask where she could help. Lisa asked her to work with Connie in food production and the kids went off with Sophie to help clean the crèche area.

***

On Friday when Sharon Long from Wales Radio turned up there was a real buzz around the place. It was a beautiful day and there was a real positive atmosphere that you could almost feel. Yahweh surely was with them. Lisa took Sharon to see all the projects that were going on and introduced her to everyone concerned, then took her back to the house for the actual interview.

They sat comfortable in the lounge. Sharon turned on her recorder and began.

"Tell me Lisa, how did this all begin?"

With a smile, Lisa began the story. Fortunately, she had expected most of the questions that Sharon would ask and was able to give her the abridged version of events, which were unbelievable enough themselves, never mind the full version. She asked about The Ark and how it got its name, which allowed Lisa to promote people coming to stay and also the fact that storms were coming, and people would need to be kept safe. She didn't hold back. She told it how it was. She just didn't use phrases like, "You are all going to die if you don't get here," she left that for people to work out for themselves. It was difficult to not come across like a weirdo, but somehow Lisa managed to do it. Yahweh said he would give her the words to use and He most certainly did.

Sharon tried to trip Lisa up several times, as all journalists do, but she always seemed to have the right answer. How people would react to her message though, she didn't have a clue. She had tried to put herself in other people shoes when she had been thinking of the answers to questions she might be asked, and it seemed to be working.

As Sharon seemed to be wrapping up, Lisa said,

"Can I just say a word, Sharon?"

"Yes of course," Sharon replied. Lisa continued.

"If people listening to this are asking themselves and other people if this is for real, or we're crazy, I would just like to say this: If you are a believer then please just pray about this and see what God has to say. If you have any questions give us a call, by all means. If you're not a believer, then you have two choices right now. You can either dismiss this as foolishness or find out about it. You see I am either telling you the truth or I am lying, but I can assure you of this fact: I am not living up here in the mountains with my two young boys and a growing community of people, just for fun or to make money. Please come and visit us. Come and see what we are doing here and why we are doing it. You will be made to feel very welcome!"

Sharon finished off by giving her thanks to Lisa and all the people at The Ark for talking to her and showing her around that day. She wrapped up.

"This is Sharon Long with Wales Radio."

Well that was it. All over. Sharon shook Lisa's hand and congratulated her on her interview and being so eloquent. She gathered up her things and put them in her car and left.

"You were fantastic," said Jenny and the rest of the gang, as they had all been listening to the radio in the bunkhouse, "Well done!" There were hugs all round. Lisa was totally exhausted by now. Jenny made her a well-deserved coffee, and everybody sat around chatting with one another about the show.

They were now public. The next few days would reveal the success or failure of it all.

***

The reality was that the radio interview caused mixed reactions. The good news from Lisa's efforts was that the phone seemed to now ring endlessly, and new people were coming to stay at The Ark just as she had predicted, or rather, as God had told her.

At the same extent, however, bad press was growing too. Occasionally they would get an angry caller online, calling them 'heretics' or 'lunatics' and the all-expected word, 'cult'. Generally, though, the good far outweighed the bad. At least it did for a while anyway.

***

The weeks ahead saw all areas of life grow at The Ark: The buildings themselves took on new life; Charles, Sam and the gang had completed the second bunkhouse, which had some people living there now; the food manufacturing plant was becoming just that, with Connie and Carol producing food for people. Bread was now readily available and other stuff was now starting to flow, although they were still dependent on ingredients from outside suppliers.

The crops in the fields were miraculously starting to show; when they had only been sown about ten days and the wheat was standing about five inches high. Even the maize, which was put in the ground only forty-eight hours before, was popping up out of the ground. The cows were in full production, all three of them, producing nearly thirty litres of milk each per day, which was a great start, but they knew they were going to need more if they were to have the numbers there they were expecting.

The bond that everybody had between one another was beautiful, totally supernatural. They were all living together how you would want a close family to be, which never seemed to happen to anyone in the 'real' world.

Everyone felt such peace there; it was truly tangible. The

214

love between Lisa and Charles was growing deep in their hearts; spending what time they could together. Their relationship was being put together with God right in the middle. It was beautiful to see.

Even the school and crèche were growing. Ben was teaching about twenty-five children now and Sophie had seventeen younger children whom she was caring for. They would follow her around like little ducklings, learning about God's world and the beautiful things nature provided. Sophie was a real natural and was loving her work.

News came from Officer Scholman that a restraining order had been put on Christopher Adams and although he was at large again, he wasn't allowed to come within five miles of The Ark. Not that he could cause much trouble in the scale of things, but it certainly gave Lisa a good feeling to think that he couldn't come anywhere near them anymore. Saying that, Lisa firmly believed that some of the 'crank' callers had something to do with him and his minions.

They had to focus on the positive things that were happening all around them and learn not to dwell on the expected negative responses that were bound to happen. What was to happen next, though, would have taken the most stalwart of Christians by surprise.

Chapter 19

A Traitor in the Camp?

It was a beautiful day at The Ark; people were busy running around, getting their work done. The sun was shining; it felt good to be alive. To be able to work in and around the incredible scenery there was itself a wonderful blessing.

An early morning prayer and praise meeting had been held that morning and had left people feeling totally inspired about their work and the whole ministry up there. Songs were being sung and people whistling tunes, all over the estate. Yahweh was being praised in the fields, in the workplaces, from every mouth.

It was about ten-thirty when Sophie burst into the house where Lisa was working, leaving an army of little ones waiting for her on the porch. She had a newspaper in her hand. Lisa was talking on the phone but she could see by the look on Sophie's face, that she needed her attention immediately. Lisa told the caller that she would call back and hung up.

"What's wrong Sophie?" asked Lisa. Sophie was shaking.

"Look at this!" she cried and laid the newspaper on the table. It was the Hightown Herald and it read,

'Mountain Cult kidnap families!'

"What?" Lisa exclaimed. 'Where has this come from?" She carried on reading. "What? Who?" she shouted. "Have you read this, Sophie? Apparently, someone who lives here has made out that we are holding people against their will!"

"I know!" Sophie replied, almost in tears. "Who could ever

say something like that?"

"Sophie, can you get the 'Seven' together? I've got a phone call to make."

Sophie ran outside, took her class back to the helpers in the crèche and rounded the gang up. Lisa picked the phone up and rang the newspaper that had printed the article.

She spoke to the editor concerned.

"How can you make allegations like this?" She listened then went on to say, "I don't care if they are living here or not, that is all lies. Who said it anyway?" She listened again. "Confidential? Right! Get up here right now and interview me and I'll give you the truth. In fact, I'll get all the other papers too!" She slammed the phone down just as the others rushed into the house.

"Look at this, Charles!" she exclaimed. "We have a traitor in the camp!" Charles took the newspaper from Lisa and everyone gathered around.

"What?" cried Charles as he read the article. Lisa responded.

"This time, I'm going to say something." Lisa took the phone and started to dial.

"What are you going to do?" questioned Jenny. Lisa answered,

"I'm going to get the truth out there, that's what I'm going to do. I'm going to call as many journalists as I can find."

"Is that wise?" Jenny questioned again. She looked at Jenny with a confused but friendly expression.

"The truth, Jenny, will set you free!" Lisa replied calmly and carried on with her phone calls. Charles suggested that they all keep calm and sit out on the porch and asked Jenny to help him make coffee for everyone.

In the kitchen, Charles said to Jenny,

"She's got a lot on her plate here, Jenny. She keeps very close to God. She has to."

217

"Yes, but do we have to agree with everything she says?" she argued back with obvious annoyance on her voice.

"Well," replied Charles quietly. "She is the leader here, she's only human and therefore can make mistakes, but that is why we are here, to help, to support, to pray, to be her friends not just when she gets it right, but when she gets it wrong too!"

"Well, I wouldn't have done it this way," Jenny said as she took a tray of coffees towards the door. "I'd have let it settle and go away of its own accord." Charles sighed, opened the door for her and said,

"We can all have our own opinions and views, we are human we are not going to agree with each other on everything all of the time, but we have to show respect for those who God puts in a position of leadership." Jenny huffed as she walked through to the porch.

When Lisa had finished on the phone she joined the group again on the deck. She stood before the table with her hands on her hips and said in a firm tone of voice,

"We're going to have a bunch of reporters here soon, so if you can all carry on with what you are doing and let me deal with them, that would be great." Everybody agreed and had a group hug.

"Come and sit down for a while and relax," said Charles. It was unusual to see Lisa's feathers ruffled so.

"I know, I'm sorry guys," said Lisa, pulling up a chair. "I just can't believe anyone here would say such a thing, and so public too. Isn't everyone told to come and talk to us if they have a problem with anything. This has to be the enemy telling his dirty lies through someone. If only I knew who it was! I'd…." Charles interrupted,

"That's probably why you don't know." They all laughed. Lisa smiled and held her hands up in surrender.

"Yahweh is smart, isn't He?" she admitted.
They all laughed again. When they had finished their coffees, everyone went back to work with the agreed pretence, as though

nothing had happened.

Lisa took the newspaper and went for a walk to find Eli and company. She figured that she might need some help. She found them sawing tree trunks into planks and framing timbers in the workshop. She walked in through the door to meet a wall of noise and sawdust. She waved to get their attention. Jonah saw her first and switched the noisy saw off. As the noise died down Eli walked over to her, pulling up his goggles as he did. He stood in front of Lisa and without a question said,

"It's Jenny." Lisa was quite taken aback with his abruptness. Then asked,

"What is?" Eli continued.

"It's Jenny who has lied about you to the newspapers." Lisa gasped and said,

"Who told you about this?" He replied,

"Yahweh did. Who else? Before we even came here we knew and now you are scared." Lisa just looked at him.

"Do not fear, Lisa," he continued, his eyes looking deep into Lisa's. "Your Father will give you the words to say. Be bold, be strong and know that He is with you. Do not say anything to Jenny, we will deal with her for you. She is just being used by the accuser. She will be fine!" Lisa wanted to ask all sorts of questions but all she could say was,

"Okay." She walked from the workshop and back up towards the house completely calm, saying 'Hi!' to people as she walked, chatting and encouraging them in their work.

As she approached the house she noticed two parked cars near to Jim's RV and another one coming down the drive. Suddenly, from what seemed out of nowhere, four reporters and several photographers descended on her, firing a barrage of questions at her, taking her completely by surprise.

"Hold on, gentlemen!" she shouted. "Come and sit on the porch while we wait for everyone to get here!" Within a few minutes

219

she had a whole crowd around her, some sat at the table with her and the rest on the steps and around the deck.

Lisa stood up and silenced the hubbub. She cleared her throat and looked around at them all in front of her.

"I think everyone is here now!" she said. "Before we start, ladies and gentlemen, I'd like to thank you all for coming so promptly and giving me the chance to answer these allegations that have been made towards us all here at The Ark."

Suddenly, Jenny burst out of the house and shouted,

"Let me speak first! I am the one who knows what the truth is! I am the one who spoke to the Herald in the first place." Lisa wanted to interrupt with everything that was inside her, but she remembered what Eli had said. The reporters all looked to Lisa for approval and she just raised her hand and said,

"Yes, you go ahead Jenny!" The reporters then turned around to face Jenny with their microphones, notepads and cameras. Jenny braced herself and started to speak. As she opened her mouth a funny, slurred sound came out. She tried again but then nothing came out.

"What did you say?" asked one of the reporters.

"Say that again," said another. "I didn't quite catch that." Everybody laughed hysterically. Lisa looked down the yard to see Eli standing watching the whole thing. He must have been fifty feet away, but he was just staring at Jenny. Lisa shouted above the ruckus,

"Go ahead, Jenny, tell them what we've been doing here." Jenny tried again but again nothing came from her lips. No matter how hard she tried to force out her words all she could produce was the occasional slurry squeak, which made the reporters laugh more than ever. She had been struck dumb, literally. She tried and tried, but nothing! She got so frustrated that in the end she stormed off in temper. Lisa felt so sorry for Jenny for making a fool of herself in front of all those reporters, who were falling about, laughing at her.

220

Halfway down the steps she turned around and tried again to blurt something out and again nothing but a feeble squeak came out, which again led to even more fits of laughter. Jenny kicked the ground which made a dust and broke the heel on her shoe. She turned away and hobbled off across the yard, feeling humiliated. Everyone felt concerned for her but knew that she needed some space.

This gave Lisa the whole stage. Everyone turned back to Lisa. The first question came.

"So, can you explain, Mrs Jeffreys, why you've been accused of holding whole families against their will?" Lisa replied,

"I'm sorry but I cannot explain that. Everybody that comes here comes for a few days at first before deciding, and on top of that they are all free to leave at any time. Ladies and gentlemen, when you are finished with your questions today I need you to do something for me. Walk around, meet people, ask questions to anyone and if you find anything untoward, you have my permission to publish it!" Another reporter asked,

"So, what about this impending disaster that you say is going to hit us all on the coast. Tell us about that?"

"Yes, of course," she replied confidently. "God has told us of a meteor storm that will hit the earth, not just the coastal region. There will be tsunamis and earthquakes too, but he told us that we would be safe here, so we should tell as many people as we can about this and give them the choice to stay here if they wish." Another reporter fired at her.

"Did God tell you when all this is going to happen?" Lisa replied with a smile,

"We have no idea! All we have been told is that it is soon." She spoke so elegantly and with such authority that she even surprised herself. They fired all kinds of questions and allegations at her and she was able to handle every single one with ease and even made them laugh in the process. When they had finished she took

221

them all on a guided tour of the place and as she had requested gave them a free run of the place. They seemed to be there for hours but one by one they left The Ark that afternoon, satisfied with the answers they had been given and totally consumed with the work that was going on there.

Several of the reporters were very much tongue-in-cheek with the whole rescuing humanity from a natural disaster and even the mention of Jesus returning made their eyebrows rise, but there was no way they could make, or stand by, any of the allegations that had been made by the Herald. In fact, the Herald reporter had been there and was going to suggest to their editor that there should be a total retraction of the article and that a public apology be made.

That which had been an attempt to sabotage the work of God by the Enemy had indeed failed. Lisa asked the leaders to gather everyone together in the yard, men women and children. She needed to speak to everyone. They gathered in the yard in front of the house and Lisa sat on the top of the steps. It was really the first time Lisa had seen everyone together. There was now nearly two hundred people at The Ark and from where she sat it looked like a thousand. She talked loudly in a kind, clear voice.

"I just wanted to encourage you all and praise you for the fantastic work that you have been doing! No doubt you saw all the journalists that visited us here today and I thank you for being polite and kind to them all." She went on, "As you know, when God asks you to do anything for Him, Satan always tries to stand in the way with his lies, but Yahweh stood up before the wicket and knocked Satan and his lies for six!" People clapped and cheered. Lisa continued. "Remember, if you ever have a problem here, come and talk to someone. There should be nothing hidden here, ever. The word 'occult' means 'hidden' and we certainly don't want that here!" Then she paused and said,

"Does anyone fancy a barbecue?!" Everyone cheered again and immediately people started to organize things. It was amazing to watch.

The 'Six' got together to talk about Jenny and where to take it from here. No-one had seen her since she had been struck dumb and stormed off, not even Ben, who was deeply concerned for her by now, as were the rest of the group. Nobody had the slightest animosity towards Jenny. In fact, all they were concerned about was where she was. How she had ever come to think such things would be dealt with later. All Lisa wanted was to help her see the truth in what they were doing there.

"But she already knows!" Ben said. "I can't imagine what got into her."

"I think you hit the nail on the head there, Ben," Lisa replied. "Something has got into her. But I've been assured that she will be fine."

However, it was agreed that they should organize a search party. Charles suggested that they ask the four Angels to intervene and went to look for them. A few minutes later he came back with Noah. They all stood around Noah as he explained that there was nothing to worry about. He said in his broken English,

"My friends, everything is under control. Eli has taken Jenny to be, erm, how do you say it? To be restored. When she comes back she will know the truth."

"What does that mean?" asked a concerned Ben.

"It means," continued Noah, "that she will be just how she was before she was attacked. She will be the Jenny you all knew before. In fact, she may not remember some things that have happened, so when you see her again be patient with her." They all looked at each other and shrugged their shoulders. At least they knew she was in good company and safe.

Lisa's phone rang just as everyone set off to search for Jenny. To Lisa's surprise the voice on the other end of the phone was that of her father.

"Hi Dad," said Lisa, inquisitively. "Is everything okay?" she asked.

"Everything is good, Lisa," replied her father. He continued. "Look, I've never been great at this so just let me say what I need to say. First of all, I have no excuses so all that I can say regarding how I have treated you is that I am sorry. I know that doesn't make it all okay, but it's still needed to be said. I know that things could never be between us as I now wish they could be, but you can at least know this: I love you, I am proud of you, and I could not have wished for a more incredible daughter. If you could ever find it in your heart to forgive me that would give me great peace."

Silence followed his slightly awkward but emotional speech and eventually, after allowing the lump in her throat to disperse, Lisa replied,

"Dad, I only ever wanted to be Daddy's girl. I felt like a complete disappointment to you. But you know what. I have dreamed of this moment so many times. Sometimes I thought it would remain only a dream. The bottom line is this, Dad. I forgive you, of course I forgive you, and I love you too!" She could hear her Dad trying to hide the fact that he was weeping.

"Lisa, I did not expect you to be so forgiving and gracious. I can't take the credit for you being such an incredible young woman, but I can be proud of you. I don't want to take advantage of your good heart but I want to leave you with something to think about; I want to be a part of your life again, and a part of my grandsons' lives." Lisa interrupted.

"Dad, I don't need to think about it, this is a dream come true for me. What is past is past. Now let's plan the future. Starting with buying yourself a new suit because I have a feeling you could be giving me away soon." She told her dad all about Charles and what God was doing in her life. They cried tears of joy together over the telephone as Lisa told him about the wonderful things that had been happening to her. When she got off the phone she could hardly find the words to express her gratefulness to God. Feeling

224

completely overwhelmed and filled with joy at this miraculous restoration she simply lifted her hands to God and whispered,

"Thank you! Thank you, thank you, thank you!"

After composing herself she went to join the others in the search for Jenny.

"So where is she exactly?" asked Lisa. Noah replied,

"Oh, she's here."

"But where?" said Ben.

"Yeah, we've searched everywhere," said Sam.

"She is here, guys!" Noah insisted. "She's just here before it all happened." He turned and started walking back towards the workshop.

"But…" spluttered Ben. Noah kept on walking. He stopped turned around and said,

"Trust me, my friends, she is in safe hands. Trust Yahweh!" He smiled then carried on down the yard. The rest just looked at each other.

"It's all we can do," said Charles. "I'm sure she'll be back soon."

By now the barbecue was well on the way; people were milling around, laughing and having fun. It was a great sight to see as Lisa leaning against the banister on the porch. She looked around and smiled to herself; it was all hugely satisfying. The boys came up to the house with a sandwich for mummy.

"Oh, thank you, my angels!" She said as she took it from them. "And just what I like! Well done!" They sat with her at the table and ate their food. Charles came up the steps, burger in hand.

"Do you mind if I join you guys here?" he said.

"Not at all," replied Lisa. "I wouldn't have it any other way." They sat for a while, not saying anything, just sitting, watching the festivities, reflecting on the days' events and the absolute beauty of the place.

"You know something?" said Charles, breaking the silence.

225

"It doesn't get much better than this. Although it's been another challenging day, it's been so rewarding too. And just look at all their faces. HalleluYah!" Lisa agreed and felt for Charles's hand under the table. Charles pulled it away saying with a grin on his face,

"Now, now, Lisa! You know what we've agreed."

"Yes, I know," said Lisa. "But I had some other mail today. I would have said earlier but with all the craziness here, I wanted a time alone with you." She paused for a second then continued. "I'm a free woman. My divorce came through!" Charles threw his arms around her and kissed her on the cheek. The boys joined in and hugged their mummy, not knowing why, but it seemed like the thing to do.

"It will be so fantastic to be a real family. I can't wait!" Lisa said excitedly.

"Me neither," said a grinning Charles. "Me neither." They hugged again. Lisa half-expected Charles to pop the question there and then but he didn't. The gentleman and romantic that he was had other ideas.

Happiness could be seen everywhere, on every face and in every conversation. All apart from Ben, who naturally was still a little concerned about Jenny, who still hadn't appeared.

Suddenly, Sam came running up to the house, almost out of breath, shouting, "I've seen Eli! I've seen Eli! He's back! He's on his way up here!" Ben and Sam climbed the steps to the house where Charles and Lisa stood to get a better view.

"There he is!" shouted Ben, pointing at the tall figure they all knew so well, winding his way through the throngs of celebrating people.

"Praise Yahweh! HalleluYah!" shouted Charles. They all cheered as Eli wandered up to the steps. He said,

"You guys all seem very happy. What is going on?"

"All the better for seeing you, Eli," shouted Lisa. "How's Jenny?"

Eli replied, "She's fine. Haven't you seen her?" There was a small pause in conversation. Ben replied worriedly,

"We thought she was with you. Where is she, Eli?"

"Oh, she's here," answered Eli. "I just don't know quite where."

"You mean she's here, here? Right now, here? In now time?" asked Ben, getting excited again, trying to make as much sense as possible.

"Oh yes she's here alright!" stated Eli, smiling.

"Let's go find her, guys!" shouted Sam, leading the posse.

"I'm just going to get a jacket and I'll be right with you," shouted Lisa, hurriedly walking into the house.

"Wait here for me." Lisa went to find her jacket as the others gathered a few helpers. "Now where is it?" she said to herself, then remembered she'd had it in the office, so she went to get it. As she opened the door to the office the first thing she noticed was the light had been left on, breaking all the rules of frugality. Then as she walked in she nearly hit the floor. There was Jenny, sitting at her desk on the telephone. Jenny smiled and signalled to Lisa that she wouldn't be a minute. Lisa backed out of the office in complete amazement. She gathered her thoughts together and went to tell the others. She went to the front door. The others were just at the bottom of the steps waiting for Lisa. She walked to the top of the steps and said,

"Ben, she's in here! She's in the office on the telephone."

"What?" Ben shouted in joyful surprise. "How long has she been in there?"

"I've no idea!" replied Lisa. Just then Jenny popped her head around the front door and said,

"I'm sorry, Lisa, did you want me? I was just following up an enquiry we had earlier."

"Jenny!" they all shouted and rushed up the steps, nearly knocking Lisa over and all group hugged her. When she was able to come up for air, Jenny excitedly questioned,

"What's up with you lot?" Lisa, remembering what Noah had said, replied,

"Nothing Jenny! We just love you and wanted to show how much we appreciate you." Ben joined in,

"Yes, and I've missed you."

"Aw thank you," said Jenny, and kissed Ben on the cheek. "I've just got a couple more calls to do and I'll be with you crazy lot. It looks like quite a party out here. What's the celebration?"

"Oh, just how great God is!" interrupted Charles.

"Indeed, He is!" replied Jenny and with that, she went back into the house, closing the door behind her.

Ten minutes later, Jenny joined them as they celebrated how great life really was and how great God constantly is.

As the evening seemed to be ending, Charles and Lisa were dancing together in the yard when suddenly there was a huge bright light shining from inside one of the barns. It was so bright that the rays shone through all the gaps in the timbers of the walls. Sam came running out of the barn, shouting,

"Lisa! Charles! Come quickly!" The music stopped, and everybody followed Lisa and Charles as they ran towards the barn. They opened the big double doors and the light hit them. They put their hands over their eyes to deflect the light and walked into the barn. Sam shouted,

"Come and look at this!" They walked towards the light where Sam was standing. Suddenly, the great light went out and everything was black. All the people gasped with surprise and laughter could be heard all around.

"What is going on?" cried Lisa. As their eyes adjusted to the light she noticed that, standing on a table, there was a small candle lit, and something near the candle was twinkling in its light. She walked over towards the table. Everybody was silent. As she got close she noticed the small object that was twinkling was a piece of

228

jewellery. It was a ring. She picked it up and looked at it. It was the most beautiful thing she had ever seen. Charles, who was standing right behind her, put his mouth to her ear and whispered, "Will you marry me, Lisa Jeffreys?"

Lisa turned around with her mouth wide open in surprise and cried, "Charles! Is this for me? Yes, yes, yes! Of course I will!" Everybody cheered, and Charles picked Lisa up and swung her around. They kissed, which produced more cheering. Everyone gathered around the happy couple and congratulated them. The music started again, and the celebrations continued. Lisa whispered,

"Thank you!" into Charles's ear.

"Thank you, Lisa," Charles replied. "You've saved my life, in more ways than one."

Chapter 20

The Wedding Feast

In the days ahead, no-one said anything to Jenny regarding the incident with the Hightown Herald. Eli told Lisa everything he'd witnessed during Jenny's restoration. He got to see it all in vivid technicolour. He told her that Jenny had first come under demonic attack at the church open day when Christopher Adams had been ranting at her and then bit by bit they had been chipping away at her causing her to begin to doubt and then rebel and ultimately an attempt to destroy what God had built there at The Ark. He said,

"She has been completely restored now, Lisa. Yahshua has completely brought her back a cleansed woman. She is like brand new now." They both smiled.

"Thank you, Eli," said Lisa.

"It's all part of the service, madam!" laughed Eli, bowing his head. Lisa slapped his shoulder and they went on with their work.

The bunkhouses were all but complete now and they were just having a lick of paint to finish them off and then they would be ready to be inhabited. Half of the bunkhouses were full, and they had enough room for about another two hundred and fifty guests. Everybody seemed to be happy and comfortable with their surroundings even if at first glance they looked like something out of 'The Great Escape'.

The food production was now in full flow. Connie and Carol and their crew had things running like a well-oiled machine and although food tasted different to how it used too, people were saying that they were feeling much better, physically. Charles reckoned that they were nearly eighty-five percent self-sufficient now and that in the next few months, by autumn they would to be virtually there.

As Eli had said, Jenny was completely back to normal and still none the wiser about the whole episode, but for everyone else it had been a real warning as to how real the enemy is. It was very easy to think that Satan just attacked the mind and didn't affect the physical, but this incident and many others had proved to them all that he could attack anywhere, any time, and usually in an area where you are vulnerable.

***

Lisa woke that morning with the sound of rainfall on the window pane. It was something that they hadn't had enough of recently and they had all been praying for it.

"HalleluYah!" she shouted, as she went to the window and looked out across the yard. People were running around outside looking up at the heavens praising God. It was amazing how real Yahweh was in people's lives now, when they had to depend on the land for your food and not the supermarket.

She saw Charles outside pulling a churn of milk on a trolley. What an awesome, true man of God he was. She couldn't wait until they got married which had been arranged for the coming weekend. They had decided that they wouldn't have a big party as they wanted it to be more intimate, between the two of them and Yahweh.

God had shown Lisa a vision of a triple braided cord, saying,

"That is how I want you to live, Lisa. The cord represents you, me and Charles, all as one. As you know, a triple braided cord isn't easily broken. We will be one forever!" When she told Charles, he was really excited because God had given him exactly the same thing in a dream.

She was just about to knock on the window when she heard a voice say,

231

"If you prepare it, He will come!" It took her back a little; it was quite out of the blue.

"Yes, Father!" she said as she fell to her knees. "Of course, but prepare what?" The voice said to her,

"The harvest will be ready soon and I want you to prepare a feast, a feast fit for a King! When you do, He will come!"
Lisa replied,

"Yes Father! Who will come?" There was no answer. "Who will come, Father?" she asked again but still no answer. She got up off her knees and got dressed. She ran outside into the pouring rain and found Charles turning on the spot with his arms out.

"This is just what we needed, Lisa," shouted Charles. "HalleluYah!" Lisa joined him in his spin and said to him,

"Can you come inside? I need to tell you something. God has just spoken to me." With that he stopped spinning and they walked up to the house.

***

"Who will come?" asked Charles as Lisa explained what God had said to her.

"I have no idea," replied Lisa. "But he must be important and certainly part of the whole plan here, so I guess we just get it done, what say you?"

"Absolutely," responded Charles. "The crops will be early, especially with this much-needed rain, so I guess we'll be looking at about four to five weeks as long as we get plenty of sunshine from now on, and with these Angels we have looking over the whole thing, I'm pretty sure things will go to plan, if not sooner."

It was agreed that they would have this feast prepared by the end of the following month which gave them about thirty-five days to prepare. The feast was to happen when the harvest was in, as in biblical times in line with the Yahweh's Feast of Trumpets. A celebration of thanksgiving.

232

A meal was arranged for the leaders that night, which would include Connie and Carol, who nowadays tended to totally be responsible for food supply, and Jim who was generally looked on by themselves as a founder. They loved getting together as a group anyway, but Lisa really felt that this was very significant to their whole existence there, so it was important to get right. She also invited the Angels, even though she guessed they'd already know about the whole thing, she thought maybe they could throw some light on who was meant to be coming.

***

Ben led the prayers before they ate. It was evident that the Holy Spirit was with them as it took almost twenty minutes to say grace. Along with everything that was happening, Jim's shoulder, which had been really causing him a problem, healed instantly. A burn that Carol had in kitchen that day, completely disappeared. Eventually, they started to eat.

The wedding at the weekend was high on everybody's agenda. Families were coming too, which was amazing as they would get a first-hand look at The Ark while they were there, with the
possibility that they would then decide to stay. That was what they all hoped anyway. Lisa was particularly excited that her parents were travelling across the country to be there. Her Dad was going to give her away and her little brother, James, who she hadn't seen for years, was going to be her page boy. It was going to be a great weekend.

Only Charles and Lisa knew about the forthcoming feast. It was lovely for Lisa to see everyone else so happy. Even though it was going to be 'her day' on Sunday, everyone was genuinely excited about it.

"The first wedding at The Ark," said Sam.

"Yes, wouldn't it be great to see a baby born here too," said

Jenny, smiling and looking at Ben as she did. Everyone laughed.

"Yes, if we have time," said Ben in his defence.

"Surely we'll be here for nine months!" replied Jenny.

"That, we'll never know!" interrupted Lisa. "Which brings me nicely on to the subject of why I asked you here this evening. Has everyone finished eating?"

Everyone had, apart from Sam who loved to finish everybody's leftovers as well as his own meal.

"Mmmm, yes even me!" Sam said, swallowing his last mouthful and putting his knife and fork down. Lisa announced,

"Yahweh spoke to me this morning!" Charles, as instructed, checked the expressions of the Angels as Lisa talked. It was only when she said the words,

"He will come," that their expressions changed. They all smiled at one another almost knowingly. The question of who was coming was speculated by the whole group. Some suggested that someone else was going to join them. Possibly another Angel. Others thought that they were going to see a massive movement of the Holy Spirit. Sophie even suggested that it could be Yahshua, Jesus Christ himself, which was quickly put down by the rest of them.

"As amazing as that would be," said Connie. "I cannot imagine Him coming here in person to see us."

"What do you think, Eli?" asked Charles with a smile. "You've been keeping quiet over there. You should know how God works."

"I do, Charles," replied Eli. "We all do. And one thing is for sure is that the Father only lets you know what you need to know. There will be a reason why He hasn't said and it's not really for us to try and even guess. We should prepare this feast as no other we have ever prepared and do our part. He will do the rest."
Everyone agreed with Eli instantly.

"But it's just so intriguing." said Sam smiling. "It's alright for you Angels. We're human, we're inquisitive." Sam looked around the table for agreement.

"I know," said Eli, smiling back at Sam. "That's what got you into trouble in Eden. If only you had just listened to Yahweh back then!" Charles interjected and changed the topic of conversation at that point; although they were smiling at one another, there was an element of sarcasm in Eli's tone of voice and he could sense
friction building up in Sam.

"Well, what should we do to make this feast fit for a King?" he asked, getting back to the subject in hand. One thing was for sure, it was going to be a special event. Ben suggested that they have a dry run for the feast at the weekend for the wedding.

"But I thought we were going to have a simple day," laughed Lisa.

"It won't be with two hundred guests!"

"Oh well," replied Charles. "It'll be fun!"

"Yes, and who's going to cater for all these people in three days' time?" asked Connie knowingly, joining in the fun.

"Oh, you'll manage, Connie," said Jim. "You always do." Connie playfully slapped Jim on the head and everyone else laughed hysterically.

"Yeah it'll be great! We'll all help," said Noah. And so, it was agreed.

The next few days were crazy. People seemed to be running around constantly, making it all happen. Apart from all the food preparation, Lisa was having a dress made, tables were being built and decorations were being created. It was fantastic to see.

By the time Sunday came The Ark was looking wonderful. The grass was all cut and the decorations and bunting flags were all up everywhere, fluttering in the gentle breeze. Family members had arrived and were being given tours around the estate and introduced to everyone. It felt amazing for Lisa to have all her family there, something which, up to a few weeks prior, she could never have imagined.

It was a beautiful day; the sun was shining, and the sky was a wonderful deep blue. Everything was spick and span and looked even more fantastic than ever.

At the appointed time everybody gathered together in the meadow behind the house, where the ceremony was to be held. The meadow grass was like a carpet of pretty, little flowers for the bride to walk on.

Everybody was dressed in their finery, looking spectacular. Even though it had kind of been a rush in the end somehow, with the last-minute decision to have everyone present, the whole scene looked amazing with the backdrop of the mountains and the valleys below, the beautiful cloudless sky and the flowers in the meadow, that seemed to be praising God and congratulating Charles and Lisa.

There was a murmur of voices at the back as Lisa appeared in her wonderful handmade gown of white satin, encrusted with sparkling stones and edged with pearls. She had a traditional veil and a spectacular diamond tiara. How a dress like that had been made in such a short time was just another of the many mysteries that happened at The Ark, which were by now almost common occurrences.

She made her way across the meadow to the crowd and slowly walked between the people who parted to form an aisle of friends. The whole thing was so natural, so organic. It was wonderful. Lisa looked incredible in her wonderful gown as she walked through the people with her proud Dad. It was a true royal wedding. Lisa was the princess walking to meet her prince, who was standing at the front of the gathering with Sam, his best man. Sophie was the chief bridesmaid, walking behind Lisa with her brother James. The boys skipped behind them, not really sure what they were doing, but they were having fun. Eli had been given the privilege of actually marrying them. Nobody argued or dared to say that he wasn't qualified to do so, being an Angel of Yahweh.

The whole scene looked like something in a fairy tale. Lisa stood with Charles and they made vows to one another in front of the congregation and in front of God. Lisa remembered the tough times she'd had and how Charles had truly rescued her. It brought a tear to her eye.

Charles reflected, as Eli spoke his words, of the times and incidents they'd experienced together and how he too had been rescued.

When Eli spoke the words,

"…and what Yahweh has brought together, no man can divide!" he paused and looked around the congregation menacingly before continuing. "I now pronounce you as one with each other and one with Yahweh!" He draped a triple braided ribbon around their hands as a sign. He paused again, as if waiting for something.

Out of nowhere, flakes of snow fluttered down like confetti from the deep blue sky. There wasn't a cloud in sight. It was the middle of summer, but they still came. Eli boomed,

"Yahweh, mighty Yahweh, the highest Elohim, sends this as a blessing to you both and as a symbol of purification! Charles and Lisa, you are now husband and wife and you may now kiss the bride!"

As they kissed, everyone cheered at the top of their voices, so loud that it must have been heard miles away across the valley. Charles picked Lisa up in his strong arms, spun her around and carried her back through the crowd and across the meadow with everyone following them.

They got to the house and he put Lisa down. They both felt physically different. They were truly married in the presence of God. As one.

Charles turned to the crowd following them and shouted,

"Let the celebration begin!"

Everyone cheered, and the party started. The food was superb, and Connie and Carol's army performed fantastically in catering for everybody there. There were no traditional speeches, only a word from Lisa and Charles, who joked about thanking everybody for coming, after all it was only meant to be a small wedding and ended up as a banquet.

"I love you, Charles," Lisa said, gazing into his eyes as they danced later on that evening. "What a perfect day!"

"Yes, it has been just that. And I love you too, Lisa Michaels," replied the proud husband.

"Oh yes, I can finally call myself that," laughed Lisa. "Thank you, Charles."

"No, thank you Lisa, for giving up your name and taking mine," Charles responded.

"That's okay," laughed Lisa. "I never did like Jeffreys anyway!" They laughed and carried on dancing.

It had been a great day for everyone concerned and they all cheered and whistled as Lisa and Charles walked up the steps to the house, waving to everyone. Charles opened the front door, picked Lisa up and carried her across the threshold and into the house as husband and wife.

During the next few weeks everything seemed to pick up speed; more and more people were coming to The Ark, so much so that they completely filled another bunkhouse. Sam was concerned with the increase in growth, that they would soon be full and in the position of building more bunkhouses. Had they just not thought big enough? The scroll had only shown ten bunkhouses but was that just a template to show what to build?

Nobody really knew but decisions were going to have to be made.

Lisa and Jenny were working on new campaigns to get the word out and in the meantime teams of people were putting flyers out all over. Lisa herself had actually being asked to appear on several local

TV stations. One way or another they were going to make sure that people knew about the tribulations to come. It was up to the people to decide themselves once they had been warned. New people were now turning up daily and the phone hardly stopped ringing. Lisa and Jenny even had assistants now, trained and manning the phones.

The crops were flourishing in the fields and food production was on the increase. Charles was now starting to suspect that they would have to bring the date of the feast forward, which was in turn increasing the urgency to get more done. They generally saw things grow at a supernatural rate. Even though they now had over three hundred people staying at The Ark, everybody was busy working in one capacity or another.

Preparations for the feast were well on the way; the menu was decided, even though it was going to be buffet style. Feeding all those people was not a simple matter and the numbers seemed to be increasing on a daily basis.

Tables and benches had to be constructed to seat everyone and marquees were being erected to house all the food. Then everything had to be decorated with flowers and bunting.

With the crops ripening rapidly, the date for the feast had been talked about being brought forward. Charles inspected the crops daily as the time of the harvest was so critical. He was convinced that their harvest would be way earlier than others, locally and nationally. He would sneak a look at the neighbouring farmers' wheat now and again, whose grain was just turning from green. Theirs at the Ark was almost ripe, very yellow and almost hard. It was amazing to see the fields full of the ripening grain, particularly the barley, with its long whiskers swaying in the breeze.

It was very satisfying for Charles, as he had been there from the very start and was a man with a spirit of excellence. As he walked the fields with great pride, he pondered on the feast and the significance of it. He stood for a while gazing of the vast acres of crops.

Suddenly, he heard a voice say,

"When you prepare it, He will come!"

Charles immediately fell to his knees.

"Father!" he shouted. "I hear you! I am here!" Even though he knew God was speaking to him on different occasions, it was usually in his head or a gut feeling, he had never actually heard an audible voice. This was so awesome. As he knelt in the field, he instinctively lifted his face towards the sky. Feeling a powerful radiance, he held his hands out as if ready receiving something. He felt empowered. The voice said,

"Well done, Charles. You are a true man of faith. I love you!" Charles fell face down.

When Charles opened his eyes and lifted his head he was looking directly into the face of an angel who was lay on the ground, on his front resting his chin on his hands. It was Jonah.

"Hey dude," said Jonah casually. "Was that good?" He stood up and helped Charles to his feet. Jonah said, "He's certainly given you something powerful, Charles! You even look taller!"

"That was amazing," said Charles dusting himself off. "I've never experienced anything like that!"

"I know," said Jonah. "That's what it's like, living with Yahweh." They walked together through the fields, back to the farm, chatting about Yahweh and his grace. Charles felt on top of the world.

When they got back, Charles went into the house to see Lisa.

"What has happened to you Charles?" she asked. "You look radiant." Charles sat down at the table and explained his encounter in the fields.

"How awesome!" responded Lisa. "I'm jealous. I wonder what he imparted to you?"

"I don't know but I'm glad he did!" Charles replied.

"You should see yourself in the mirror!" Lisa exclaimed. "You look almost sunburnt."

Charles dashed off to the bathroom and came straight back out laughing. He ran out onto the porch and shouted at the top of his voice so that everybody could hear. Everyone gathered around.

"Yahweh, most high, the mighty Elohim says, 'Prepare for the feast! The harvest is ready and plentiful! Gather the crops and let the celebrations begin!'" Everyone cheered and danced for joy. Sam came running up to Charles and asked with a concerned expression on his face,

"Are you sure, Charles? It wasn't ready yesterday when we went to check."

"Well it is today, Sam. I didn't say that, Yahweh did. Get on the phone to the contractors and get them here today. Let's go!" Sam asked no more and did as he was told.

Lisa couldn't believe the way Charles had spoken.

"And we wondered what He had given to you, Mr Prophet! That was amazing!" she said with total excitement.

"I know," replied Charles. "And it wasn't even on my mind to say anything!" They danced around in circles, holding each other's hands, praising God and shouting for joy at the top of their voices,

"God is good, All the time!"

Chapter 21

The Feast of Trumpets

Within hours there was two combine harvesters coming down the drive, followed by a convoy of tractor and grain trailers. The contractors came immediately as they had no other work on with it being so early in the season. They weren't expecting any either, not for a several weeks. They were amazed to see the fields so far advanced; so much more than others in the locality. The silos were all cleaned out and ready to be filled. The barns were ready for the bales of straw. It was all systems go.

In the meantime, preparations for the feast were almost complete. Everything seemed to be running smoothly. There was great wisdom in Eli's words suggesting they use the wedding as a dry run a few weeks prior. People were well trained in their knowledge of what to do to manage such a feast.

That morning, Lisa was at her desk as usual, where she always seemed to be these days, planning their next strategy to spread the word to more people, which involved all the local TV stations. She smiled as she read an e-mail from Sharon Long, confirming that she was willing to accept the voluntary job at The Ark that Lisa had offered her. She had always come across as being interested from a journalistic point of view but Lisa knew that really, she wanted to come and join them there, but pride and worldly reputation was stopping her. So, Lisa had asked her if she would help with Media marketing, an idea which Sharon jumped at, although Lisa's real intention was to talk to her and invite her and her family to stay. One way or another she would see her saved. Since the wedding, another bunkhouse had been completely filled and half of the last one, so Lisa knew that this would impress Sharon and maybe convince her to come and stay. She would be there in an hour; her desk was all tidied, waiting for her.

Lisa was sat at her desk reading about the Feast of Trumpets in her bible when there was a knock at the front door which made Lisa jump.

"Wow, she's early. She must be keen!" Lisa said to herself and walked out of her office towards the front door. She opened the door expecting to see Sharon but instead was greeted by a man wearing something like a floppy cowboy hat. The sun was shining extremely brightly, and Lisa had to put her hand up to her brow to even see him.

"Hello, can I help you?" Lisa asked politely.

"I've come to see The Ark," said the man in a gentle voice.

"Oh great!" replied Lisa enthusiastically. "Let me get Jenny for you and she will show you around." She shouted across the yard, "Jenny! Are you there?" A voice answered from the stores, "Yes Lisa! Coming!"

"It's you I've come to see, Lisa." the man said. "You've been expecting me."

"Oh right," said Lisa thinking she must have spoken to him on the phone. "Come on in then." There had been so many calls lately that she couldn't remember everyone, even though she tried to. He stepped inside the door.

"Thank you," said the man.

"That's no problem," she replied. "Here, let me take your things." He took his hat off and handed it to Lisa. As she took it from him, she could see his features for the first time. He was, she would have guessed, in his mid-thirties, with light brown, shoulder-length hair and his eyes were so striking, almost turquoise. They instantly mesmerised her. She had never seen such love in someone's eyes. She felt a power bolt through her body, which turned her legs to jelly and she fell to the floor. Jenny was just walking up the steps to the house and saw, through the half open front door, Lisa fall in a heap.

"Lisa!" she cried, followed by. "Charles! Come quickly!" Jenny ran into the house and knelt down to tend to Lisa.

"What happened?" asked Jenny. The man answered,

"Don't worry, my child, she'll be fine."

"What do you mean, 'don't worry'?" She turned her head, looking up at him, somewhat annoyed. Her eyes met the man's and she too collapsed on the floor. Lisa regained her consciousness and sat up just as Charles was running up the steps followed by Sam.

"Charles!" she exclaimed. "He's here!" Charles ran into the house and ran into what felt like a force field of love and before he could say anything, he joined Jenny on the floor. Sam came in, looked at Lisa sitting on the floor, looked at the man and buckled at the knees, falling on top of Charles. The man helped Lisa to her feet. She looked into his eyes again and said,

"It's you. You love me!" All she could see, somehow, was the man's eyes and his mouth.

"Yes, it's me, Lisa," he replied. "I told you I would come." Jenny stirred but couldn't move, as Charles lay on top of her arm. "Get off, you lump!" she moaned at Charles, who was starting to come around.

"I can't," groaned Charles. "Sam is on top of me." Sam was out cold, so Charles rolled him over and got to his knees. Jenny tried to get up using Charles as support but had no strength in her legs so sat back down. Just then Eli dashed in with the other angels in tow. He saw the man and fell to his knees.

"My Lord," he said and bowed his head in reverence. The others followed suit. Lisa, still staring into the man's eyes and holding his hand, said quietly,

"Charles, Jenny, this is…. your Saviour and King, our

244

Messiah, Yahshua, The Messiah! He has come as promised!"
Connie came through the door, asking where everybody was and fell
instantly as she stepped through the door. Jenny and Charles
followed the angels and bowed before their maker. It was the most
incredible scene. Almost unbelievable but it was happening. Just as
Sam was reviving, Sophie and the boys tried to get in through the
door and fell immediately. Bodies were now littered all over the
place, even outside the house. It looked like a scene of carnage but
in fact it was just the opposite. People were falling down because of
the power of the anointing of Yahshua Jesus Christ, the Holy Son of
God, their Creator.

As people began to realise who He was, Yahshua's very
persona began to change; his face took on a glow that could only be
described as glorious. It was all quiet in the house. People were
either on their knees or lay prostrate before Him.
Yahshua spoke in a calm voice,
"Hello everyone."
"Hi," said Jenny, almost automatically, and then put her
hand over her mouth and shut up, realising who she had just said hi
to.
"Can you all get up off the floor?" asked Yahshua with a
broad smile. "I think we have a feast to enjoy!" Yahshua walked
outside, with Lisa still holding his hand. Everybody got up instantly
and followed them out.
People came from all corners of The Ark and gathered
around Yahshua. They were weeping and cheering all at the same
time. Emotions ran wild as they realised who he was.
"Let's have a feast!" shouted Yahshua. "I will meet with you
all in due time!" Lisa attempted to get everybody refocused on the
meal and the celebrations. Everyone seemed to be in a complete
daze, which wasn't surprising since they were all standing in the
presence of the Creator of the Universe.
Just then a car came down the drive. It was Sharon Long.

245

She got out of the car and Jenny went to meet her.

"Hi there," shouted Sharon cheerfully. "I've come to see Lisa."

"Yes, I know," said Jenny. "I'll tell her you're here but she's with Jesus at the moment."

"Oh, she's praying?" questioned Sharon.

"No, I mean she's with Jesus. In fact, let me introduce you." Sharon, looking completely puzzled, followed Jenny as she led her to where Lisa was chatting with Yahshua.

"Lisa, sorry to interrupt you," said Jenny apologetically. "But Sharon Long is here." Lisa turned around and said,

"Sharon, great to see you!" They hugged one another. "Let me introduce you to a friend of ours. Sharon, this is Yahshua. You might know him as Jesus Christ." Yahshua turned around and Sharon immediately hit the floor.

About thirty minutes later she was still there. Charles went over to her to help her up, but she seemed so happy that he left her there. When she finally got up out of the dust she joined everyone in the preparation of the feast.

Yahshua seemed like such a normal, everyday person. People had noticed that he was wearing trousers and a regular shirt, which seemed amazing, considering who he was. He was dressed for the world He had come to visit. He spoke normal too, even though some expected him to talk using 'Thee, Thou and Thus!' as though he was straight out of the King James Bible.

They walked together through the yard towards the meadow where they were holding the feast and as He walked He began to transform before their eyes. His worldly clothes changed to a magnificent white, princely robe and the glow He had to His face intensified as His Glory shone out, just as it was described in the scriptures. His hair, almost pure white, flowed as it moved in the fresh mountain breeze. They were witnessing a second transfiguration, just as Peter, James and his brother John had witnessed when Yahshua last walked the Earth.

As they walked past the animal pens, the sheep, cattle, pigs and chickens all fell silent and appeared to bow their heads. It was incredible. Everyone was in awe. It was a real wonder to behold. All of creation was indeed bowing down before Him. He walked across the meadow and the plants and flowers seemed to move out of the way of His feet every time He took a step. There was no mistaking what this man meant to them. This man was God. Yahshua and Yahweh were as one.

Tables were dragged out and arranged in a huge circle, where Charles and Lisa had been married. They had all, somehow, expected to have some further notice for the feast to begin and have had everything out ready, but He was there, He had come, so everyone mucked in to help.

Connie, Carol and their team had the food prepared in what seemed like no time at all. The chairs and benches were put out and the feast was ready. When everyone was sat down it was a real spectacle. It was amazing to see five hundred people all sat in a circle facing each other and Yahshua. Lisa could see Sharon Long almost right opposite her. She seemed very happy, if not a little bewildered.

The teams served the masses of food and drink. It was a feast beyond all others, truly fit for a King.

When everything was put out, Yahshua stood up. Everyone fell silent. He raised his arms, looked to the sky and cried out,

"Father! Bless you! Thank you for this food and the harvest. Bless all the people who have been involved in the preparation of this feast. Let us celebrate and eat!"

Everyone cheered and settled down to enjoy their meal. Lisa sat reflecting on the whole scene. There she was in the middle of a beautiful green meadow with wild flowers all around. The sun was shining, it seemed with joy, praising God. The view was beautiful beyond compare and so were the men sitting on either side of her; Charles, her loving husband and Yahshua, her master and friend.

She thought back to her days in Hightown, just six months ago. It was like a dream, beyond her wildest imagination. Was this a dream? It felt like one. She almost had to pinch herself to believe it was really happening. But it was.

"Are you not eating, Lisa?" asked Yahshua.

"Yes, I am," she replied. "I was just marvelling at what was going on here today."

"I understand, Lisa," said Yahshua. "But this is just a mere taste of things to come for you. Are you excited?"

"Yes, I am, my Lord, I am indeed," she answered.

"Good, my child," Yahshua went on. "You should be." He smiled.

As the meal was coming to an end, for everyone apart from Sam, that is, someone's mobile phone rang. It was Sharon's. She looked so embarrassed that it should be hers, but everyone laughed, and she joined in.

As she searched for it in her bag, Yahshua gestured for her to answer it. He said to Lisa, "Let her answer it. This is a call for everyone here

It was the station manager at the radio station. He screamed at Sharon, demanding to know where she was.

"I'm at The Ark at my appointment," she answered.

"Still?" he erupted. "I need you back here at once!" demanded her boss. "We've had reports that Jesus Christ, yes can you believe it, Jesus Christ, the Son of God no less, has been seen at over a hundred locations around the world in the last half an hour! Apparently, he is having a feast at a hundred different places at once. He's one clever guy. I need you to fly on down to London and rip this whole thing apart."

"Okay," said Sharon. "But there's no point."

"What do you mean, Mrs Long?" he shouted back. "May I

248

remind you who I am? I command you to go!"

"There's no point, Jack, because He's here!" and with that she hung up her phone and switched it off. Yahshua asked,

"Would you like to tell everyone about that call, Sharon?"

"Yes, my Lord," said Sharon. "I certainly will." She stood up and addressed the whole gathering,

"Yahshua has been sighted at over a hundred events all over the world today and my station manager insisted that I fly to one of these places and tell the world how foolish people are to believe such a thing."

Everyone chuckled.

"I told him," she continued, "That there was no point in me doing that because He was here with me now!" Everyone laughed hysterically as Sharon sat down. Yahshua stood up. The laughter subsided. He said to the whole crowd,

"Thank you, Sharon. You are correct of course, I am here. And," he paused and looked around. "I am there, too!"

People stared at him intently.

"That's the great thing about being omnipresent, you can truly multi-task!" Everyone laughed. Lisa was amazed at how awesome he was at speaking to crowds. She thought to herself, 'He even tells jokes!' He continued,

"Well done to all of you for being here, even you Sharon, albeit very briefly. But you have inspired many with your phone call. Thank you all for such a wonderful feast; it was most satisfying, and if that's any reflection on your harvest, you are in for a mighty one!" Everyone cheered and applauded.

Yahshua continued with authority,

"Let those who have ears, hear my words!" It all went quiet. Nothing could be heard. Even the birds fell silent. "I have commanded you to not be afraid and I ask you now to be strong! You are about to face tribulation in this world, like you have never known before. There will be many disasters and many trials will need to be taken. Some of you will be protected and hidden from danger, while others will have to face the tribulations to come and fight for me. All who are here now, who stand firm to the end, will be protected. Some of those who aren't yet sealed will be killed and will be beheaded for the sake of my name. Some will be called to face adversity beyond anything that any human has ever had to bare. But I ask of you to hold on, be bold, be strong and know that I am with you and I am waiting for you, preparing a life for you, in a place beyond your dreams, where you will live for eternity with the Father, myself and the Spirit, along with all the believers who hold on to Me and to The Fathers commandments until the end. You have all read of these times. That time is now!

> 'Stand at the crossroads and look,
> Ask for the ancient paths,
> Ask where the good way is
> and walk in it.
> There you will find peace for your souls.'

"Always remember that I love you!"

As he finished talking, there was a mighty rumble and the sound of a mighty Shofar, a mighty trumpet blast. The ground shook. Everyone fell to the floor. It was impossible to stand. There was often a slight tremor near the coastal regions but nothing ever like this. It was an earthquake like never before. They could see trees crashing down with the shaking accompanied by hideous sounds of destruction, and then as suddenly as it began, it stopped. People picked themselves up off the ground and looked at each other to make sure everyone was okay.

Yahshua had gone! The Angels had gone!
They were on their own.

Suddenly, there was an enormous flash; an explosion which lit up the whole sky. They all fell down on the ground and hid their faces. The belt of Orion had exploded.

It had begun.

To Be Continued....

ABOUT THE AUTHOR

Ian C. Jervis was born in 1963 and is married to Lisa. They live in Northern Ireland with their two boys, Ian and Oliver where they are currently embarking on a project to establish a Christian Media company to help and encourage others to express their own artistic gifts. Both Ian and Lisa have been involved in music ministry for many years and are currently working to produce a new album. More recently they worked for Revelation TV as prayer co-ordinators in Spain. They returned to the UK in 2017 but Lisa continues to assist Revelation TV with their social media pages. Both Ian and Lisa are currently involved in other projects as authors.

Printed in Poland
by Amazon Fulfillment
Poland Sp. z o.o., Wrocław

61836059R00148